Code White

Debra Anderson

Library and Archives Canada Cataloguing in Publication Data

Anderson, Debra, 1974-
Code white / Debra Anderson.

ISBN 1-894692-11-X

I. Title.

PS8601.N43C63   2005C813'.6   C2005-904245-1

Copyright © Debra Anderson 2005

Editor: Ann Decter
Copy editor: JP Hornick
Cover design: Suzy Malik
Cover illustration: Heather Schibli
Inside layout: Heather Guylar
Author photograph: William Scott

All rights reserved. No part of this book may be reproduced in any manner whatsoever without written permission, except in the case of brief quotations in critical articles and reviews. For information contact McGilligan Books, P.O. Box 16024, 1260 Dundas Street West, Toronto, ON, Canada, M6J 3W2, e-mail info@mcgilliganbooks.com; www.mcgilliganbooks.com. McGilligan Books gratefully acknowledges the support of the Canada Council for the Arts, and the Ontario Book Publishing Tax Credit for our publishing program.

 Canada Council   Conseil des Arts
for the Arts   du Canada

This is a work of fiction. Any resemblance to persons living or dead is coincidental.

Printed in Canada

*To Linda and Paul Anderson.
Your support and encouragement have
meant more than you could know.*

*And to William Scott, with all my love.
This is for you.*

one

I'm cold. A big hook in the back of my neck is slowly dragging me through the deepest, darkest parts of the ocean. Salty parts, water so thick with seaweed it barely parts for my heavy body. I want to keep lying here. My bones are too big. They're twisted and cracked, splintered outside my skin. Glowing with a pulse as bright as tiny flitting neon fish.

I don't know how long I've been here. Asleep in this blank, black way. Like someone covered all the windows with black tar. Unplugged every phone. Layered the walls with foam. And still it wouldn't be as silent. Wonder when I'm coming back, if every piece is still here. Is this still me? I never want to sleep like this again. It's not really sleeping when you've died at the bottom of the ocean.

This seems to be a doctor's examining table. My body isn't mine. It's made out of sticks that haven't been moved in a long time. The doctor's table looks as if a horde of vandals attacked it while I was sleeping. The wood is nicked all over. Tiny burns like someone went at it with their lighter. I sway without meaning to. Waves still having their way. The ratty, brown vinyl cushion underneath me gapes open. Ripped in too many places. Scars that haven't healed yet.

There's mud on my legs, like a blotchy coating of my grandmother's uneven foundation. My regular skin comes through in fragments. I don't remember how it got there. Why is the mud still there? Why didn't I wash it off?

My jean shorts look ragged. Too short. My thighs poke through, overly fleshy. My red spaghetti-strap tank top suddenly seems too tight. Skimpy. My tits threaten to rip through the fabric. The straps little licks of fire keeping me together. My cleavage too brazen for this room.

I look ridiculous, covered in mud. No shoes and not even sure where they are. This room makes what was okay, obscene. Takes what was acceptable and makes it trash. I sway on the doctor's table. Why couldn't I be wearing a nice sweater set from Talbot's when I got dragged in here? Something that says, *I know how to behave*. I know how to make myself small, they don't have to try and do it for me. These clothes make every word out of my mouth invalid. Nothing sinks in, they've already stuck me in a binder. I check for something I can use to carve my initials into the examining table. My pockets are empty. I wonder where the things in them disappeared to.

The walls in the room are grey. No windows, no art. Nothing but concrete right up to the tall ceiling, which goes up at least three stories. I'm locked in a concrete closet. And I'm freezing. They took my sandals. I have no shoes and I'm locked in their ugly closet.

I go up to the yellow metal door with the tiny window in it. I cringe with each step since my feet are touching the dirty floor with nothing on them for protection. I want my shoes back. I never said anyone could have them. I tap gently on the door to get the man's attention out there. He jumps. I smile at him. He doesn't smile back. *Screw him*.

"Can I please have a blanket? I'm freezing in here," I ask politely. "And my shoes? I need my shoes back."

He doesn't answer.

My tongue feels hot; heat spills down my throat like someone packed my mouth with cinnamon hearts.

"Hello? I asked you a question? I'm really cold. Please get me a blanket. And my shoes," I say. This time he doesn't turn around. The heat in my mouth expands, like I ate a hot pepper and it's warming my chest. The rest of me is still cold. I want to speak to his boss. Lodge a complaint. I knock on the door, harder this time. He ignores me. The heat is jumping out my mouth and smashing against the window, yelling about blankets and shoes and my rights. He can't just fucking ignore me. It all clatters against the glass and lands on my naked feet. He doesn't turn around.

And then in a bright flash, like someone took a picture of me from before I fell in the ocean and passed out, I'm holding a Polaroid in my fingers, shaking it to make the image come clear. There is dirt I'd never ordinarily have around my fingernails. I'm in this same room. The grey concrete walls are pressing even closer. They're wet slabs of clay someone's sliced off with a bright copper wire. About to swallow me. With me is a tall man with curly brown hair. He wears a long white lab coat. I stand in the corner. There's nowhere else to go in the room. No one will let me leave. Someone has stolen my shoes. He won't tell me who.

"Please get up on the examining table," he tells me.

"No," I say. I stand, so I'll be on his level. So he'll see we're both human beings. Equals. He shouldn't be trying to tell me what to do. He shouldn't keep me in this room when I don't want to be here. Or steal my shoes. I know it was him.

He is a bird, one with a big, pointed nose. He chirps at me repeatedly. He doesn't know I'm up high, near the tall ceiling. The closest I can get to the sky. The furthest away from him. I'm a bird, too. I'm flying higher than him, circling the ceiling. I can do that for a long time. He doesn't realize how strong I am.

"I need to give you this needle, Alex. You have to get up on the table. They're waiting," he says.

CODE WHITE

Suddenly, I don't want to be up by the ceiling anymore.

"There is nothing different about you and me," I explain. Beneath his patronizing look of agreement I can see he thinks otherwise. "You can't just make me get a needle with some drug in it that I don't even want to take," I tell him. He doesn't look convinced. "I don't even know what it is!" I say. He just stands there. Like he can wait me out. He doesn't tell me what is in the syringe. I guess I don't get to know that. "I have rights. You can't just keep me locked up in this room and give me needles," my voice rises. "This is Canada," I holler, "You can't keep me here against my will! This is illegal!"

A policeman quickly looks in the room, unlike when I was shouting for help and they all refused to acknowledge I was speaking. I guess it's different when I talk too loud to the doctor, instead of pleading for help. Apparently, they can only hear me sometimes. The doctor and I aren't really the same after all. The guards only come running at certain times. Only to protect one of us. I guess we are different.

Suddenly a line appears between the doctor and me. A thick line under my feet, like under your name on a form, under my name right now on the form on his clipboard. And there are big X's all over me, the kind that go over a mistake. Something crossed out because it's wrong and useless and you need to start over to get it right. The X's coat my body, sticky like sand covering you at the beach. Getting into places you didn't realize.

The line under my feet roots me to the ground. Keeps me in place. I am a patient. That's all I am now. Anything else has been crossed out. The doctor's bottom line is the needle. He's not leaving the room until he gives it to me.

"I'm fine," the doctor says to the policemen. They go back

debra anderson

to their places outside my door. I smile at him so he knows I am a friendly person. I'm not a troublemaker. He looks like he thinks I'm a con artist.

"I just really want to leave. It's all a big mistake. I don't even understand why I'm here. I don't belong here," I explain. But every word is blocked by those discounting X's covering me. He seems to listen; although, as I talk longer, I notice he's just pretending. He nods in most of the right places. Smiles and appears sympathetic, but I know he's faking. He keeps fondling the needle in his lab pocket. He thinks if he pretends to listen to me long enough I'll run out of the letters holding me up. Each stick poking up and down in my skin like an alternate spine. He's waiting so that, deflated, I will plop down on his examining table in exhaustion. Let him stick it in me.

The concrete wall is cold and hard. My shoulder blades press against the flatness of the wall. I wish I could disappear through it. End up miraculously somewhere outside, where none of these assholes could find me. The whole thing is some sort of weird misunderstanding. A joke. A nightmare. It always ends up explained away in movies. I press harder. Feel my tailbone grind against the concrete. The wall isn't going anywhere.

"Listen," he whispers to me. Friendly.

"Yes?"

"You see all those police out there?"

"Uh-huh."

"The thing is...," he says, and suddenly he seems shy.

"What?"

"The thing is I have to give you this needle, Alex. I'm sorry you don't want it. But, it's going to make you feel a lot calmer –"

" – I *am* calm."

"Okay, but it will make you *more* calm. And sleepy. You

will have a long nap. I was supposed to have given it to you already. And if I don't give it to you in the next couple of minutes, all those police outside the door are going to come in. You're going to find it very upsetting. It'll be much better if I just give you the needle. Quietly," he says.

I'm not really sure whose side he's on anymore. If this is a trick. Maybe he is trying to be nice to me in the limited way he can. Trying to help me. I think about what he's said. I know those policemen aren't going anywhere. They're here for a reason. And the doctor isn't going anywhere until he gives me this shot. Maybe someone else, someone higher up the chain sent him to give the needle. And he can't leave until he gives it to me.

Except, I am not supposed to be here. I am not supposed to be locked in some room. I don't need a needle. But the people in charge think something else. And in order to get out of here with most of myself intact, I need some sort of strategy. The thought of all those policemen grabbing me, laughing as they force me down while the doctor tries to put the needle in makes me sicker. Either way I'm getting this needle. Either way I'm forced.

But this doctor is giving me a choice. Sort of. I look into his eyes, behind the reflection of his glasses. He seems to be seeing me. Not just another patient standing on top of a black line on the other side of the sharp tip of a needle. Perhaps.

He is giving me a choice. Sort of.

The sheet on top of me feels so cold it's like a thin layer of ice; I expect each fold and wrinkle to crunch as I slowly move it off me. I don't understand why this place won't ever give out

debra anderson

blankets. I've been at the bottom of the ocean again. My muscles don't listen when I tell them things. I try to sit up for what feels like hours. I can't seem to make it happen. The fog is thick. My head is a windowless bathroom where a shower's been running a long time. It's hard to string words together. I think of a sentence, but lose half the words in the mist.

I'm still wearing my red tank top and jean shorts. When I finally sit up on the bed, my sandals aren't on the floor. No one's returned them. I've been upgraded from the closet to a new room at some point. Who moved me? How did I get here? My body is a piece of old luggage a stranger carts around. I take comfort in the fact that I'm still wearing my clothes. I try not to think about it. I'm here now.

This room is a little pod, smaller than a normal hospital room. These walls are also unfinished grey concrete. I have trouble climbing down from the hospital bed; my legs are all rubbery. That's all the furniture there is, other than a chair. No windows. No real door, only a sliding glass one that takes up one tiny wall. Enmeshed in the glass is a layer of chicken wire, like we used in grade school for papier-mâché sculptures. The wire isn't there for decorative purposes, but breaking the glass wasn't on the top of my list of things to do, so I don't care. It's not like it's blocking a great view of anything. There's a sheet you can pull across the glass door for privacy. Mine's open. Outside the pod are little tables in the middle of the room with chairs. A TV on the side. Along the walls are more pods for other patients. A nurse rushes right up to me. Not like she's glad to see me. More like she was expecting me to remain in a coma for another fifty years. She seems surprised to see me wobbling around.

I try to walk, but my legs won't work. One leg trails behind me. I pretend this isn't panicking me, even though before that doctor's shot I had full use of all limbs. Eventually I sit down. The patients flit around me. A bunch of moths attracted to a bright, burning light. My mouth stops working, too. Then I really do panic. I'm in a horror movie. Piece by piece, my body is breaking down. My tongue is thicker. Not quite attached at the root. I'll never speak again. I make myself keep talking. Concentrate on the movements each word makes even if what I'm saying doesn't sound like anything.

The nurse keeps coming by with a little white cup and a pill inside. I slur, "No."

But she keeps coming back. A fly in my face. The nurse brings ammunition: more nurses from behind a big, white desk. They form a wall. There is nowhere to go. All of them are talking at me. Flapping their hands. Wind chimes on a porch. The moth patients stare at me. Their pupils are the wrong size.

The nurses say, "You have to take it, Alex. Just swallow this pill. You'll feel much better."

I've heard that before. And I am not falling for it again. It's the nurses' job to make all moths take their medication. I'm setting a bad example for the big eyes watching from every pod. Watching someone refuse a nurse. Refusing to take medication. I am not a moth. The nurses need to understand. They have lots of other things to do. Deliver medication to other moths. Write out charts.

"It's just Cogentin, Alex. Take it," a nurse says.

I don't know what Cogentin is. No one explains it to me. I don't think they understand it's my first time. The nurse shoves the little plastic cup in my face. I try to back away, but my neck's on a stretchy marshmallow band. I try to tell her, *No,* but my tongue won't work. It's too big for my mouth. I am heavy. Full of pancake syrup. It slowly drips down into other parts of my body. I'm so coated I can barely move. My legs are melting. When I walk, they bend in ways I've never seen. I stuff my fear under my swollen tongue. Down my dry throat. If I don't admit what's happening, maybe no one else will see. Maybe they'll still let me leave.

The nurse is still there with her plastic cup. I want to explain the cup won't hold nearly enough water to quench my thirst. But I don't waste energy talking to her. She isn't on my side. I wave her away like a pigeon at a picnic. I know not to take anything else they try to give me. They are trying to poison me. The nurses drag a doctor over and take me into a bright, white room for a meeting. Not to discuss why I'm being made to stay there. Or that I don't want any of the medication they keep forcing on me. But to force me to take this pill. The meeting is to gather all the staff in one room to more easily gang up on me.

"You are having an allergic reaction to the shot you were given earlier," the doctor says without looking at my face. "Your mouth and tongue are swelling so severely that soon you won't be able to breathe at all. You could die if you don't take this pill."

I try to ask why they gave me a needle that could kill me, but my tongue is hanging past my chin. I watch the tip of it curl like Gene Simmons'. I pinch it to make sure it's real. It is. I want to stuff it back inside my mouth. I'm convinced it's going to get so big it will fall off at the root. Break like an icicle. I'll have to carry a notebook to communicate. I will need a massive supply of pens.

There's no way to be sure if the doctor is telling the truth. He can make up anything. Maybe he's making up the allergic reaction story to get me to take more medication. I want justice. The other doctor who did this to me should pay. Instead, this doctor holds a clipboard. Stares at it. He sits across from me as I try to make my body work to stand. No one's offered me a chair.

"You need to take the Cogentin. You'll feel much better," the doctor says and knocks his knuckles twice on his clipboard. Sharp.

My feet are stuck to the black line on the floor. My tongue curls out of me. A long, hunk of meat. I want someone to put it away. My lips are stretched around it. Pulling. The doctor writes on my chart. I no longer fit. I want him to look at me. See who I was before I got stuck on his floor. But he won't look up. There's comfort in forms. In typed facts and blanks waiting to be filled. I want to answer, *No*. I want to resist. I attempt to form the word, but nothing comes out.

"Everything will keep swelling. Unless you take the antidote," he says.

What will this pill really do to me? Will I end up needing some other medicine to fix the side effects of this pill? No one in the room warns me about any other things that could potentially happen. The staff here likes to hand out Band-Aids. Stick them on you whether you want them or not.

I don't want to die here. It's an Alice in Wonderland moment. I don't want to eat a piece of this cake to get smaller. Drink this to get bigger. But I want my body back. And my shoes. The only offer on the plate is Cogentin. I don't really know what else to do. I want to live. I take it.

When I wake up I'm back in my pod, under the thin sheet. All the runny pancake syrup's gone. I can feel my lips. I can talk again. The nurses and the doctor are instantly sorry I can talk. None of them seem to like a single sentence coming out of my mouth. I don't care. It's not like I chose their company.

A man comes over wearing squeaky running shoes. He's an orderly. The nurse tells me to go to the washroom and clean up. She hands the orderly a toothbrush, toothpaste and soap for me. The toothbrush isn't in a package. I hope she isn't recycling it from another patient. There are two washrooms, one for men and one for women. Each has a toilet and a sink. Except for the sign on the door they're the same. I want to use the men's washroom. If the washrooms only hold one person, it shouldn't matter who goes where. They're just washrooms. The orderly blocks me when he sees which washroom I'm headed towards.

"Go to the other one," he nods like I'm stupid. I don't even know why he's following me around. I know how to use a bathroom.

I still try to head for the men's. He shakes his head like I've asked for access to the doctor's secret lab where they invent the poisonous drugs that make patients sick.

"Look. When I go in there, the door will be shut. No one but me will be in there. There's no point in having gendered washrooms. We should all be working to break down the differences between people that society enforces. Highlight our similarities. When people connect, that's how revolutions are started," I explain.

"No," he says. "Go use that washroom." He gestures to the women's.

I haven't needed permission to use a washroom since I was in grade school. And I don't need supervision. Does he plan on listening to every fart and splash of urine through the door? If his whole point is that women and men need to go to the washroom separately, then why is he parking on top of me while I do my business? Doesn't that go against his whole argument? That the world would fall apart if people pissed in rooms without labels? Except, in this twisted place, apparently it's fine for a strange man to count in his head how many squares of toilet paper I rip off because he can hear it unraveling through the door. It makes absolutely no sense.

I walk around him to the men's washroom. Peer in. Inside is a grey-green tile floor with too much grout seeping through. A toilet wearing a black seat. A white sink with silver taps. And a scratched mirror riding above the sink. There's a white metal paper towel dispenser on the wall with heavy brown paper towel feeding through the bottom. Nothing mysterious that I shouldn't be seeing. Nothing so incredibly masculine that exposure to it will damage me or change my life.

The orderly clamps his hands on my shoulders like a bracket. He redirects me to the women's washroom, three baby steps over.

"This is stupid," I tell him.

Every moth eyeball is glued on us. He stops me in front of the door. Points at the stick figure wearing the triangle skirt on the sign. It's the ugliest skirt ever. I wouldn't be caught dead in that skirt. He nudges me forward. Gender behaviour re-education at its finest. The gruff man in the hospital scrubs and squeaky sneakers is retraining me on how to be a woman. Why make a big deal? No one listens to anything I have to say here. I go inside.

I piss. Ball the cheap one-ply paper in a wad. I brush my teeth into a rabid, foaming mess. Drip wads all over the sink. The mint sparkles against every microscopic surface in my mouth. I've never felt so clean or beautiful. My mouth is filled with shining diamonds. I breathe a hissing stream of mint. It's the best thing ever. I brush my teeth again. Think about how toothpaste would feel frothing up on my face. What's the difference between fancy exfoliating lotions and expensive peels and the cooling, tightening sensation of the toothpaste?

I make tiny circles with the tips of my fingers. Careful to keep my eyes pinched tight. It's like rubbing my face with heaps of sharp snow. Every flake crushing against my skin makes me realize I've had a dead face until now. My skin was turned off. Now I'm waking it up. A bright light switch. I flick until my whole face shines. As I rinse, the orderly knocks repeatedly. I ignore him. This is a WOMEN'S washroom. He has no business coming inside.

I check for toothpaste marks. The kind that look like saltwater stains. My skin is tight. Every pore as minute and nonexistent as a multi-decimal calculation of the mathematical equation of Pi. I notice the mirror isn't real. The knocking switches to banging. The mirror is actually a thin sheet of silver-coloured metal screwed into the wall. With rounded edges. The surface is covered in scratches like an old coffee table. I can't see myself very well through all the marks and cuts.

The door opens. There's no lock. It's the orderly. What if I was on the toilet? Yet, when he sees the bathroom, suddenly it's me in the doghouse. He's not smiling like before. When he could raise his eyebrows and roll his eyes thinking I wouldn't notice. Saving every "weird" thing I did to turn into a great story to his friends about the crazy people he has to take care of. When people get a kick out of you it's one thing. It's another deal entirely when people are just fucking fed up.

"What's that smell?" he barks.

"What?" I answer, looking confused. Like all women's bathrooms reek of Winterfresh toothpaste so bad you'd choke on it. He gets more mad when he sees the toothpaste. It's on the sink ledge, squished up like a tube of paint. Frothy blobs coat the bowl of the sink. An uneven blue line runs all over the white enamel and faucets. Colouring outside the lines by mistake. Or on purpose. Hard to tell, standing in the doorway.

"Go sit down out there," he spits out. "It's time to eat."

I sit at a small group of little plastic tables that look like they've been stolen from McDonald's. Behind the big shoulders of the orderly, I see Max. I'm surprised to see her here. But I'm also not. Like another Polaroid developing in my hand, I remember at some point screeching repeatedly, *If I'm going to be kept prisoner, someone needs to know I'm here. I can make one fucking phone call. Otherwise, I could die here. Disappear forever.*

There's another snapshot of me, standing by a payphone. Finally. A bunch of guards surround me. Sulking. I put in a quarter someone has to give me because everything I have is gone. I stand for a second, not sure who to call. I don't want to call my parents. They've taken my purse with my daybook inside. Every phone number lost. They won't give it back. The guards keep moving, waves around me. Choppy and restless. If I don't make a choice immediately, they'll take me back. I won't get to make my call. I pause, take a breath and send out an invitation. Open and deliberate. Numbers press firm against my heart. They travel bright, like a branding. I'm singed. I dial each number slowly. Pray the ringing stops. Make the person answer. I know the guards won't let me try again.

Then there's a photo of my hands. Curled around the black nicked plastic of the receiver. Max's voice small and tinny. Pouring out the holes into my ear. Warm rain rushing down.

"Hello?" she says. "Alex, where are you? What's going on?"

"Will you do me a huge favour?" I ask, my voice trembling. I haven't even seen her in a while. The group we used to hang out with sort of dissolved. I've missed her. But I never really knew what to do about that without looking like a total ass. Before today, I'd dial her number, but never let it ring through. Scared she wouldn't want to see me. And now I send this awful bomb of a phone call. About to ask something so huge. Way worse than just an ass. Captured and contained. Crazy. Not exactly the look I was going for. And needing help. What I hate most of all.

"Alex, are you alright?" she asks. Her voice is so caring. It's too much. The softness runs over my rough spots like sandpaper. Rubs me wide open instead of making it better. I am such a fucking bother. None of it makes any sense, but I know I'm about to cry. Something is about to tear.

"Hey, listen, it's okay. What do you need?" she asks. Spilling over with concern. I don't deserve this kindness. I'm going to cry any second. I can't let her hear me crack open like that. Everything leaking all over the place.

"Will you come help me?" I croak.

A photo of my bare, dirty feet against the tiles of the floor under the payphone.

"You won't believe what's happened. What these assholes are doing," I stutter, trying to throw fireworks. Camouflage. The sky is blazing. It isn't falling down.

I'm so fucking scared.

The last photo is dark. My lashes squeeze tight against what she might say. A flutter.

CODE WHITE

In the fake McDonald's a woman in a pink polyester dress comes by, the kind you see on people who are cleaning hotel rooms. She pushes a cart and puts an orange plastic tray down on the table. On the tray there's some cold white toast, a hard-boiled egg, a little paper carton of milk, a few pats of butter wrapped in wax paper, a couple of miniature tubs of strawberry jam sealed with plastic and two rectangles of cheese swallowed up in plastic and impossible to peel open. The cutlery is plastic. There's also a little round fruit punch juice cup. It has a tin foil lid you peel off by a tab.

I'm not hungry. I don't remember the last time I ate. In here or out there. My body doesn't feel like it runs on food anymore. Max nudges me from her seat beside me.

"Eat up, Alex," she says.

"Why?" I ask. It's rude to eat while Max is here.

"Because you're going to need your strength while you're here, hon," she says, and tries to smile. Her smile looks like it got lost. I try to think of a good way to cheer her up, but I can't. I offer a piece of my styrofoam toast. She smiles bigger this time.

"You're very sweet, but I'm not actually hungry. It would really make me happy to see you eat it," she says.

So, for Max, I try to eat little bites. Dry bits crumble against my tongue. The butter is salty and greasy. The cheese tastes like orange chemicals. Plasticine. I even drink some milk, a warm coat of paint. I stopped drinking milk years ago because it hurt my stomach. I wonder if I'll have farts that'll stop traffic now. If I do, I hope they come after Max leaves.

Like any stereotypical girl, I'm embarrassed to eat when no one else is. Like every bite instantly puts more pounds on. I wish Max were eating something, too. Or had her back turned so she couldn't see. But the more I eat, the happier she looks. I swallow my stupid pink shame like swirls of icing on a cupcake and just eat. Put food in my mouth without thinking about what I look like. I eat like a man, without apology or explanation. When the food is gone, there's a pile of plastic wrappers and crumbs. Empty containers in a heap on the tray.

I stand to throw it out, but the orderly tells me, "Sit down." He uses a curt voice like I've done something bizarre, bordering on the obscene. Stuck panties on my head and run in circles barking. All I want is to throw out my garbage.

"Someone will be around to get it. Don't bother," he says.

Back in my pod, Max keeps explaining what's happening in a quiet voice.

"You're going to have to be here for a while until things settle down and they take you off the form they're putting you on," she says softly.

I don't think Max really understands. I'm going home really soon. Whatever she's saying about being transferred to another floor and needing to get someone to bring stuff from my house isn't necessary. I don't need stuff. I'm not going to be here. I appreciate her trying to look out for me. I keep trying to explain so she'll get it.

"Thank you so much for coming here, Max. I can't tell you how grateful I am," I say.

"It's fine. Don't worry about it," she answers and blushes.

"This is good. Maybe soon we can hang out. Like wander around Kensington Market. Or go sit on a patio. Something fun."

Her face has that far off look again. Like her smile crashed somewhere else, even though the rest of her is right here, in front of me.

"You're going to have to protect yourself while you're here," Max says. It feels like she's giving me a hug, though she isn't.

"I'm fine," I say, even though I'm not really that sure.

"You'll get through this. In the meantime, keep to yourself. Get lots of sleep. Eat whatever they bring you, okay? And I'll be back to visit you tomorrow, to check on you. Remember that, Alex?" Max says, making sure each word is bright. A shining light between us.

"I know you can do this," Max tells me. I wonder how she knows. If this is just one of those things you say to someone in this kind of situation. Basic pep talk. The kind of thing a football coach says in the locker room to pump everyone up. Maybe Max is saying, *I know you can do this*, because she wants me to know she's rooting for me. Whether she actually believes it or not. What is she supposed to say? *You can't make it through this, you piece of shit. Why are you here in the first place, you fucking loser?*

Max quietly puts her hand on my knee. I'm sitting on the bed facing the windowless, concrete wall. I watch Max, how calm she stands. She is really here. She came. Max is on one side of a slender needle and I'm on the other. Her arm is the thread between us. Stretching through the tiny eye to reach out to me. Something tugs. Maybe I will make it to the other side. Off this bed and to where Max stands. Her eyes quickly scan above my shoulder through the circles of wire in the glass of the balcony door, to check who is watching us.

"I have faith in you," she whispers. Reaches for my hand. Holds it. Gives it a squeeze I feel across my whole body.

I swear I'm going to remember this. I'm not going to let any of them take this moment away from me like they're taking away everything else. And then Max drops my hand fast, like it's covered in something disgusting. I wonder if I did something wrong. If Max is sorry she came. The doctor rushes into the pod. His slacks whine loudly. He grips a clipboard.

"I need some details from you to complete this form," he says.

"Okay," I answer. He seems surprised I agree.

"I'll need your address, phone number, full name, age," he declares, pen poised.

I want to show him the hospital bracelet clamped around my wrist. All the essentials already there. Doesn't he know I already gave this information eons ago? Max nods imperceptibly. So I give him my address. Again. If they can't keep track of their own paperwork, far be it from me to suggest a new filing system.

"I need a name for your next of kin," he says, and waits. Except, I don't know what that really means. What if I pick the wrong person?

"It's a name for the doctors to know who to keep in touch with. You think about it for a minute. I'll be back to fill it out," he says. He thinks I'm not only crazy, but stupid. Excuse me for not ever having been in this situation before.

"The next of kin is responsible for making all your decisions once you're formed. The doctors will decide you're no longer able to make decisions for yourself," Max fills in blanks that the doctor left empty.

"But I can make decisions for myself. That's bullshit," I sputter.

"*You* know you can make decisions for yourself. And *I* know you can. Sort of. But the doctor is going to decide you aren't able. Your next of kin acts on your behalf. They talk to all the doctors and nurses and find out what medications they're giving you and what treatments they want to give you. How much longer they'll keep you. They won't always tell you all of that. They tell the next of kin. They don't tell anyone else," Max explains and then the doctor is back.

"Have you decided?" he frowns.

I want someone good. Someone who'll be on my side. Someone who isn't going to turn on me.

"Her. I want her to be my next of kin," I say. Max doesn't actually move, but it feels like she jumps.

"For the first few weeks," he turns and addresses Max like I've left the room, "you'll be the only one who is allowed onto the ward to visit."

The doctor must be making a mistake. I'm only going to stay a couple days, max. Long enough for this stupid thing to get sorted out. And then I'm out of here.

"Are you sure, Alex?" Max asks softly. "You sure you want me to be your next of kin?"

"Yes," I say. The doctor gets all the specifics from Max: her name, address and contact numbers. Then he leaves the room.

"Are you sure you want it like this?"

"Yes. This is the way it's supposed to be," I answer. "Is it okay? Is it too much?"

"It's fine, Alex. I'm just worried maybe there's someone else you'd rather have. Your parents. Or someone you're closer to. One of your other friends – "

" – No. I want it to be you. Unless you don't want to," I say.

"I'm honoured," Max says. I can't tell what she's thinking. I'm sure she'd say no, if she didn't think it was a good idea.

Something in me just knows it's supposed to be her name riding that black line. I don't care if it's strange. It's that same feeling that burned in my heart when I pressed each digit in her phone number. I didn't know who to call. Her number came immediately. Pushed itself right into the red messiness of my chest. Held itself there when I could reach out to only one person. All because I fought to get someone to help me in this place.

Max pulls out a tiny notebook. Writes something down, rips it out of the book and hands it to me. It's her name and pager number.

"Call me any time, Alex. I'll be here tomorrow to see how things are going, but if you need me, call. Okay?"

And then Max pulls out her notebook again. Rips out a bunch of pages from the front with her writing on it. Then she gives it to me with one of her pens. A blank book.

"I want you to have this. It's yours. However hard this will be, you can write anything you want in this book. No one can stop you. Remember how beautiful you are, Alex," Max says.

I don't want to take Max's notebook. But I don't have anything. Not a single thing. The idea of being able to write things down, have a little space of my own where no moth eyes can see, is really tempting.

"Are you sure?" I ask.

"Take it," Max says, smiling.

"Would you do me one more favour?" I ask. "Would you keep this necklace for me until later? I'm afraid it'll get stolen."

I wear a silver necklace everyday. I don't want it tainted by being here. Max nods like she's staring at a bunch of scrabble tiles and can't figure out how to pick the right ones to form the sentence she wants to say. I hold the back of my hair up. I don't want to take my necklace off and I don't want to stay. If I have to stay, I don't want Max to leave. I know it's not the best time, but I wish Max would wrap her arms around me with my necklace deep inside one of her fists, the other hand touching my face. I want her to handle the back of my hair as she undoes the clasp. Bend down and kiss the back of my neck. Stay a minute, lips pressed against that place.

Max never seemed very interested in me before. She's not going to like me now that I'm covered in mud and stuck on a mental ward. I don't even have my own shoes. Not the best time to try for a date. I'm not too far gone to see that. But, I wish things could be different. I like to think in this flickering fluorescent light Max does, too.

I close my eyes when Max reaches for that soft spot on the back of my neck. I feel the length of her fingers brush against the sides of my neck; move all the hairs I haven't managed to capture out of the way. The smooth tips of her fingers work the clasp and move against my skin. She laughs and clears her throat.

"Sorry, I've never done this before. I hope I'm not hurting you," she mumbles.

"You're doing fine," I say quietly. I know she's blushing behind me. The heat is like a sunburn against my skin where she touches me. I wish I could turn around. She finally opens the clasp, separates the chain. The open space is a dropped towel. Her fingers quickly slide along my neck to grab the chain. She drags it and it's gone. Her fingers, too. I'm standing, neck bare. Nothing. I clench my eyes tight; try to capture this goodness inside. I turn around.

"You know, you're my next of kin now. You have to come back," I say, afraid that this is it. That I will never, ever see Max again.

debra anderson

"I will," she says. "I'm coming back."
I want to believe her.

When I wake up I'm tucked under the frozen sheet, still wearing my red tank top and dirty jean shorts. There's no sight of my shoes. I'm afraid I'm developing a circulation problem because I'm so cold all the time. I have no idea what time it is. Someone's stolen my watch. I climb down off the high bed, careful not to slip. My head tingles. If all I'm doing is sleeping, why am I more tired than I've ever felt?

I saunter out of my pod. There's a giant in front of the TV. He's wearing jeans and has a great ass. He's also wearing a white undershirt. It shows off tiers of muscles in his arms. Despite myself, I feel like grabbing them. He's barefoot, too. He looks at me and grins. I know what he sees — a typical hole to bang. I could show him there's more than that if I felt like it. He checks to make sure I'm watching and drops to the floor. Push-ups. The fastest I've ever seen. No breaks. It's incredibly hot. Who knew? He carries his entire weight on his bulging arms. Muscles in his back tighten and knot underneath the thin fabric of his undershirt. I want to rip it off. It's as if his big hands are pressed up against me, I can feel the heat of them spreading through my skin.

Part of me thinks it's funny. His display of sweaty gym prowess is supposed to make me, a dyke, fall swooning into his beefy arms. In a mental hospital, no less. I watch him with an ironic smile meant to distance. Except, part of me is pressed up against the spine of my shorts, interested. I had a realization this week. There is beauty everywhere. It shines in disguises, but it's still there. Gorgeous. New. If only I'm open to it.

If I turn down the beauty, I close off joy. Why would I want to do that? This message keeps laying itself in front of me. A welcome mat to step on.

He presses up and down. Smiles at me. Not in a gross way. It's actually rather sweet. With each thrust downward I get what he's saying. It's my body he's placed underneath himself. So that, in front of the nurses, doctors, orderlies and other moths, he's fucking. He looks at me again. *Is this okay?* I blush. He asks again with his eyes. Who am I to say no? To not enter this room placed in front of me? There's a reason I'm having this connection. Nothing is a coincidence. And nothing bad can happen.

If we all communicated so easily about what we wanted, the world would be a better place. I sit in my McDonald's chair. Watch him get off on being watched by me. On doing the imaginary me. I try to see if he has a hard-on through his jeans, but the angle I'm sitting at isn't working in my favour. I imagine grabbing him, dragging him into a pod and pushing him against a cement wall. I pin him and squeeze his ropey arms at the wrist, burning my face on his stubble. Yank a handful of his hair. Tilt his head back to kiss him.

I take away his stubble for a second, like I have an eraser. Cut away his bulk. He is a hologram. He's a woman, not a man at all. He looks like a hot butch, wearing a sports bra instead of the undershirt. And then the light changes again and he looks like he did when I first saw him. A giant full of stubble. A man. The hologram tilts back. He's a female version of himself again.

This keeps happening lately. I look at certain people and can't tell whether they're men or women. Or they keep changing. No one stays one gender. There's a lesson here. We all have parts of both inside us, no matter what body we're born into.

We need to honour those parts, that energy, regardless of the sex we walk through the world as.

The orderly comes by. The sharp, scissor noise of his sneakers cuts between me and the giant. Cuts whatever we were doing across the room from one another. The orderly makes the giant go into his pod. The giant brushes the dirt from the floor off his hands, and winks when the orderly isn't looking. He has a big hard-on that fills the front of his jeans. I smile. The orderly spins around with a loud squeak.

"You," he tells me. I know he wants to point his finger. His hand shakes. "Turn around in your chair. Don't look at him. Keep away from him."

I long to point out that I was keeping away from him. But why should I? Won't talking to other patients prevent my social skills from disintegrating?

"Just stay away from him, Alex," the orderly warns.

I try to imagine what it would be like to be the orderly. If I had to go around intimidating people all day. Would I be more or less tired than I am now? I want to open a dialogue with him. About why he is so angry. Why he doesn't feel enough power in his own life that he has to grab so much here. Help him figure out life doesn't have to be this way. But he's in a pod, telling a moth what to do.

I start talking to the moth sitting in front of me. His five o'clock shadow looks smudged on with dark blue charcoal. A nurse who could use some highlights in her hair comes by and puts him in his pod.

"Don't talk to anyone else," she says, like it's some sort of threat.

If someone doesn't want to talk to me, they can tell me themselves. The nurse swishes off to her white desk where everything has its place. I can see her white underwear through her white polyester pants. They are big and high-waisted. Not exactly panties I would choose to show off. Behind the desk I can see her writing something down and pointedly looking at me. So what. We can all write things down. It doesn't make us any more or less important. Being in the McDonald's alone is boring. Like when you're watching television, but someone else holds the remote.

Later, after I wake up in my pod, I come back and sit in McDonald's again. Watching TV. The orderly makes sure I stay away from the giant. The giant has the remote and we're watching music videos. Charcoal Face keeps laughing. I don't know about what. It sounds like gravel spraying from a big truck. I don't want any of it to get on me. The giant changes the channel fast, about a million times. He leaves it on a steady stream of commercials. Even I can change channels better than him. Everything is too loud, too bright. Like someone's pelting me with buckets of jewels. The colours hurt my eyes. No one will stop.

A moth shuffles back and forth by his pod. His feet are sandpaper against my back. Charcoal Face swings his McDonald's chair around one way and then the other. It squeaks worse than the orderly's shoes. He goes faster like on an amusement park ride. Why does the fucking TV have to be on all the time here? I need a cigarette, but to get one I'd have to ask that nurse's permission. The underwear nurse. She has my cigarettes and my lighter. I'm not sure how that happened. Only one moth at a time can have permission to go into the grey pod cave where we're allowed to smoke.

Last time I was in the smoking pod, it was so cool and quiet. Everything grey. Beautiful. No moths, except the ones fluttering at the glass. They pushed their faces against it. Bumped their bodies with dull thumps. Left smears. I ignored them. I wanted to keep sitting there once my cigarette was finished, wondering where all the smoke went. The pod was completely shut. No windows, just like all the rest. A sliding glass balcony door closed tight. I tried to open my lungs, like a bright red secret box. A lid no one but me knew about. A box I could open and close whenever I wanted. Slip whatever I chose inside and push deep. I tried to breathe in every last wisp that had escaped out the end of my cigarette. The orderly tapped on the glass. A sharp sound I couldn't ignore.

"It's time to go," he said.

"Go where?" I asked.

"Don't be smart." He squeaked away across the floor.

When I sleep again, it's like someone's pulled the plug. I can barely slump across the floor to my pod. Before I crash, I have many heartfelt conversations with moths. The nurses and the grumpy orderly repeatedly break them up. But so many moths need help. They're broken, but not so broken they won't benefit from a helping hand. I am all set to pitch in. The moths want my input. Each waits their turn. Sits down in the chair across from me.

None of the staff is on board with the guidance I offer. In the middle of each session, the orderly interrupts the progress I am making with the moth, tells me to go sit somewhere by myself. If this is a place to help people, why does the staff stop all the incredible breakthroughs the moths are having with me? They exude such a beautiful light, sitting across from me. When the orderly makes me leave, the moth always looks so upset. Asks the orderly if I can sit there a little longer.

"No," he spits out each time.

But it doesn't matter where they make me sit. Every moth is drawn to me. They creep slowly around so as not to draw attention from the staff. One by one they come. Attracted to the great shining light inside me they can't help but see. The next thing the nurses know, everyone is sitting in a big circle around me. Like a planetary constellation. All the moths drawn by my light. Little satellite planets revolving on the charge from my sun. I am the apex.

Then, all of a sudden, I'm not there anymore. I'm in this other place. I don't remember how I got here. It's all pancake syrup. Blurred and sticky. There's no more giant. No squeaky orderly. No Charcoal Face. No pods either. I have my own room. It's small, but mine. It has windows across the whole wall. And concrete walls painted white. And a door. There is no more Cogentin.

Now, nurses bring me cups filled with lots of other pills. I have no idea what they are or what they're for. They won't listen when I say I don't want them. I have a few other clothes now. Max says my parents dropped them off for me. And, finally, my sandals. Before, it bothered me how dirty the bottom of my feet were. Now, I like it. My own personal pair of shoes, made out of dirt. A history of every step I've taken in this awful place. I don't want to wash it off. The nurses keep trying to get me to shower.

There are only women's washrooms here. In this place there are only women.

"The doctor from the other floor thought this would be the best floor for you. Because of how you were behaving with the male patients. He said it would be in your 'best interest' if you were on an all women's floor. More 'appropriate,'" Max tells me and we grin.

I'd much rather be on an all women's floor if I have to be here at all. I don't want some asshole peeking in my room when I'm changing. I just find it funny that the doctor who thinks he knows everything thinks it's "better" for everyone if I'm on the all women's floor. Even though I'm a dyke. Who is now totally surrounded by women.

I look at Max and we both burst out laughing. It's hard to stop. And not just for me.

"Now, try to behave yourself," she wheezes out with a wry smile.

"I can't promise anything," I say and Max shakes her head. "Just kidding," I add, but I'm kind of not. Right now I can't promise anything. About anything. I just want out of here. Since that can't happen, I'm really glad Max is here for the moment, visiting. I try to find something in me to pull up. Anything to hold on to. I don't want to cry when she leaves. The flowers she brought are the best thing in this shitty place. The only spot of light, beaming brightness back at me in this awful room. Each pretty head is held up by a delicate green stem that looks too thin to do the job. Petals surround each center like hands held out for a hug. I wonder how long they'll last before they die here. Brown petals dropping off and curling. I try not to let it sink in that I'll be in here that long. That I can't just pick up Max's bouquet and walk out of here. Unwrap the gorgeous smells and colours once I get home.

I stare at the flowers, vibrant and alive. A sign Max was thinking of me outside the locked doors of this place, carrying me with her, out there. I stare at her smile, aimed directly at me, press it into my chest. Press it flat like a dried flower.

I want to believe they mean Max is coming back.

two

August 22, 1999

The pillow they gave me is so thin. It reminds me of that skinny sliver of soap curving into itself someone left on the wet sink ledge. This thin curve. Nothing you'd want to lie down and rest your face on.

August 22, 1999

I keep trying to stay focused, but it's impossible. It's like someone else is holding a remote control for my head. Every time I have my thoughts steady, someone flicks the remote. Then I zap a thousand continents away and can't find the path back. Sometimes, I don't even know whose thoughts are showing up. They don't seem totally mine. But I wouldn't tell anyone that. Where am I in all these channels? Where are they coming from?

August 22, 1999

I need to tell my office not to tell anyone where I am if they ask. I don't want them giving this number to anyone. I wish I could get a cell phone. Or a pager. That way no one would have to call for me on the horrible payphones they have on the ward. One right by the ward door. One across from my room. And one in no-man's land on the other side of the horseshoe hallway where no one ever goes. What shows up on call display when I call from here?

August 23, 1999

Ever since I got here I'm so hot. The nurses insist I have no fever. They won't give me any Tylenol or Advil. So I've devised my own plan on how to cool down. If I take a few dry tea bags from the kitchen and put two inside my shoes, they press against the bottom of my feet and I can feel the tea leaves working their cooling magic all the way up through my ankles. Sometimes even higher.

The only problem is, I have to remember to change them often enough. If I don't, the coolant powers get stale and my feet get too hot again. Another thing that works are mints. Every time I pop a mint, my lips go tingly. Every word I say becomes icier. Slowed down. The nurses tell me to go easy on the candies, but they don't get it. I don't even fucking like mints. I just eat them to reverse the heat.

Menthol cigarettes are good, too. The smoke goes deep inside my chest. If I inhale hard enough it hits my stomach and cools me right out. When I'm too hot and things feel fast, I avoid eating anything red. No cinnamon hearts. Even a red apple is iffy. To change the balance, I'll eat or drink something blue. Something cooling. Blueberry Snapple smoothies are my favourite. I drink one, suddenly, I'm chilling out in front of a big fan.

Sometimes other patients make fun of me. Especially since if I can't get anything blue I can eat I'll just grab something blue and hope that works. I'll even hold a blue pen and start scribbling. I don't care. As long as the heat washes away. I sit in the corner while they poke fun at me. Let the words flow in heavy blue ink. Let the blue take affect.

August 24, 1999

The meds here come in little foil jackets. The nurse stands in a small closet to undress them for us. Each pill tumbles into a miniature plastic cup, the kind that comes with liquid cough syrup. The way the nurse takes off the jackets, she never touches a pill. She doesn't wear gloves when she does it. We touch our pills with our hands when we pick them up to swallow.

Only once the nurse touched my pill. It popped out of its jacket and landed on the wooden shelf on the top of the half-door that says, *KEEP OUT! STAFF ONLY!* As if I'd ever want to get more pills. I'm being forced to take enough.

I've been having some problems with the nurses. So I made a small list of all our concerns. The nurse I met with wrote in my notebook: *Inappropriate clothing/touching*. So I'd remember later. According to her, I'm not supposed to wear certain things here. I don't get that. Don't they have better things to do than censor my wardrobe? Like open more foil packets? Then she went on about how ANY time I touch ANY patient in ANY way, like even a *Hello, how are you* kind of handshake, it is ALWAYS INAPPROPRIATE and I should NOT do it. EVER.

"Under no circumstances. Do not touch anyone, Alex," she said.

It wasn't clear if this was the rule for everyone or just special for me. And if it was a rule just for me, was it because I'd been excessively friendly? Had I really managed to creep out everyone by infringing on their personal space? I've never done that in my life. I wondered if the rule was made specifically for me because I was a dyke. Perhaps no one wanted to be within two centimeters of me in case of contamination?

I listened to the nurse's diatribe, nodding with a bland look on my face as if my head was a slick, boiled egg. Underneath the shell, I was outraged. What the hell kind of place was this? After the nurse left, I changed her note in my book to read: *ALWAYS inappropriate clothing/touching*.

It was immature. I wasn't going to traipse around in my best lingerie, heels click-clacking against the halls and grabbing people for heartfelt hugs. The nurse didn't have to worry. Even I knew what was obviously INAPPROPRIATE. I didn't need a jerk in a lilac acrylic sweater to write a note to tell me so. But changing her note made me feel better. So what if no one wanted me around?

I was tired of being told what's appropriate and what's inappropriate. All of a sudden, total strangers were measuring my acceptability. I'm sure before I got sick, most of the things I wore, read, said, did, thought, who and how I touched would all be thought as inappropriate by staff. That was when I was "healthy." When I had "full powers of discernment" on my side, unlike what they believe I'm operating under now. Here, there are all these people who I have nothing in common with and they're the ones who get to determine what's okay for me. I really appreciate a nurse who wears a banana clip in her hair telling me the clothes I'm pulling on for breakfast are not suitable.

When it's my turn to talk, Lilac Cardigan pretends to listen.

"There weren't enough carrot muffins for everyone. Everyone fought over them. It was really sad. Very bad for morale," I said. "The whole thing could be avoided if the kitchen made more carrot muffins. Then everyone would be happier," I explained.

Her eyes glazed over like a door closing. We had made a deal: I'd listen to her issues if she'd listen to mine. But she could give two shits. She could walk out the ward door and buy herself a carrot muffin any fucking time she wanted one. She'd never have to fight for her share. Have that sick feeling in her gut. So why would it be important to her?

"The food is under the kitchen crew's jurisdiction. Or the nutritionist. If you have any concerns with food, take it up with them," she said in a clipped voice and stood up. With the buck passed, she said again, "Please only wear APPROPRIATE clothes. And cease all INAPPROPRIATE touching, Alex."

And then she left, a greasy lilac blur out the door.

August 24, 1999

I didn't want Max to go today. I'm afraid to be left alone with the nurses. They don't like me. I can tell. I don't care if that sounds paranoid. Just because I'm here doesn't mean I can't tell someone hates dealing with me.

Every time Max comes to visit everything seems a little better. Like a big plateful of cake in front of me. Of course, Max always has to go. I feel like I'm saying weird shit that ruins things. Stuff that's going to make her not want to visit anymore. But she keeps coming back.

I felt so sad today. I can't remember why. One minute I was really happy. Everything bright and intense. Even Max's teeth were really shiny and white. Her blue eyes two sharp circles punching at me. I wanted to grab them inside my palms and hold on. We were laughing about something so hard I had to cross my legs tight. Max was bent over holding her stomach. Her hair looked so nice. I wanted to run the palm of my hand over the shortness. Feel each hair poking soft out of her scalp like a little prickly fountain. But I'm not supposed to touch Max. Those are the rules here. And those are also the rules of Max. That's what she tells me. Sometimes shyly and sometimes sternly. Except, even when she says it sternly there's this smile deep in her. I can feel the warmth of it like putting my hands close to a candle. I know she likes me. That one day, Max and I are going to be. Just not now, when I'm here. Not like this.

The next minute it was as if a nurse touched a dimmer switch. Everything low. Slow motion. It was hard to move my arms and legs. Max looked choppy, as if someone was flipping channels and she was on every one. I didn't understand why everything was darker. Stained in cola. *Drip*. My face was wet.

"Alex, why are you crying?" Max asked sweetly, leaning forward.

I hadn't realized. The cola was dripping right out of my eyes. Max dug in her knapsack for tissues. I was going to scare her away if I kept this up. But I couldn't stop. Someone's hand kept playing with the dimmer switch.

Max talked to me. I followed the blue of her eyes. Felt calmer. It was like we were sitting in a forest or something. Our own quiet spot. Even though I knew we were just sitting in this crappy room. And then Max's eyes filled up. I thought for sure I'd done something wrong.

"I know this is a hard time for you," she said. "But you're going to get through this. Please don't be afraid of how absolutely amazing you are," she told me.

And not a bit of it was under the dimmer. Full light, no cola sludge. Every letter settled. Lodged tender in my ragged heart, swollen like an old lady's ankles.

August 25, 1999

I don't get it. They won't let me keep my eczema cream in my room. They make me take the most toxic drugs a zillion times a day, but I can't keep a simple tube of skin cream to use when my hands get too dry from washing off the germs this place is crawling with. What do they think I'm going to do? Eat it? Take a big gob and swab it all over my crotch?

August 25, 1999

Only after I begged her fifty times did a nurse write the name of one of the drugs I'm on in my notebook. It's a "mood stabilizer" called Epival. I drew a picture of what it looks like. That way I can remember its name. It's a horse pill. Peach-coloured. With a lowercase letter "e" carved on one side.

I don't care if they don't want me to know what drugs I'm taking. If they want to keep it a secret from me. I'll fool them and figure it out. I'll get the nurses to tell me. Even if it's just one by one. I'll log it in my notebook.

August 25, 1999

I need to find my calling card. I temporarily misplaced it somewhere. When I find it I should call my work. Let them know some good times to visit.

August 25, 1999

Maybe this sounds granola, but I'm really sensitive to colour right now. Every colour has a specific vibrational frequency. I feel it so acutely sometimes I can't feel anything else. I can't feel whatever I was feeling before I put on my red shirt other than red. Or I can't feel anything other then the greenness of the salad at lunch or the blueness of the sky pulling me through the locked window. If anyone had tried to explain this before it happened to me, I'd have thought they were a total flake. It's getting to be too much. I want to turn it off. But how do you turn off colour?

CODE WHITE

August 26, 1999

The greatest photo exhibit would be to take a photograph every five minutes of whoever's in the smoke room. The same spot, same angle for days. *Click, click.* It'd be so amazing to see all the photos. All the stuff that goes on in that room. I wish someone would let me do it. But they won't. NO CAMERAS ALLOWED on the ward. Even if they were, none of the patients would want their photos taken. The more good ideas I have, the worse it puts me with the nurses. Whenever I have ideas to make art, or to improve myself, they're sure it means I'm worse. That I need more meds. Stay here the rest of my life.

Since when does wanting to take photos mean someone's crazy?

August 26, 1999

What kind of a hospital performs bloodwork in a room with no beds or cots, only chairs? There's no juice after, either. This morning I don't feel up to having my blood taken. I don't like sitting in the patient line up. Everyone falls asleep in line. Like cows in a meadow. The psych assistant prods us awake, hauls us back upright. The vampire nurse is worse. Bright slash of lipstick. Mostly on her teeth. Barely says two words to any of us. Like we aren't human beings. Just waving arms to tie a rubber tourniquet band around tight. Jab us to fill her required amount of vials. So she can leave and get to the next floor. I don't want to be part of someone's quota.

Waiting in line for my turn, fear wells up in me like a fountain. Sparkling through me until I can't keep it inside anymore. Crying. I can't have the needle poke me today. Something bad will happen. Out of nowhere, the vampire labels my tears "resisting."

Doug, the psych assistant, asks, "Are you resisting? *Yes* or *no*?"

A pathetic hot trickle burns down my face. My little shoulders shake. It's not like I've linked hands with protestors, laid down on the street in front of the riot squad. I'm just sitting in a chair, leaking anxiety in salty streams. It's not an act full of spice.

"Are you resisting?" Doug asks again.

His voice a hand on my back. A hard push. I hate looking at things, *True/False*. *Yes/No*. Never any room for my own answers. I am not a box waiting to be checked off. One or the other. Out of the two choices the decisions are never mine to make anymore. They can't have everything. They can't have my arm. Not today.

The vampire nurse jiggles three empty glass vials between her fingers. Like the foam spacers women jam in between their toes so the nail polish goes exactly where it's supposed to. The tubes are empty. They need pieces of me for people to analyze. So other people paid to do so will make decisions about me.

"But you do it so well," the vampire nurse croons.

I used to possess useful skills. Real talents that made me someone to admire. Not like now, when the only thing I'm good at is letting a nurse take my blood to analyze how much medication another nurse should keep feeding me. I'm not even told what medication it is. Or what side effects to watch out for. Short-term or long-term.

"Not today," I say.

"We don't agree with your decision. We aren't taking responsibility because you've refused to have your blood taken,"

Doug says, fast tires on a grey highway. Everything he says is exactly the same as what you see out of the window of a speeding car.

"*Yes* or *no*. I need a *yes* or *no*," he orders. Doug sounds panicked. That prickly, wet underarm feeling. For once, someone is actually interested in something I'm trying to say on the ward. It's a peculiar feeling. Whatever is going to come out of my mouth has the most unexpected and unreasonable weight. Unlike so many other things I've really needed to say here. I'm almost afraid to open my mouth. It feels so heavy.

"Are you refusing?" he asks.

"Yes," I say simply. It feels scary. But good. If it can't be on my terms or on agreeable terms, then I've had enough. Enough of everything being on their terms on this ward. Always. The vampire nurse purses her lips in disgust like she's just watched me lasciviously strip off my panties and spread my legs. She can go fuck herself. No one's chasing her down for blood all the time. She doesn't have to live here.

"You realize that not allowing her to take your blood constitutes a bona fide threat to yourself," Doug adds. I think I see a thin sheen of sweat on his face.

I can think of so many threats I want to make. To everyone in this place. For how they treat me. For every last thing they've taken away. But I never do. I just want to leave. Get out of here so I can make decisions again. For now, I've decided: *no more*. It feels good.

All day, I examine my arms. Clean and unbroken. No sticky Band-Aid. No bruise spreading across the crease of my inner arm like ugly mould. No ache reminding me of what was taken. How different I am. I'm me. The whole day. Sort of.

Later in the day, my nurse talks to me. She lays worries

thickly as if placing delicate doilies across me. I can barely see through the little white stitches holding them together. When she leaves my room I'm frozen to my bed. What's going to happen to me now that they don't have my blood to analyze? I still have to take all their stupid medicines. If they aren't monitoring that, every pill they give me could make me sicker than they say I already am. Even refusing isn't really a choice. No choices left in here at all. They're not going to stop making me take their pills just because I won't let them have my blood. I stare at my doorknob from my bed. Make no move to touch it. Will something to change.

August 26, 1999

    I'm sitting with my parents at one of the kitchen tables where we usually eat our meals. I've already shown them the activity room, the smoke room, the lounge – which is actually part of the kitchen – the laundry room, the hallways, and my cruddy room. There isn't really much else to show. They've brought me more clothes. A few books. My Walkman and some music. Magazines. A blank notebook. Some pens. A bunch of get well cards from other people in our family and friends. There's a big plant sitting in front of us with orange flowers. The plastic pot is wrapped in blue foil. Someone else has given them a little stuffed dog to give to me for good luck. The carton of smokes and bunch of bottled water I asked them to bring is on the floor. I'm too afraid to drink tap water here. There's something wrong with it.

    One of the really bizarre patients wanders by. Opens the patients' fridge. Closes it. Looking for a good snack. Starts humming really loudly. My dad starts to laugh. I wish all the patients would go sit in their rooms until my parents leave. I wish my parents would just leave. The woman breezes out down the hallway.

"You're much better off than her," my dad says. I don't really know what to say. If I'm so great, why do I have to be here at all? "You'll be out of here in no time. Look at the company you're keeping," he says.

The orange petals look incredibly soft. What would one feel like against my cheek?

"Soon, the nurses tell me you'll have passes. I'll come and pick you up and we can go to a movie," my mom says. Puts her hand over mine. Soft, but firm.

"Yeah," I say. "Like a matinee. That would be fun. Thanks."

And then there's too much in our heads to say anything at all. Nothing small enough to fit out our mouths and into the thick, hot air of the ward, filled with all the crazy sounds of every woman living on it.

August 27, 1999

When will the nurses notice that thumping noise coming through the door of Tammy's room? Most of the thumps are muffled, I can only count the loud ones. She has the Close Observation room across from the nursing station with a huge window in the door. Tammy rigged up a sheet she stole from the laundry room, so no one can see in. I don't need to look to know what she's doing. I should tell a nurse.

Except I haven't been outside in over two days. There's always some kind of "emergency" or a short-staffing crisis when it's supposed to be my turn for a fifteen-minute accompanied courtyard trip. It's actually more like ten minutes when you take into account the time it takes to get the elevator to come to our floor and then get to the bottom. There's the second loud bang from Tammy's room. Even though it's only ten measly minutes, it's always the best ten minutes of my day when I get to go, other than a visitor coming.

When I don't get to go outside, I go to my room and pound my fist on the plastic-coated bed. It makes a pathetic crinkly noise. I cry until my face and pillow are covered in snot. Heaving so hard I don't know how I'll get my chest to ever be calm again.

My nurse, Susan, promised I could go with her to the patio downstairs in three minutes. Now Tammy has ruined it with her thumping. I know she can't help it. And I know what they do to "calm her down." But I haven't been outside in forever. There she goes again. I just want to get out of here. Even for a minute.

I long to breathe fresh air. See the sky, hanging huge and open. Even if there still are four walls. It reminds me, one day I'll be like that again. Sprawl in large spaces I used to take for granted. No one to contain me. How can staff not hear the noise from Tammy's room and clue in that the self-harmer in the Close Observation room is at it again?

As soon as the nurses notice the thumping from Tammy's room they're going to call a ward "emergency." Code White. It's like bullies on the schoolyard. White medical coats trying to shove one person slightly closer to normal. Sanctioned by doctors. I know I should tell Susan before Tammy bashes in her eye or something. But I hate the way they call Code White over the PA system. It's like being in school when your name was called over the loudspeaker to go to the principal's office. Everyone knew you were in trouble. Except here, you don't get called down to an office because you can't go anywhere. It's a locked ward. They call for the Principal to come punish you.

CODE WHITE

When they call a Code White over the PA system, the first six psych assistants who arrive from any floor will bust into Tammy's room. Hold her down. One of the nurses will give her a needle while Tammy's in restraints. I can't decide if Tammy's better off bashing her head into the wall or restrained to her bed by six men and drugged unconscious. Why should I have to decide? Why should that be my job? All I want is to go outside. For once.

There's another loud thump. Number nine. Nurse Susan is almost right in front of me. I keep my face neutral, like I didn't hear. I know Tammy is in a trance. She doesn't know she's bashing her face in right now. I can't believe I'm even deliberating. I won't be able to live with myself.

"Okay, let's go," Susan says.

I take a deep breath. "I've heard at least ten thumps from Tammy's room," I tell her and stare at the floor.

"We'll have to postpone. It's a ward emergency. Go to your room," Susan says.

I hate watching the men come. Hearing Tammy scream when they pin her. If they were in an alleyway, wearing different clothes and ski-hats over their faces, it would look the same. Even though they're supposedly doing it for her own good.

Nurse Susan doesn't have to tell me to go to my room. I prefer to hide there with my headphones on and cry than watch. But I don't like being ordered like a little kid. The only choice I have is to refuse. Then they'll call a Code White on me. A double on the ward. I'm already on enough drugs against my will.

Tears stream down my face because the sun is shining a hard yellow smear across the sky today. And I could have been outside to feel it. For the first time since I've been on the ward I had put on my sunglasses. Now I have to take them off again.

I'm not a violent person, but I think this ward is making me turn into one. I want to throw my sunglasses at Nurse Susan's face. I want my old life back. Go outside any time I want. Never have to ask anyone. Didn't have to be accompanied. Didn't have to earn any privileges. I deserved to do what I wanted because I was me. It was my right. My behaviour wasn't policed by the threat of a Code White. People appreciated my help. Thanked me for it. Didn't order me like a three-year-old to be quarantined in my room.

I hear the eleventh thump. Nurse Susan runs toward the nursing station. Nothing is ever going to be okay with anyone of us on this ward. Nothing is going to be okay ever. Then I hear Nurse Susan's voice, as calm and steady as I am shaky and out of control.

"Code White, Code White, Code White."

If Tammy wasn't already a goner, she is now. I go to my room, shut the door and take off my sunglasses. Put on my headphones and turn on the music real loud. I'm too tired to hear anything else. I don't want to move until tomorrow. I don't want to see Tammy's window de-sheeted. Witness her strapped to her bed. Every pretense of privacy stripped away, again.

August 28, 1999

I woke in the same position I fell asleep. Like I rode the same spot on a record player all night. I had the worst charlie horse ever. My whole body was so stiff I could barely uncurl. I tried to roll over, but my room multiplied. Playing cards flipping. Still dopey from last night's sleeping pill. I kept hearing someone call my name, over and over. A fly I would swat if I had the energy to lift my heavy arms.

Something hits me. I realize this whole thing isn't a dream.

I'm really here. I'm institutionalized. Someone's calling me to the payphone down the hall. By the locked ward door. I feel like I'm going to vomit, but I push myself out of bed. Limp down the hallway. One leg crumpling underneath me.

I get to the phone. No one's standing there. The receiver isn't hanging upside down like it usually is when someone's coming to pick up a call. I ask at the nursing station. They look at me like I'm crazy. No one's called for over an hour. I feel stupid. Limp back to my room, my leg still threatening to collapse. The nurse who came out of the station watches me wobble back to my room. Doesn't ask about my leg. I feel like an idiot. That I'd think anyone would ever call me here.

August 29, 1999

Sadie was here for a little visit today. I'm now allowed one or two visitors other than Max and my parents. We sat at one of the tables in the kitchen. Across the room in the lounge someone was watching TV. I tried my best to follow our conversation. But there were too many distractions. The voices on the TV were so loud. People kept walking around us. Opening and shutting the fridge. Making tea. Pulling out chairs noisily, sitting down for only a second and then scraping the metal legs against the floor. The payphone kept ringing. People would answer. Write messages on the chalkboard. Holler for people. Nurses and psych assistants circled restlessly, like small moons around a large planet. How are we supposed to find quiet within ourselves and get better if it's always so loud on the ward?

I felt a hand holding mine. It was Sadie. She was still there. Her eyes big and warm.

"Hey," she said softly.

"Hey," I said. She leaned back in her uncomfortable chair. I tried to take back my hand, but she wouldn't let go.

"So, I see you get a lot of privacy here. A lot of quiet time to think?" Sadie said and burst out laughing. So did I. For a second it felt like I wouldn't stop. And then I felt Sadie's grip. Like something slipped from her calm eyes down the length of her strong arm, into the palm of her hand and through the skin of my wavering one. Suddenly, I felt a tiny bit different. My feet flatter on the floor. Something. Sadie had me. And even if it wasn't okay on the ward, it just was. It could just be. At least for the rest of Sadie's visit.

"You want some feedback on how to get through this, sweetie? I can see what a hard time this is," Sadie asked.

No one except Max had asked me what I'd wanted about anything. Definitely not the nurses or doctors. They talked for me or right through me. When everyone treats you like you don't exist, it's hard to remember you actually do. That you're not a ghost. It's weird when someone sees you. I tried not to cry.

"It's okay, Alex. Breathe."

I nodded.

"So the first thing – you have to calm down. Until you calm down no one will hear what you have to say. Know what I mean? It all works together. People will listen to whatever you say, once you are calm," Sadie said.

"I shouldn't have to be anything to get anyone to listen to me. You don't have to be anything to be heard. I never had to either. Why should I now?"

"I know, I know," Sadie said. "But life is about playing games. You know that. I know that. What you're really pissed about is being stuck here in the first place. Everything else is a by-product. Am I right?"

I didn't say anything.

"Just try to settle. Too many choices are making you manic. I know you don't want to hear this right now, but you need to slow it all down," Sadie said.

She was right. I didn't want to hear it. I hated Sadie at that moment. Wanted to pull away my hand. Send her away. What did she know about it? She was on the outside. Did whatever she wanted.

"You might want to think about withdrawing a bit at a time like this. Think about who you're reaching out to right now."

Flames raging. How could Sadie suggest I hole myself up here? I was supposed to stop all social contact? Because I was an embarrassment?

"What I mean, Alex, is there's a big difference between taking space out of shame, and taking space. Give yourself a buffer of privacy. You might really be thankful for that privacy later on. That's all I am saying."

We wound the visit down. I wondered when Sadie would come next. If she would come. I watched her leave, until the cluster of patients hovering by the payphone, arguing over whose turn it was to use it, blocked my view.

August 30, 1999

This is the truth. When I smell my armpits, each one smells different. One reeks of raunchy male sweat. The other of dainty female perspiration. No one will believe me, but it's true. I check every day, and every day the left is male and the right is female. I put anti-perspirant on both sides, so I don't know what gives. I tried to tell the nurses, but they just looked at me like I'm crazy.

I discovered my bi-gendered sweat two days before Jamie

arrived. I was in the kitchen when I first saw her come in the ward door with two nurses. Then three others swarmed her. I was wearing my checkered old man pants, my pink plastic soapbox stuffed down the front to represent the dick I thought I should have, and a Metallica T-shirt I'd slept in. My hair was matted in the back because I'd forgotten to brush it for a while. And even though all my instincts were now telling me the most unfamiliar fact that I was a boy, I still couldn't give up some of my old femme habits. Eye make-up from the day before, which I'd been too tired to wash off, was now riding a much wider surface area.

I watched the nurses explain some ground rules to Jamie, whose name I already knew from the outside, it being such a small queer community. I didn't know Jamie personally. And she didn't know me. But I'd seen her around. I wondered if she was nice. I wondered if we'd get along. I wondered what she was in here for. What was wrong with her.

I crammed ketchup-flavoured potato chips in my mouth. Licked my fingers, which were stained a salty red. Every time I came to a break in snacking, I'd whip out my compact. Reapply my bloody red lipstick. And then smear it off with more chips. I'd crunch extra hard, as loud as I could. Andrea, this bitchy anorexic girl who always got dressed and never wore her pjs during the day was trying to watch Oprah in the open-concept lounge. She kept turning around to glare at me. I didn't care. I wasn't here to win a popularity contest.

The gaggle of nurses blocked my view. *Is there ever a time when they don't get in the way*, I thought, just as they split. There was Jamie again. Resplendent in butch glory. I hoovered in her image: men's white dress shirt, tie, sweater vest, black pants and black cap. It felt like forever since I'd seen a dyke. Not one that was a friend, visiting out of pity, but a hot butch. Potential for something. Maybe. Not someone I wasn't allowed to flirt with because I was in a mental house, like Max. I wondered how Jamie smelled. I looked a mess. I checked my lipstick in the compact. Felt the soapbox with my other hand. Jamie looked at me just after I decided to hide in my room. I stood up too fast. Tripped. I'd forgotten I'd taken off one of my flip-flops under the table. It's hard to keep your balance in only one platform shoe. By the time I put on my shoe and stood up properly I could tell my face was bright red. My hand was shaking. Andrea was laughing at me; Oprah was on commercial. But Jamie was still looking. I made my way past her. That's when she winked. She winked at me. And then mouthed one word: *Later*.

The night nurses did their checks every fifteen minutes like they always do, noisily opening everyone's door. Shine a flashlight in your face. Not the greatest for people with sleeping problems. I tried to time the length of relative privacy I had until the next one came back. I jerked off hard thinking about Jamie's handsome face and small hands. I assumed she packed; it was just a question of what her dick looked like. I came in thirteen-minute intervals that night for hours, until the sleeping pill, exhaustion and bliss finally made me pass out.

August 31, 1999

I tried calling my work today from that annoying public payphone by the ward door. I should have used the one across from my room. Less traffic. Instead, three goddamn bitches were hovering, trying to get me to shut up and get off the phone, almost before I'd dialed. I couldn't believe how pushy they were. No concept of waiting their turn. You'd think I'd been on the phone for a marathon conversation. Going at it for hours all hard and heavy with a girl. But I wasn't. I was trying to have a professional conversation with one of my bosses to update him about my situation. From a mental hospital. Tentatively trying to see if I'd have my job when I got out. Those pushy bitches kept screeching how they needed the phone. Even though I'd only been on it for thirty seconds. They wouldn't stop yelling all this weird, crazy shit. I couldn't tell if my boss thought some of that crap was me. As if I couldn't control myself while talking on the phone with him for thirty stupid seconds. That I was that far gone. Not really the angle I was pushing. Trying to sell to my boss that I was normal, that I have always been fairly normal, and I'd be returning soon to work in his store again – normal. Yay, normal!

I kept waving in their faces to get them to quiet down. I wished I had a torch or a stick or something. I was trying to avoid yelling, *shut up, shut up* at them. For sure my boss would think I was crazy aggressive violent on the psych ward. Never work for him again. Goddamn phone hags.

Of course, they refused to go anywhere. And got louder. I couldn't understand why there was no psych assistant to escort them away. Someone on staff must've brought up a carton of doughnut holes. I couldn't hear a single thing my boss was saying. By the time I'd figure out what he had just said, he'd be onto something else. And then he was on to call waiting.

"Alex, I have another call. This is really important. Thanks for calling. Stay in touch," he said, and hung up on me.

The bottom sunk like an elevator going down really fast. I pretended to talk for a bit longer because I didn't feel like handing over the phone to any of those fuckfaces huddled in front of me. I didn't care if they could tell I was faking. I didn't have call waiting at my house. Could you fake an in-coming call, just to escape the one you were on?

I guess either way it didn't matter. My boss didn't sound sad our conversation was over. He hadn't sounded happy I'd called in the first place. And he didn't apologize that he cut me off short. All bad signs. I'd become another person, stopped being the amazing worker who'd been with him for years, and become a fucked up mental case who was never coming back. Good riddance.

September 1, 1999

We're sitting at one of the kitchen tables, me and Sunshine. Her real name's actually Edie, but I like to call her Sunshine. It sounds cliché, but if you ever saw Edie in action, you'd know that's how it had to be. Her mess of blonde dreadlocks waves around her face like the arms of the sun.

Sunshine caught me writing in my journal and insisted on a whole page just for her. She made me write down a whole bunch of stuff about her future as a rock star. Sunshine's going to be famous someday. She's convinced.

"Just you watch," she tells me. "You'll be able to say you knew me when."

I doubt if Sunshine gets to be famous that she'd really want me spreading stories about how she was in a mental ward. Even if they're true. But she's right. Whenever Sunshine does get famous, I'll be able to say, *I knew Sunshine when.*

After all the rock star stuff and some really weird songs that didn't make any sense, Sunshine wanted me to write about this friend of hers, Sage, who she's worried about. Sage is this junkie who somehow ended up living with Sunshine and Sunshine's kid.

"But she's not like a real junkie," Sunshine qualified. "She is so cool. She's the nicest junkie you'd ever meet. But she uses. That's the only thing. We try to mellow her out with pot, but it never works. She always goes back to the bad stuff."

I wonder where Sage keeps her needles. If Sunshine's kid ever found any by mistake. Poked himself. There was all this other stuff that kept coming out of Sunshine's mouth. Faster and faster. I put down my pen when I'd had enough. She leaned across the table.

"You need to finish. This needs to be documented, man. We need to write this down," she said, her eyes bright.

It was hard to keep up. I didn't remember applying to be her secretary. She kept rapping what she wanted me to write down. I was laughing too hard to hold the pen. We'd crawl awkwardly onto our hands and knees looking for the pen, giggling. The nurses kept looking at us. After a while one of the psych assistants, Anna, came and sat in one of the cube sofa chair things, half-watching us and half-watching the TV. As though if she was there we'd just go somewhere else and be quiet without her actually having to say, *Tone it down*. It just made us laugh harder.

Then Sunshine's eyelids started going half-mast. Pale pink covered her eyes like a puffy pillowcase. I could see tiny blue and purple delicate veins on the pillowcases, a fishbone pattern. I couldn't see Sunshine's eyes or the light that always streamed from them. She'd become zombie Sunshine. Not really there.

Except she was, because her mouth kept moving. Faster and faster. I couldn't distinguish one word from another. Like she wasn't speaking words at all. She told five stories simultaneously, staggering through them all. Winding them like threads turning on one of her friend's hair wraps into a tight, brightly coloured cord.

"Sage is into the full graffiti action. She sprays and spits onto the walls of the streets: *Beauty is our only weapon.* That's Sage. She's even gotten my son into it. We do the graffiti in our apartment, too, all of us. All over the walls. Fuck it, the landlord is a total prick. What do we care? We wrote on the floor, but that didn't work. We had to wash it, but Sage was out scoring by then, so I was left to clean the floor. We're trying to transfer all this graffiti into a book so everyone can admire our stuff. I'm a huge rock star, don't you know? I'm a rock star with a sore throat. I have to get better in time to record all my music."

I missed whole chunks, my hand was killing me. Sunshine was talking so fast I couldn't follow anymore. Every sentence an iridescent bubble catching the sunlight before the next word of hers popped it. It didn't add up to much. If Sunshine was on a stage, in a fancier costume, with people dancing around her there wouldn't be any difference between her and the rock stars in videos on TV. She was that charismatic. Her sparkle shone in your eye and led you towards her. Left a sweet taste in your mouth and made you want more. When she wasn't freaking you out. But it was the same light as all those famous people. She just wasn't famous. And she couldn't turn it down. Not a single bit.

As I watched her, babbling across the table from me, her arms waggled in the air and even though there were only two, it seemed like more. That there was so much more of her. Everywhere was decorated. Her wrists were covered in bracelets made from coloured embroidery thread, beads, boondoggle, leather strips tied through heavy shells. Quick dandelion gold floss fingers.

"We gotta give Sage love," she advised me, as if I could do something. "There's no other way. Sage needs love or she'll fall apart."

September 2, 1999

I finally found out the name of another pill I take. The blue one is called Lorazepam. It dissolves when I put it under my tongue.

September 3, 1999

Now that I'm so sensitive to colour, I can see gold shading around Sadie's head. I don't care if anyone thinks that's crazy. It's not. At least not to me. That cloud follows her everywhere. I watch it when we talk. It never leaves, not even when she walks out the ward door. It follows her out this shithole to the other side. Sometimes when she visits Sadie catches me staring at her head.

"What the hell are you looking at?" she says. "Is my hair messed?"

"No, it looks good," I say.

"Are you sure?" she asks. "Cause I can take it if I'm having a bad hair day, Alex. I would rather know than walk around looking like crap."

And then I have to make sure Sadie knows her hair is great. I don't explain about the gold smudges, even though I bet Sadie would understand. I don't want to chance anything. Don't want to lose the few people on my side. I don't want them to look at me and see only this ward and me on it, needing to be here. I'm still Alex. Even if I'm on this side of the door right now. So I keep it to myself. I wonder what happens to the gold when Sadie washes her hair? But I don't need to know all the answers.

"It's not for you to revolutionize this place. You aren't here to redesign how they run mental houses. Though I'm sure you have great ideas. They don't want your ideas. They want your subservience," Sadie says.

"But – "

" – It's your job to get better," Sadie says. Her eyes take up all the space instead of anything I want to say next. I don't want the job she's talking about. I want something better.

"Trick them by playing their game. Then you'll be allowed to leave. Until then, you have to keep your opinions to yourself. No matter how smart you are, this is not the place for it. Don't talk to anyone," she warns.

I disagree. I refuse to willingly let this place squelch everything out of me. I start to rant. And then suddenly, we're surrounded by one of her gold clouds. The shine of the metallic pixels energizes me. Somehow, I know it will all work out. I'll be okay in here. I know I'll get out. As long as I play the game Sadie has laid out. Don't tackle every snake in my path. Find every ladder I can. Even though it goes against my instincts. Sadie is trying to show me how to get there. In camouflage.

September 4, 1999

Jean sings *Ave Maria*. Her favourite song. Slashes of yellow stream brightly out of the activity room. A sharp, lemony yellow cutting into you. Slicing through whatever you were in the middle of thinking. Coating you thick canary yellow. Flutter of wings in your face. The threat of fierce beak at any second. The sound of Jean glares a piercing sunshine in my eyes, a shrillness in my ears. Her yellow is everywhere, ringing in the halls. It won't stop.

September 5, 1999

    I made the nurse write stuff down in one of my notebooks so I can keep track of things. They feed me pills non-stop. Five minutes after I take one pill, some lady taps me on the shoulder with a little plastic cup of water and more pills. I'm surprised I have any room left to eat with all those pills stuffed down there.

    It's the same with meals. I never know when it's time to eat. Sometimes it seems like weeks between lunch and dinner. But sometimes I've only managed to have a smoke and they're already serving dinner before I've even summoned up a fart from lunch. You'd think in an institution like this they'd do things the same time every day. But so far I haven't figured out the schedule. Someone needs to give me the *TV Guide* for this place so I can get organized.

    They write the day of the week in a squeaky, smelly pen on this white board in the lounge near the nursing station. Every day one of the nurses wipes off the day before but yesterday is never fully gone, only scattered in strange inky specks across the board. For all of us who can't retain the logical sequence of information from the day before, the nurse squeaks in a red or green or blue marker whether it is a Monday or a Thursday and completes the pattern. She also fills in what month it is, and the date. Often in the smoke room, one of us will ask what day it is, but none of us ever remembers. Almost every day is the same on the ward.

    "Go check the board," someone will say and we just nod.

    There isn't any other marker here for me to keep track of the days, other than my journals. A document of what happens when. Of what makes a day what. If the nurses wanted to screw with us, they could write it all wrong on the board some morning. We'd think it was a Friday when it was really a Wednesday. I don't know how many people would catch on.

I can't keep track of when they do the blood tests here, either. The blood nurse wears plastic thrift shop jewellery. Latex gloves she can never just quietly slide on. She always has to put them on with a loud snap. I sit in the chair. It's dark behind my eyelids. I usually fall back asleep sitting up. Occasionally I wake up from the nods. Loose head on rubbery neck. Hungover from whatever drugs they gave me. The snapping sound of her gloves calls up all the latex gloves I've put on in my life before I slipped into some hot girl. Latex gloves are never going to be the same again. Ever. They are not one bit sexy. Especially when Bernice the blood nurse wears them. Her fake gold bracelet frames the top of the furled glove in a cheap jangle. Bernice wears glasses on strings around her neck. The strings are neon orange. Her glasses perch on the tip of her nose, like they're about to fall off.

I make a fist for Bernice. She uses one hand to push up her glasses. The nosepads clutch her nose like tiny bird feet on a branch. She lightly slaps the pale crook of the inside of my elbow with the tips of her fingers. Like tossing dough. Her long, copper nails flutter like the wings of some exotic bird taking flight. I hope she finds what she's looking for. I turn my head when she brings out the needle.

"No offense," I tell her every time. "I'm not being rude. I just don't want to faint. I don't like the sight of my own blood."

"No problem," Bernice says.

Bernice is a woman of few words. She changes vials. I know because I can hear the second one clink in her lap as it lands and her nails click together in the complicated twisting process. *Flap, flap.* Each vial has a different-coloured lid. I wonder what the code is.

When Bernice is finished, I always feel dizzy. I'm seeing spots. The room is sinking. Sliding from side to side, like a boat. I go back to my room. Hold tight to my pillow. Will the spots to disappear. Make everything slow down. Usually I fall back asleep. Someone wakes me for breakfast, whenever that is. I check my notebook. I got one nurse to explain to me. She wrote down they only serve muffins for breakfast on the weekends. Not any other days. *Don't ask for them,* she said. There's a lot in here I'm not supposed to ask for. Not supposed to want. One weekend day, I haven't figured out which, they serve blueberry muffins and also corn muffins. The other day they only serve bran muffins and carrot muffins. Who decided what should be paired together? I like the carrot. I always check to make sure there are no raisins. If I'm late for breakfast the carrot ones are eaten. Then there's only bran muffins and I have to wait until lunch to eat. I hate bran muffins even more than I hate raisins.

One time I asked a nurse to write down when I see Bernice. It seems like I'm summoned all the time. But I know that can't be true. What would they need so much blood for anyway? If it were true, I'd have pinpricks running down my arms. Big splotchy bruises stained all over. I'd look like a blueberry muffin cut wide open, without the butter. Berries bleeding into the batter.

I forgot what the nurse told me. I rifled through my notebooks. There are several of them now to sort through. They multiply like coat hangers. Then I find it written in strange handwriting. Lots of squiggles, like a teenaged girl reapplying her lip gloss in a food court. *Check Epival level every Tuesday – blood test.*

CODE WHITE

I can deal with once a week. Every week, see Bernice's birds take flight. But then I wonder, have I already seen Bernice this week or am I going to see her soon? I can't remember. I forget what day of the week this is. And I'm nowhere near that white board to check. It's really hard to be organized in here. It's frustrating. And I'd also like to know how many more days until I get a carrot muffin. On that day, I don't want to be late for breakfast. I guess that's what they call incentive here.

September 6, 1999

Tammy has excellent boundary skills. Puts up her walls super fast. Not even a tentative shrug of apology. Utterly inspiring. I wish I could be like her. Blunt and to the point. A sharp knife slitting through a soft slab of butter. All back-off-and-no-one-near-her, toughness I want to wear like a weathered leather jacket that's been somewhere. Even if she likes the person, Tammy will bark, "Leave me alone. I'm in a fuckin' bad mood," if she thinks they want something from her or just feels like it.

Then Tammy turns her moon face to the wall. I watch Tammy do this over and over to people. That's what she needs to do. There aren't a lot of places on the ward where you can be alone. I wish I could be like Tammy the next time someone wants to talk to me and I just can't bear to open my mouth. Or have their words press down on me. I want to tell them not to say one single thing to me. Drag my wooden workhorse in the middle of the dirt road. Drape a bunch of caution tape. Go sit behind it.

September 6, 1999

I have to remember Max is like a turtle in its shell. Rather than coax her out, I need to engage her when she comes out. Otherwise, she's too shy. Has to hide or leave. I don't want scare her away.

I think about her all the time. Yet, when she visits, I can't stop acting like the biggest idiot. I don't know what's wrong with me. Every single thing I do and say horrifies me. Like I'm standing there with my pants pulled down, a yellow puddle at my feet. She always sits there and takes it. Smiling that same beautiful smile right at me. I have no idea why. Anyone else visiting me would have stopped a long time ago. Max has a lot of patience.

September 7, 1999

I thought I had it bad. I was at the gym with Tammy and two psych assistants, Anna and Doug. I bounced a basketball around the gym, trying to calm down using the repetitive rhythm. I don't know if that trick works or not. Tammy sat in the corner. Hugged her knees to her chest. A small group of patients from another floor came in with their own psych assistants. This one guy didn't have shoelaces in his sneakers. He ran around like he was on speed. His shoes were too loose. The tongues flopped all over. He kept tripping. His shoes almost looked like they weren't shoes at all, but something different. Something that framed his feet, but left them undone. Vulnerable. I could see his white socks were grey with dirt. Then he almost fell into me. Landed on the floor. I offered to help pick him up. You never touch anyone in a mental ward without asking first.

"Are you okay?" one of his psych assistants called out. It looked like a hard fall.

"Sure," he said and brushed off his hands like it was all part of his plan.

"Why did you take your shoelaces out if you keep falling?" I asked him quietly.

"I didn't take them out. They did," he said, motioning to the psych assistants. "My nurse confiscated them."

I didn't get it. Why would a nurse want his gross laces? He read the confused look on my face. Grinned. One of his front teeth had a tiny chip at the bottom. I wanted to touch it.

"I might use them for something they aren't intended for." He said it like he was proud. Like it was this huge accomplishment. And then he ran away and almost tripped again.

He could tie his laces together. Choke himself with them. All a nurse would find during her fifteen-minute check was his dead body. A puffed blue face. And empty shoes. Now his shoes won't stay together, but he's still alive.

Gym time over, chauffeured back upstairs to the smoke room. No one else here for once. At least they didn't take my shoelaces. I'd have no dignity left if they did. Before I went to the gym it felt like I didn't have any dignity left. I guess I do.

I think about the boy from the gym. Running into walls like he was trying to get out. Caged. Not caring how much it hurt because he was already gone. Crazy sloppiness the nurses deem order. I look down at my laces and smile. They're mine. I wouldn't give them up for anyone.

September 7, 1999

Candice is a volunteer here. She has a laminated piece of official-looking hospital paper that outlines what each of the codes mean pinned to her shirt. I've heard so many codes being called over the loudspeaker that I'm hungry for them. Hungry for knowledge. I want to taste her smooth laminate on my tongue. Transfer the codes like a sublingual pill. Let my saliva dissolve the colours until I'm swollen with forbidden, classified information.

I ask her if she can stay with me for a couple of minutes. If I can have her permission to write down the codes from her tag in my notebook. Candice is a laid-back volunteer, more amused than frightened by the antics of the "crazy" patients. Fodder for stories to tell her friends on the weekend at the pub. She opts to humour me. Sits while I copy down the coveted information. The information that unlocks the hidden language of the ward. **Black** – Bomb Threat. **Blue** – Medical Emergency. **Green** – Evacuation. **Red** – Fire. **White** – Disruptive Behaviour. **Yellow** – Missing Patient.

I think about all the colours that are missing. Things that could be on this list, but aren't. Many are behaviours I realize they would just deem "disruptive." I think about how Candice, a volunteer, knows that if they call Code Black on the loudspeaker it means a bomb threat and all of us patients on the ward wouldn't know shit. We wouldn't know our lives would be in danger. Candice thinks it's funny I'm so interested in the codes. That I care at all mystifies her. The look on her face is the same one people get when their puppy does something cute and unexpected.

I want to be a Code Yellow. Go missing. Where would I go? Where could I call home? Who could I let know everything about me and not be afraid, not have things as loud and obvious as the sound of my meds rattling in their pill bottles between us? Maybe I don't want to be missing. Maybe I already am. Absent. But I really don't want to be a Code White. I don't ever want to be a code called on this floor. To be figured out. Pinned down. Managed.

Candice watches how hungrily I write down the chart. She

says in her annoyingly perky voice that is meant to engage me, "I feel privileged I know the colours."

"You are privileged in a lot of ways," I tell her. I am jealous, but resigned.

"Thank you," she answers politely, completely missing my point. Just like most of the staff, every time I open my mouth. She just doesn't get it. But it's okay, I'm getting used to being invisible.

"I have a fear of fire. Also of heights. I hope there's never a fire here. That they never have to call a Code Red," Candice shares.

Candice isn't locked in a ward without a key. She doesn't have anything to worry about if there is a fire here. I clench my teeth.

"Thanks for letting me copy down your codes," I say and smile. I don't tell her what I really think of her and her stupid velvet shirt. Or of her fucking codes that box me in until I can't breathe. Even without a fire. I don't say anything, because I might need something from her again someday. That's just how things work around here. I guess I'm afraid of fire, too. I don't want to burn my bridges now that I'm thinking a bit more clearly. Now that I see I won't be leaving for a long time.

ced # three

September 8, 1999

Woke up before breakfast freezing and covered in sweat. Soaked through my hospital bottoms and my sheet. Totally gross. I didn't want to leave my bed for breakfast, except I was starving and so cold I couldn't keep lying there. I tried to get dressed before anyone opened my door. My whole body shivered. Could feel the crank in me coiled tight, ready to snap in anyone's face if they got too close. What made me most sad was trying to remember what I dreamed. I couldn't remember anything. I reached deep down. Came up with soggy handfuls of mulched paper. Snapshots from the night before, soaked too long in those hard to reach places. Left with a feeling I can't shake that a lot of things are being erased. I don't know if once I leave I'll be able to get any of it back.

September 8, 1999

That weirdo lawyer guy's been bugging me ever since him and the naturopath came to visit Sunshine. They were watching me on the other side of the ward door when I was on the phone with someone. I don't remember who. A patient was buzzed out so I dropped the phone for a minute. The receiver clanged against the wall as I poked my head out and barked at them, "What're you looking at? We're not animals at the fucking zoo, you know."

Then I ducked back inside the ward. I didn't want to be considered trying to escape and have a Code White called to subdue me. I continued my phone call thinking *that was the most outside the ward all on my own that I'd been since I got here. Telling those assholes off felt like throwing firecrackers.*

I guess the lawyer guy liked what he saw because now he keeps calling the ward to talk to me. Sunshine must've told him my name, which I don't appreciate. I don't have anything to say to him. I think he's a lot older than me. In his forties or fifties. All I do is read him off lists of things to buy for me, like nail polish and office supplies so I can get organized. I have a lot to do.

Today on the phone he says, "I really appreciate you giving me these things to do. It's nice getting things for you."

And I was like, "Why? What do you want from me?"

He had some non-descript answer. Something about how he finds me a very "interesting" person. And enjoys talking with me.

I wondered if he understood properly what the deal was. That I was locked up in here, so there was no chance I was going to fuck him. And that even if I wasn't, there still was no chance I would sexually service some creepy lawyer in exchange for Post-its, Scotch Tape and lipstick. Not in exchange for anything. I'd take whatever he wanted to give me and that was it.

"I think it's odd that an older man like yourself is paying all this attention to a younger woman in a mental hospital. Buying me all this shit even though all we ever do is talk on the phone. But if it makes you happy, then go to town. Just don't expect anything back from me. I'm not interested," I said.

I didn't bother adding I was a dyke. That was my business. I'd already piqued the oddball factor for him. I didn't want him to get visions of girl-on-girl shows as some sort of gratuity for all the office supplies and attention. Then I hung up. It felt as firm as a spanking when I smacked the receiver down.

September 8, 1999

The thick cardboard crinkles when I pull it out of the envelope.

"Go on," Max says. "I didn't bring this for anyone else. Open it!"

The weight of the paper, heavy in between my fingers makes me shy. It's all too substantial. I can't picture Max, off this ward and in her apartment, thinking of me in her bedroom, cardboard and scissors and glue and pencil crayons laid out across her duvet. Sitting cross-legged, hunched over this card. Wasting time on me. Making something she doesn't have to.

"I know I'm not a very good artist, but seriously. I'm starting to get insulted here, lady," she jokes.

I pull the card Max made for me the rest of the way out of the envelope. It is beautiful. Bright colours and flash that almost hurts my eyes. Too good to put on my wall here and let anyone else ever see it. I know I'll hide it somewhere safe in my room. Sneak peeks at it constantly. Trace the abstract design with my finger.

"You're going to get out of here, Alex. Just remember that. Even when it's beginning to feel like this is all there is. It isn't. There's more. You're going to get there," Max says, her face flushed. "I know it."

I stare at Max's face for too long. I wish I was already out of this place. A million times over.

"Thanks, Max," I say, and gently touch her thigh, which is right next to me on my bed. Something jumps.

"Don't be silly," she says. "It's nothing," and lightly

CODE WHITE

punches me in the arm, throwing my hand off her. "Here," she shoves a pile of magazines at me that she's grabbed out of her knapsack. "I brought these for you. Help you pass the time. Figured you're probably really bored in here."

My hands are full of magazines. A stack. Sharp, glossy paper cutting into my palms and threatening to slide to the floor.

"Thanks, Max. You really didn't have to go to the trouble," I answer, afraid she'll stop coming if it means she has to keep bringing things and buying a whole bunch of crap every time she comes.

"No trouble," she smiles. "Enjoy."

September 8, 1999

In the washroom there are boxes of toilet seat protectors on the walls. They even have a sheet of instructions mounted on the wall next to the box. I never realized before that people need to be told how to use a toilet seat protector. Any time I ever used one, I just grabbed one and laid it out on the seat. No instructions needed. Usually I hover. But that's just me. I wonder if this list of instructions is displayed in every public restroom? Or is this special for mental patients? Are we particularly incompetent?

PLEASE FOLLOW INSTRUCTIONS FOR USE:

1. Pull up and then down.
2. Break the perforation in middle of sheet.
3. Lay on toilet bowl with centre flap of sheet in the bowl.
4. Flush sheet after usage.

Seems simple. I decide to add my own helpful toilet protector hint to the sheet.

5. Beware of tiny limbo dancers coming under the door while you are trying to use toilet protector!

September 9, 1999

I made this sign on the door to my room. It was up for maybe twenty minutes before some nurse took it down. Then she chased me to discuss why it wasn't "appropriate." Each word was a burst of light. Only, she couldn't see it. All my positive intentions. And now she won't let me keep the sign up. Some people put up homemade, "Do Not Disturb" signs on their door, if they don't want people to bug them. I decided I really want people to talk to me. People should reach out if that's what their instincts tell them. We're only on this planet a short time. If people want to embrace each other, they should. And if the person people want to embrace is ME, I want them to know they're welcome to knock on my door any time. So I made this sign saying: "THERE'S NO SUCH THING AS DISTURBANCE. I welcome being 'disturbed.' I will always have time for everyone who needs it! I promise."

"You need to concentrate on yourself, Alex. And develop better boundaries. You're not here to be constantly available to other patients. You're here to get better. And so are they. We all just need to work on ourselves," she said in a patronizing way.

My sign started out as a good thing. Now, it was heinous. At this point, I *was* feeling disturbed. You couldn't do anything good in this place. You couldn't be yourself and you couldn't offer to do anything nice. But, if you felt too sad and actually stopped talking to everyone like the staff told you to, the staff circled you like vultures. They'd pick at you to talk to other patients. So you wouldn't be isolated and lose all the great social skills you'd come in with. You just couldn't win.

I listened to the nurse bleat her horn about boundaries as she held my beautiful sign. I decided to make clearer boundaries between us. Draw thick lines between me and her in lieu of being allowed an actual wall or a lock on the door. In my imagination, I smeared them across the floor with the oily yellow pads of butter from meals. I ripped off each waxed paper top from the square packet before turning it over and making my mark with a mushy, dragging movement. My sign looked stupid in her hand. The letters looked like a five-year-old drew them. I didn't want her to take it. I had a bad feeling she'd stick it in the file they were making about me, the one in those orange binders I never got to see and figured I never would. The file that was constantly "In Progress" even when I wasn't.

When the nurse was done honking and there were enough greasy lines between us to keep her contained, I asked for my sign back.

"Could you please explain why you want it, Alex?" she asked.

I didn't want to get into it. Why was it okay for her to put me in the position of having to justify wanting something back that was mine in the fucking first place? I wanted to point out that if she was lecturing me about better boundaries, perhaps she should work on hers. That it wasn't exactly "normal" behaviour to steal someone's things and then make that person beg for it back with a huge explanation of why they deserved it. But I didn't want her to have that piece of me. So I had to promise I wouldn't put it on my door anymore. As if I'd even want to after all this. I put some pretend butter on my tongue before I spoke. Salty sweetness coated the roof of my mouth a slick yellow glow so it was, but it wasn't really, me saying what she wanted to hear. Each letter a pastel greasy shine.

September 9, 1999

I'm still not allowed many visitors. The nurses decide who gets in and who doesn't. That lawyer guy must've left the package for me at the nursing station. Inside was an expensive MAC compact I had asked for in just the right shade for my skin. Also this really ugly teddy bear with a green bow around its neck. I hate teddy bears. I gave it to Tammy for her collection. She was so happy. She named it Freddy. There was also a creepy note. I'm going to avoid his calls for a while. Maybe from now on. Except, maybe I'll need more stuff. His desire to get me things can definitely come in handy. Especially if I don't really talk to him.

September 10, 1999

I'm like a campfire out of control. The nurses tell me to slow down. Get "stabilized." Whatever that means. Thoughts leak like an accident I can't hold. I'm jealous of everyone else's privileges on the ward. How they can hold their own smokes and lighters. All the passes they get. The common goal is to work our way up the ladder with each privilege. And then get out. I'm at the bottom. Staring up. I have no gold stars on my chart.

If I were a better person, I'd mind my own business. Not care who has what. I'd focus on the work I need to do to fix myself. Then maybe I wouldn't be so miserable. Sometimes in here, I don't feel like a very good person anymore. Even though this place is supposed to help us get better.

CODE WHITE

September 11, 1999

I don't see how I could ever complain about the weather again, having gone without it for so long.

Daytime TV talk shows and evening sitcoms drone incessantly in the lounge, fan hums in the smoke room, every woman holds a cigarette, inhales or exhales, taps her ash or puts it out when she's done, begs and makes demands of her nurse, food is a bland mishmash on paper plates, thick black mould lines the bottom of every rubber bathmat. The tubs are always decorated with traveling-size, gem-coloured bottles. Bath supplies left by women trying to stake a claim. Every few days a nurse does a sweep and returns the bottles to their rightful owners. Scolds them for leaving toiletries in the communal washroom.

"This isn't your home," the nurse reminds. As if we all don't realize that every second we're here. "There has to be space for everyone to put their things out when they shower."

Liberty for hygiene. She should relax. I'm not going to break down the walls of the Bastille to get a little legroom for my Salon Selectives.

"Keep all your things in your room. Don't keep anything you'd hate to see stolen here at all," she tells us.

Where am I supposed to keep myself?

Here, I know time has passed when the shape of the pill changes. Or the colour. Or amount. Not because yesterday the sun was shining and today it's raining. But because yesterday Mary took six pills and today she's taking eight. Today Mary wants orange juice with her meds. And that's okay because she has so many new pills. In a week, even a couple of days, there'll be no more orange juice.

I miss the weather. The real marker of time. I'm becoming

acclimatized to the ways of marking things here, on the inside. It's raining if drops stream down the scratched windows that don't open. They serve the horrendous chicken stir-fry every Wednesday. Four days will pass before Mary will wash her pyjamas. Tammy never washes her clothes. Maybe in secret. Maybe she hides in her room naked until her matching windbreaker and pants are ready to come out of the drier, because she wears exactly the same thing every day. Nothing else fits her.

I want sun on my face. Rain making my hair wet. I want to be stuck without an umbrella in a downpour. Utterly soaked. I want to smell hot dog stands and bus exhaust, feel the spring of grass under my feet. The hardness of pavement. I want to watch out for shit and gum. Kick leaves. Wear shoes. I'm tired of slippers.

I want to be off the ward. Not trapped in other people's predetermined cycles of laundry, meals, florescent lights, fifteen-minute patient checks. I want to go outside. Sticky, freezing, wet, humid, sunny, icy, hot, stormy, grey, snowy, sweaty. And when I do, I'll never complain about any of it.

September 12, 1999

In the smoke room we talk quietly about our drugs. I don't really say anything. Partly because I can't remember what drugs the nurses have me on or how often they give them to me. But more, I just don't want anyone else to know. It's my business. I wrap the information around me tight, like my ratty housecoat. Even though anyone who lives here can see everything. It's nice to pretend. Especially while I'm snooping on other people. My eyes are pretty wide open on this ward.

Mary and Tammy talk about all the different meds they've

been on since they got here. It's a reeling shopping list that bounces to the floor like an old-fashioned scroll. Almost every drug they rattle off I've never heard of. Then they each bring out a new scroll. All the different drugs they've been on their entire lives. Meds for all the times they were on other wards. Or weren't in a hospital at all.

I wonder how early they developed their mental illnesses, but I don't want to ask. Mary starts laughing and can't stop. She's trying to calculate how many pills she's taken over her entire life. Enough to fill her whole body? I picture her and Tammy drowning in the Ikea ball room. No red and yellow and blue balls, instead, the room is jammed to the ceiling with all the pills they've ever swallowed. Tammy starts laughing too and pulls out another smoke. She tries to choke out the question of exactly how many milligrams of medication she's ingested in her whole life. Except she can't stop laughing.

"Do you have any idea how much a milligram is?" Mary cackles.

I actually have no clue. Tammy hoots again and I start up, too. I think about how tiny one pill really is. About how many milligrams are in some medications. Twenty-five. Fifty. One hundred. One hundred and fifty. Two hundred. Five hundred. That's just in one pill. How can you tell what's in one milligram? How can you tell what one milligram will do? I only knew grams when it came to drugs. A gram of pot, rolled up in baggy. A gram of hash, flattened onto a penny for safekeeping. Not a milligram. Would one milligram fit onto the head of a pin?

"I've probably beat the fucking world record for milligram consumption of meds," Tammy hollers.

Laughing, we roll on the floor. Our eyes are wet and our

stomachs catch. Tammy flips one of the cheap foil ashtrays with her foot by accident. Charred filters jump in an explosion of dull grey confetti. The snow coats the leg of Tammy's silky tearaway pants. A burnt mess. It only makes us all howl harder. I feel like picking up the remaining ashtrays and winging them around. I can tell the others do, too. The flash in their eyes. But, in a second, a nurse comes. Peeks in the window. She opens the door.

"Keep it down," she says and walks out. Leaves us covered in grey ash.

September 12, 1999

"Here, Alex," Max says, looking up when she's finished carefully writing on a thick rubber band she's gently stretched across the top of a book. Drops the pen in her lap, covered in those beige chinos she likes to wear. I picture Max at home, running the iron in a calm, smoothing hiss over the material to work in a crisp crease. Deliberate. I worry for a minute the pen might leak. Leave a stain. Ruin the respectable, clean look. Those tailored pants hide so many buried secrets underneath their carefully pressed fabric. This boy could iron away all her wrinkles momentarily, but I can still see inside. Max needs the beige unmarred. To keep blending her in wherever she goes.

"Hey, Alex?" Max says, ducking her head to catch my eye. Sometimes, it's hard to pay attention when Max is around. Max holds out her hand. I stare, memorizing all its parts for later. So I can imagine what it would feel like next to mine in exact detail. Max is too shy to allow me to stare at her ever. Flustered, she slips on a curmudgeonly, defensive gruff like a big, bulky sweater to hide behind if she catches me looking at her.

CODE WHITE

"Cut it out," she'll say and smile, trying not to. Her voice getting deeper. A bit hoarse.

I suck in the details before Max notices. Nails so closely cropped at the edges that what's left looks like it hurts. Sore for whatever she might touch. Thick blue veins crawl across the surface. Up past her wrists and buried deep in her forearms, which poke out of her oversized jersey. Resting on her palm is the elastic she's customized for me. A pearl riding on a black, velvet cushion. Pristine.

I feel too shy to take it. To meet Max's eyes. I don't deserve gifts. Max has already given me too much. I'm one of those parasites. Desperately sucking her host dry. It's too much that Max is still there, in my room. That she keeps coming to see me. On a mental ward. Even when I'm unwashed. Ragged and unkempt. Hair knotted and wild. Sleep probably still hanging in yellow chunks in my eyes because I'm too afraid of the water and the gross sinks on the ward to wash.

I stare at the ugly floor. Part of the crappy blue blanket is dragging on the ground, getting dirty. I don't care. I'll still sleep with it tonight, pull it over me later once I'm cold. I can feel Max sitting across from me, looking at me. Patient. Why? I'm afraid of what she'll find. Of what Max won't find. My face feels extra greasy.

I'm ridiculous. I don't deserve any of it. Why is Max still coming to visit? I'm shit. My eyes start getting wet. I think of soggy grapes leftover in a fruit cocktail cup. Bobbing in all that syrup. I dig my nails into my palms to stop my grape-eyes from spilling juice onto my cheeks. I don't deserve pearls. I'm garbage. Can't Max see?

"Here, Alex," Max says softly, leaning towards me. "Take this, it's for you."

I want to ask her to hold me, to just spoon me on my bed. Even though the crinkling from the mattress and pillow would embarrass me. Even though the blanket is dragging and dirty. Even though I'm dirty.

Each time Max visits, I try to remember she's here because she wants to be. No one makes her come. I look into her eyes. At the softness she lets me see in this particular moment. Unveiling something that hides so far back, not many people know it's there.

Every time I flirt too much with her, Max blushes and tells me to stop. I know I should cut it out, but when I see her I can't help it. I wish things weren't the way they are. Max is a gentleman. Told me last time, *This isn't the right time for you to be with anyone. This isn't the right place.* Then she filled me in on the latest gossip. It was like opening and shutting a door. Any tension that had been there just disappeared. For the most part. I laughed as she told me about what was happening with a few couples and a bunch of other people we knew. Happy to hear some news that didn't revolve around the nurses' schedule and medication times.

So today, I didn't ask Max about spooning. Even though I really need to be held by someone. Have needed it for a long time. I already knew the answer. Even though the only person I can think of in the whole world that I would feel safe lying next to, even out of all the girls I've ever slept with, is Max. I just wanted Max. But I can wait.

"See this?" Max asks, referring to the elastic band. "I know it's only an elastic, but I want you to have it. I want you to take it."

And then Max reaches out her hand. I try not to shrink as I let Max see me. Try not to be afraid she'll leave the room once it's sunk in for her who is in front of her. But Max is still sitting across from me, the hand with the elastic resting casually by her side.

"Are you sure you want to give this to me?" I ask.

"This is for you," Max starts again, and with gentle firmness, takes my wrist in one of her hands and lowers it to the bed.

Max lets go of my wrist. Like it's a hard thing for her to do. It still feels like she's holding me. I know that even though Max will leave soon, that her visit will be over, we'll still be connected. Even though I'll still be on the ward. I know Max won't forget about me in here. That we will find each other when the time is right. After I get released from the ward. Whenever that is supposed to happen. We'll find each other.

"Alex, I made this for you. It says, 'Remember Who You Are,' because I think you are the most amazing person. You are so strong and smart and funny and beautiful. And I think being sick and being in here, you are forgetting *who* Alex is. You're forgetting all the things you are that the rest of us know and adore."

I know my eyes look like the little runny pots of paint from Arts & Crafts that Colleen lets us use. I don't have a lid to keep everything inside. I don't want Max to see she's making me cry.

"Hey, Alex, it's okay," Max says earnestly.

"Mmm," I sniffle.

"Listen, Alex, every time you're feeling shitty, look down at this elastic on your wrist. Think about it. Give it a little snap, or whatever you need to do to get back to yourself. But do it. Do whatever you need to do to stop losing yourself. That would be the biggest gift you could give me," Max finishes.

And then she puts it around my wrist. I feel like I'm wearing a diamond bracelet instead of an old rubber band. Suddenly, we're both too shy to say anything.

September 13, 1999

I demand that a nurse write down the name of the medicine they've given me every night before I go to sleep, even though I don't want it. I insist I'll go to sleep on my own. But they make me take it. I'm afraid if I take a stand they'll do something worse, I'll end up forced to take something even more awful, so what's the point? After the cup of disgusting liquid, which tastes like nail polish remover, I go for a cigarette and can barely put it out. I stagger back to my room and collapse on my bed. Down into the wishing well darkness.

One night I couldn't work my hands and legs to change into my pjs. They were too heavy. I lay on the bed trying to keep my eyes open to make sure I was still alive. I had this feeling I wasn't going to make it until the morning. I tapped the tip of my tongue on the roof of my mouth. It had grown thick, like a tree root deep underground. *Tap, tap.* Then in about two seconds, my eyes shut.

Someone had sewed my eyelashes together. No matter how hard I tugged, my lids stayed shut. They were just too heavy. I fell asleep on top of the twisted covers because I couldn't work my body. No matter how fiercely I instructed my muscles, they wouldn't move. When I drink the nail polish remover medicine someone switches my body into a replica. A wax museum statue at Niagara Falls.

I hoped no one would come into my room in the night and steal anything. Or do anything to me. I knew I probably wouldn't wake up if they did. I hoped I woke up with all my clothes on. The exact same way as when I fell asleep. I wanted to set a booby trap to protect myself. So I'd know if anything had happened during the night. As everything was turning dark and then darker, like someone from very high up was pouring thick, amber syrup into me I realized I was being paranoid. If I could devise and lay out a booby trap, I could definitely get myself under the covers and didn't need the booby trap in the first place. Even so, I still wanted a booby trap. I hated sleeping on a floor full of strangers, some of whom I was supposed to trust to look after me. Who was okay and who wasn't? It would be better if I had a lock on my door. Except I didn't. At least I didn't have to share my room with anyone.

    I couldn't think of a worse feeling than not being able to move your own body. Even when you willed it to. I fell asleep trying. I refused to give up even as I fell over that edge every night. Someone pushing me hard from behind with both hands. Hurtle down onto a pool of copper pennies. Arms stuck from that cup of bitter liquid. I couldn't reach out and make a wish, even in my dreams.

    The nurse's handwriting in my notebook is written in curvy bubbles, like cheery humps of dry macaroni art. *Loxapine – for calming effect*. I examine my notebook for gold spray paint or sparkles, anything the nurse might have added to make the news look better. It's just plain ink. Now I know the name: Loxapine. I don't know anything else, except how it makes me feel. And the nurse's patronizing explanation. That I take Loxapine for a "calming effect." That explains everything. But she's right. I'm pretty calm every night, paralyzed on the tiny raft of my mattress until late morning. I'm calmer than I've ever been in my life. Every morning, I can't get up for breakfast no matter how much the psych assistant shakes me. He has to come get me. I'm stuck to the sheets in a sticky, thick film of amber. Syrup I can't rub out of my eyes no matter how much I try.

September 14, 1999

Max's visit was like stealing away to a green, sunny field with a big picnic basket. Tucked inside the basket are all your favourite treats, carefully picked out. Spread out a blanket and kick off your shoes. Talking, silence and breathing, accidental feet touching. Maybe one person's hands fall across the other's. You stare at the clouds. The blue sky hanging so clear and open over your heads, which unconsciously lean towards each other.

At least her visit was like that for me. Even though there was no picnic basket. And we were locked indoors. Max did her best to make sure we weren't touching. That would go against the NO TOUCHING rule. But I don't think it's because she doesn't actually want me to touch her. Max always gets this tiny smile she isn't aware of when she sits further back from me in accordance to THE RULE. And blushes. A red glow like a triangle of light from an open door. Spilling across the space between us. Tempting me to try to crack it further.

Later, when we can go anywhere we want, maybe Max won't have so many rules. Maybe. It's a word I hold close. I carry it on the tip of my tongue. *Maybe*. It brightens up the dark floor until I think I see the edges of Max's plain, dark brown leather shoes. Standing close by. Close enough. Maybe taking another step closer.

Maybe. That's the story I tell myself about what Max is thinking. That she's thinking these things, too. Shelved somewhere safe for later. For when I leave here. That she'll want me in spite of these visits and the things that stream out of my mouth.

Crazy shooting stars burning across the room. Max will still want me not just in spite of, but because. That she sees it all and wants more.

Mostly I doubt that could be true. That anyone could sit through any of this and ever want to come back. But there's this short breath of, *maybe*, I can't completely get rid of. So I stare at the picnic blue sky in her eyes. Try to grab hold of a piece for later. Especially in case she isn't coming back.

We sat on my bed. I wished for the zillionth time I could lie down beside her. Or she could put her head in my lap. Stroke her head. I didn't bother trying to get flirty. I knew we weren't allowed. I was feeling so ridiculous at having to be inside. Sub-human. Like no normal person would ever want me again. Never mind someone like Max. I vowed to be good during this visit. Except, each time I looked at her a volcano surged through me and made it difficult to behave, despite my intentions.

"The lack of control is the worst. It's what's making me sink," I told her.

"Alex, you need to accept your powerlessness here. As much as you hate it, that's one of the lessons you need to learn. I know that sounds shitty. I understand how frustrating it is. I think you're managing wonderfully. To go from who you've been, to this, I can't even imagine," she said.

I wanted to hide, but there was nowhere to go. If I excused myself to camp out in the washroom she'd think it was rude and leave. So I had to stay. Everything just kept crumbling.

"What's really bothering you?" she asked.

And I started to cry and couldn't stop. "I'm scared. That everything good I felt when I was manic is fading. My life is just going to be this slump. This crappy place. I don't want all the strength I felt to completely disappear. All the wisdom. And just be this loser who's institutionalized and has to take all this stupid medication."

Max offered me tissue. And then she took my hand and held it tight. I could see she wanted to hold me. But we were two dykes and she still wanted to visit. So she just held my hand. I felt embarrassed that she was doing it out of pity and tried to pull away, but she wouldn't let me. She just kept holding my hand while I cried. Our skin was pushed together hot. My brick red, chipped short nails next to hers bitten down to the quick, the whorls on the pads of our fingers imprinting something distinct. Lines on our palms criss-crossing close against each other's fate. In this place where there was no kindness, that action filled the room. The action became the room and the room drifted away.

Max spoke softly and slowly. For a long time. Her voice was like water. Waves lapping against me. My bed was a boat and we were sitting inside. Like we had gone away somewhere together, even just for half an hour. I didn't want to come back. But when I did, I was full.

"People like me and you are givers. But life is about trying for the balance. Learning how to take care of people. And how to take. You have to allow others to give to you. Without expecting you to give back," she offered.

She was right. I was almost the one who looked down. It was almost too hard to keep looking. To see Max wanted to give me something. She came to visit me because she wanted to. Because she wanted to see me. That was all.

Max came to see me even though I didn't take her out on wildly entertaining dates like I did with the girls I used to see before I got sick. She came to visit me even though I wore my pjs and hadn't showered. Even though I wasn't glammed up in my tough femme boots and short skirts and there was the NO TOUCHING rule.

All of a sudden, I don't have to do anything. For anyone. With anyone. Max comes and just wants to talk. She wants to be here for me. Something shifts, makes all those walls open up a bit more. Even though I'm locked up in here, I can see so much more gorgeous blue sky than I ever could before. Underneath my feet are the hard copper circles of pennies. Wet and shifting under me as I move to get a better position. A better foothold. I don't want to always be shut away here. I want more open sky. When I looked up, Max was still there. Looking at me. The sweetest smile on her face.

"You're going to be okay, Alex," she whispered in her hoarse drawl.

And for that moment, I really felt like I was.

September 15, 1999

There's too many rules here. My friends have called on the ward payphone and told me they tried to come. I don't understand why anyone who comes to visit, can't just visit. It's not like I'm booked up. Or have a stream of shady characters knocking on the ward door. You should see the skanky people who come to see Sunshine. Alfalfa sprout people with dirty feet that look like they haven't bathed in five months. The type of people who spread scabies and go smoke a bowl in the washroom. These sorts of people they let into the ward in hordes to see Sunshine. Granted, all my friends are obviously big queers, but compared to Sunshine's associates, they look like angels.

"You're only allowed four visitors a day," a nurse explained.

"What, exactly, is the logic behind this rule?" I asked in a friendly manner.

"You're only allowed four visitors a day," she repeated. Again and again.

"But why?" I asked. I really wanted to understand.

"Policy," she snapped. "If you want any visitors at all, you should stop asking why. You should be grateful for your four visitors each day."

"It's just that seeing people who care about me enriches my experience on the ward. I'm unhappy. My visitors really cheer me up," I explained.

She looked as if we weren't having a conversation at all. She was sitting there. And I was sitting there. We were in the same room. I was talking to someone who looked like her, but she was somewhere far away. Where she didn't have to listen to a word I said. I could relate. I really didn't want to be sitting there with her either having this degrading conversation.

"You need to make a list of all your potential visitors. Now," she ordered.

Miraculously, she was back. How was I supposed to guess, out of everyone I knew, who would want to drag themselves to this sorry place for a visit? It wasn't exactly an uplifting place. Who would bother to show up here? I could picture the nurses laughing. *Look how long Alex's list is! She thinks all these people are actually her friends. None of her little "friends" have bothered to come.* I was trapped in a mental hospital.

"If you want any visitors at all, you have to give me a list of all your potential visitors. That way if anyone comes, they'll be on the pre-approved list," she said.

I was a Spirograph toy, one of those things I'd wanted as a child, drawing circles wider and wider until there was nothing but a big blank. What if I forgot some major, important person who must visit? Attention to detail wasn't exactly my strong point right now. I'd be screwed. This vital person wouldn't be on my pre-approved list. They'd argue with the nurses to get in. And they wouldn't. The whole thing was a catastrophe.

I picked up a pen and set to work. The nurse sat and waited, pretending to be somewhere else. And making sure I knew she had other places to go instead of wait for my stupid list. Panicked, I put down names of people I was sure would never visit in a hundred years. I didn't want to leave a single possibility out. Prayed I wasn't forgetting anyone who lived in my heart. And hoped that each day, the exact right combination of four people came to see me, so I could make the most of my limitations. I prayed four people would come. So I wouldn't be so alone.

September 16, 1999

flowers in boxes

never noticed before
the sensuality of fresh air
each arm hair follicle
blowing in tandem
shaking quivers
like flowers in boxes.

flowers, properly contained,
captured in their beds
like me
tucked (not so) safely
on the ward.

debra anderson

September 16, 1999

    They're giving me a new pill at night to conk me out. Some sort of sedative. White and round. *Lily 4115.* I have no idea what that stands for. I know this pill has a full name. I'm going to find it out. For now, it's the Lily pill. When I tried to politely refuse the nurse last night, she was having none of it.

    "I'm trying to cut back," I joked. Figured a comment laced with diet innuendo would be something she'd get. Someone, somewhere had the resources to develop Lily 4115. Someone else has the resources to make me take it. To make me as small as they can get me so I'll fit into whatever mould they have. The nurse looked like someone who ate frozen Lean Cuisines from the microwave on lunch. She didn't think it was funny. She also wouldn't tell me anything about the new pill other than, *It will help you sleep better. C'mon dearie, let's go. The others are waiting.* I didn't need to be told that holding up a line is very un-Lily-like behaviour. Especially holding up a line of mental patients waiting to be re-medicated. I knew this place was working by how much of me was disappearing. Someone behind me cleared her throat. I turned. Another nurse. I didn't have a choice. I lifted my pills in one hand, water in the other. Swallowed.

    "Good girl," the nurse chirped, suddenly chipper.

    My mouth tasted like chalk. I backed away from the med station, careful not to trip on my slippers. Sending daggers to the nurse behind the counter. I could barely move when I woke up. It felt like my idea of those date rape drugs. Total paralysis. Every part of me ached and seemed strapped down with weights. Opening my eyes was a half hour process. Prying open the rusted door of a freight elevator. I don't need to find out the full name of Lily 4115 to know it isn't in the same harmless category as an antibiotic. I'm definitely in a new league now.

September 17, 1999

 I went into the washroom off the main hall. The one with three stalls. I heard the main door open and someone come in. I hate it when people can hear what I'm doing but I only had to pee, so it wasn't a huge deal. It took forever because I'd drunk so much water. I couldn't hear the person next to me going. I finished and went to the sink to wash my hands. The toilet flushed and Jamie came out, eyes glassy. This giant, lolling smile across her face. Looked sort of drunk. She kept running her hand through her short hair, making it sloppy like her face. She stared at me with her back against the stall as though that was the place to be. Everything was charged. Two candle flames sucked into each other with a whoosh. Even though we stood still. She was tracking my every gesture. The bright light from the overhead fixture reflected off her pupils. It seemed Jamie hadn't come into the washroom to use it, but to listen to me piss.

 I was figuring out a way to make washing and drying my hands look sexy. Jamie had both hands tucked into her belt, framing her centre. Still propped against the stall. I wanted to take the two steps towards her, grab her by the hair, push her hard into the wall with my leg, press into her and –

 – And I knew someone would open the washroom door any minute. A nurse. A psych assistant. A patient. Someone would find us. We weren't doing anything. Not yet. But I still didn't want to be caught with her. I didn't have time to develop my entire fantasy. Me. Jamie. The washroom. Yanking her jeans down and pushing her into a stall. On her knees, head against the toilet seat I'd just squatted over. Graced moments ago while she listened. My hand poised by her heat. I'd think about it later.

A bright fire blazing in my eyes. Jamie stood against the wall catching every quick second. Like she'd come in here for something like this. I felt the cool hardness of the lip of the sink against my lower back, anchoring me in place. The flat tile under my ugly slippers. I didn't care I was in my pjs. That I couldn't remember the last time I'd showered. I knew what Jamie saw. And it wasn't my hideous pjs.

I walked up to Jamie in a big push of air. Watched her swallow. I laid a hand on the solid bone of her chest. Above where it turned into soft girl the femme in me was used to ignoring in butches like her. I pushed my palm in hard. Laid my print. Pressed further as time passed. I held her eyes through the reflection of the overhead light. Found their dark colour. She tried to come up to the surface, past her meds. Got smaller and bigger all at once.

"Thank you," she said. "Can I call you, Ma'am?"

I let go of her chest, the tips of my fingers warm from her. I walked out of the washroom, flamboyantly shutting the door hard behind me, without looking back. I knew I carried her eyes. A fishing line. Connecting us every step as I increased the distance. Each feeling the tug.

September 18, 1999

Jean's where they hand out the meds. She tells her nurse, "I want a list. So I know what the score is."

I watch her nurse try not to smile. I try not to hate the nurse. All Jean wants is to know what medications she's taking. I don't think that's funny. A few minutes later Jean stands at my table for dinner. I feel guilty, but I don't want to sit with her. I wish she'd picked another table. I wanted to eat quietly. But I don't want to be mean. It's only one meal. I've had to sit with worse people.

Jean looks more disturbing than usual. Her shortish hair is greasy. It looks like a wig pulled on crooked. The waistband of her elasticized pants is drawn up higher than ever. She has foam in the corners of her mouth. I wish she would realize it was there without me having to tell her. And her eyes. She drops her tray on the tabletop. Other women turn in their chairs to see what the noise was. Her plastic fork and salad fall from her tray onto the table from the force of the drop.

Jean sits down. "Do I look normal? Do my eyes look normal?" She asks me in a panic.

I'm not sure what to say. What's "normal" anyway? None of us look "normal." But I know what Jean's asking. So maybe now is not the appropriate time to get into how we should all strive to accept ourselves as we are. Challenging customary conventions and all that. Besides, I'd have to say that Jean is definitely NOT a part of the norm. In any way. She sticks out wherever she goes like a bad window display.

She asks again, "Look at me!! Do I look normal? Are my eyes okay? Are both my ears the same size?"

Eyes wild with anxiety. Big and round. I can see the whites all over. Her pupils are huge. Jean's rolling eyes remind me of movies I've seen where a horse freaks out because they sense something's out to get them. Eyes humongous, rolling out of control in their head in a way you never knew possible. Fifteen minutes ago Jean was at the medication counter with her pile of pills, demanding to know what she was taking.

Before I can answer Jean's question, she grabs her fork and

spears an entire brussel sprout. Shoves it in whole. She's forgotten she's even asked me a question. We continue to eat dinner. I no longer feel hungry.

September 18, 1999

I offer her my nails.
it's her first time
and it shows.
here on the ward my nails are the longest
they've been since I was straight.
> curved edges poking off fingers.
> the base of me lost
> in sharp tips.

she tries to remove the old, chipped polish
with the rugged enthusiasm of a boot shine,
except the surface is too small.
after I've trained her
she files back and forth
asking, *Is this okay?*

we don't have much time.
I grab the board. do it myself.
then it's time to paint.
we are racing against night
med time,
that nasty night nurse,
every patient who walks by gawking.

CODE WHITE

I pick out the polish
another patient gave me,
Ruby Desire.
she tells me, *Like your lips.*
I forget the cliché,
    clear sweetness coming through her eyes
    and med talk coming out her mouth.
        I don't care, I want
to pull her face towards me
            kiss.

she brushes on colour
like my fingernail is a spot
on the wall she missed.
she goes over too many times
the colour uneven.

I like her focus,
a spotlight, hot
raining down on me.
so I don't say anything about how
the meds make her sloppy,
painting skin around my nails bright,
staining me.

the psych assistant uneasy
at her kneeling on the hard floor
between my knees.
she takes my hand in hers,
some sort of promise passed between us
though we don't say what.

September 19, 1999

I'm having a panic attack that the drugs they pump me with are turning me into a zombie. I'll never have my own thoughts again. The pills rattle around in my empty head. I can't just choose not to take these pills. And the more I take them, the more afraid I am that I'm going to disappear. Each time I tell a nurse I get a plastic jack-o-lantern smile that swallows me up. They speak in this leveling voice. As if my concerns are bothersome weeds in a pleasant garden they are busy maintaining. They take out their little trowel smiles and smooth me out. They tell me, *You're becoming less anxious. You're actually becoming more yourself.*

I'm not sure how that works. It feels like the more anti-anxiety pills I take, the more anxious I am about all the pills I'm taking. Too much electricity zapping around. As if I swallowed a huge hydro tower. And all the sharp parts of the tower press on my insides like a thousand piercing toothpicks about to go all the way through. After these quick conversations with the nurses, I feel weighted down. With a heavy sprinkling of fertilizer. Like I'm covered in a handful of smelly crap. I want to say to the nurse, *Why don't YOU take these pills if they're so great?*

But I don't say anything. I'm trying to learn when to keep my mouth shut here. Even though everything about my teeth clenched feels completely wrong. Wanting to preserve myself is a good thing. No matter what they tell me. Not wanting to disappear is actually a sign I shouldn't be here in the first place. Wanting to stay myself is a sign of not being crazy.

CODE WHITE

September 19, 1999

Terry still has no shoes or socks. She walks the ward barefoot. She's tall and fat and has long greasy hair. An aura of calmness around her. I want to catch some, but it isn't working. I asked her about not having shoes or socks. If she misses it.

"Having no shoes is the least of my problems," Terry answered. "When I get discharged, my brother'll pick me up and I'll just go in his car. Nothing to worry about there."

And it's true. She doesn't really need shoes or socks to get in a car. I used to wonder when I would get out of here. Now, I wonder if.

September 20, 1999

I came back from a fifteen-minute pass to the convenience store. The nurses confiscated the Perrier right away. Went right up to Jamie and grabbed it out of her hand. As if the green bottle was a Molotov cocktail Jamie had been planning to lob at the nursing station.

"It's glass," Nurse Dee said. "It can break. So it's dangerous. It's considered sharps."

Then she took it. It's a good thing I have unsophisticated tastes. The nurses wouldn't bother tackling my Pepsi. Plastic. Harmless. I felt bad for Jamie that she couldn't have her drink. I'd already spent her money on my pass. And I wasn't allowed out again to buy her something else. I offered her some of my Pepsi, but she looked like she couldn't swallow anything. Like all that would fit in her throat was that dangerous, glassy green bottle of Perrier. Without it there, her throat had closed in on itself. She went to go hang out in her room.

Later, Jamie came for a smoke. She had a few sips of my

Pepsi. I wasn't sure if it was because she was thirsty, or she was trying to put something else in that space to erase what had been taken.

September 21, 1999

I only have three T-shirts to sleep in. I have to wash them in the laundry all the time to have something clean to wear. They get dirty fast because I get night sweats now. Might be the medication. Or that none of the windows in my room open to let in any air. I sleep in the bottoms the institution provides. I grabbed a bunch of the ones I like best from the linen room. Shades of fading blue, with the words "Hospital Property" stamped in an erratic checkerboard pattern. It's as if they were made in a secret sweatshop in the basement of the hospital, and the workers were all patients who couldn't follow the pattern.

Each pair is absolutely threadbare. If you're not careful, the fly gaps open to show your pubes. I always wear gitch underneath. When the gap spreads everyone can see my underwear. I don't exactly feel secure, but at least it's some sort of barrier. I just pull the drawstring tighter. Washing the blue bottoms is not my responsibility. I'm allowed to drop them into the blue garbage bags near the little med room next to the nursing station. The med room has a Dutch door that only reaches my waist. The top of it is always sticky with old orange juice spilled by the patients' shaky hands. No one ever cleans it. There are layers of skanky old juice, tacky to the touch. A topography growing on top of the rings in the grain of wood.

I can also drop off my bed sheets in the blue bag that says, ONLY FILL HALF-WAY. I don't like the hospital to wash it though. I like the way my detergent from home smells. Invisible strings tugging at me. Roots I hope are still there. I want to wear that smell. Envelope myself into it in a big safe pocket. Maybe if I'm still surrounded by that smell, I'll still be that person. I want my things to smell like the calm before all this. For my things to be only mine. Even though all the pj bottoms sort of look the same, they aren't. Like each woman on the ward.

I've picked the ones that fit me exactly. Big, but not swimming. Long, but not so long the legs flap over my slippers and threaten to trip me. If I send them to the laundry I'll never be able to find those exact ones again.

Maybe I'm superstitious. I want to keep using the exact same pair of sheets, too. I lie on them every night. Spend so much time on them during the day. I don't want anyone else putting my sheets on their bed. What if they have my dreams or nightmares? Information meant for me. What if they get that thing I'm waiting for? A sign that was destined for me, filtering up through the weave of the cheap, poly-cotton blend? You could say that's crap. But what if I'm supposed to sleep on the same sheets to work through this process? Energy pulsing through me, sinking into my sheets as distinct as a fingerprint. Ready to meet me each night in a connection that one grand morning will finally reveal how to get out of here. If I give away these sheets I'd be messing all that up. I wash my sheets.

"Alex, you can just plop your sheets in that blue garbage bag down the hall. That way, you don't have to wash them yourself," the nurses tell me slowly. Like you'd tell someone who you think is stupid, verging on mentally disabled. I guess they talk that way because they've told me so often they must think I'm an idiot for not putting my sheets in the communal laundry. Just more evidence that I'm crazy. I want to do laundry; therefore, I'm crazy. Therefore, I belong here.

Every time, I say, *No*. I strip my bed and wash them myself.

And I keep rotating through the couple of lucky bottoms I picked out and washing them when they get dirty. When I walk, I put my own paces into them. I haven't told anyone, but I'm conducting a scientific experiment. I'm measuring exactly how much I've worn out my sheets and pjs by the time I leave this dump. How much I've managed to strip away the threads of every inch of sheet that stretches taut across my bed, barely making it to each corner. I try to take silent notes with my eyes every time they come out of the drier. Hot against my hands. I want to note the difference. It's really difficult to tell. Hard to see something changing so slowly, right in front of my eyes.

September 21, 1999

I'm sure this isn't a big deal, but Max hasn't been around in a little bit. I don't mean to sound clingy and weird, but I'm worried she isn't coming back. I know that's stupid. Of course Max is coming back. Why would she stop coming now? After everything she's seen me say and do, why would she be tired of visiting now?

Max doesn't always tell me when she's planning on coming. It's never been an issue. I'm always here. There's nowhere else I can go. And it's not like my schedule is all booked up. So it's fine for her to just show up when she's able to show up. The thing is, I can't remember if she said when she was coming next at the end of her last visit or not. Is she late or am I just being over eager? I guess it doesn't matter. I know Max will be here when she gets here. I won't be anywhere else. That's the problem.

I miss her. Just seeing her always makes me feel better. And she always seems to understand everything. Even before I open my mouth to explain a single thing. Max just gets it. I miss that right now. I miss connecting to someone like that. Everything under the surface, you both holding it. Together.

The girls on the ward, once you get to know them, they're mostly okay. Some of them are obviously better than others. But it's not like it is when I spend time with Max. I just wish she'd get here again, already.

September 21, 1999

Jean is wandering through the TV lounge in a drugged stupor again. She looks out one of the windows that doesn't open and says, *Oh, it's raining. I wish I were Mary Poppins.*

September 21, 1999

For some unknown reason, the nurses have upped my visitor quota to five. I have no idea what I've done to be allowed to see one more person a day. But I'm not going to get into a discussion with staff. I'm just going to enjoy that extra person. What has changed to change that rule, when I don't feel I've changed?

September 22, 1999

Tammy's being sent to ACU today. That's the Acute Care Unit. I guess she's been hurting herself too much. There are too many of us for the nurses to watch her closely enough, even though she has the room with a huge window in the door across from the nursing station.

In the smoke room Tammy complains, "They," (meaning the nurses on ACU) "never listen to me, only to them" (meaning the nurses on this floor). "It's horrible down there, if you tell the staff to fuck off they put you in restraints right away and say that's not how you talk to staff. Well fuck, they can do whatever they want. Make all the rules. They aren't the ones being restrained."

Crisp Nurse Emma opens the smoke room door, peeks her sleek bobbed head in and announces, "Tammy, now."

Then the door shuts firmly. The click of the handle is a grim proclamation of Tammy's fate. *Click.* Tammy's replanted on another floor. *Click.* A file cabinet shuts on this floor. *Click.* The ward door locks behind her.

Tammy puts out her cigarette, stares hard at the floor, then heaves herself off the smoke bench. Mumbles goodbye real quiet. I give her my real address, the one at home. The phone number, too.

"Stay in touch," I say. "Really stay in touch." But I know she won't. I'm crying already. I don't let it show because I don't want to make her upset. I give her a big hug. "Stay alive," I say. But not so loud that it stands out like a gaudy pair of earrings. All flash, no substance. She pats me on the back to soothe me.

I want to comfort her. And I don't want her to leave. I try to center myself. Shoot her positive energy to take along. But it's not enough. There's no time. We both feel nurse Emma waiting outside the door. I wish I had something else, a chocolate bar. Or a stuffed animal for her collection. But I've eaten all the chocolate everyone's brought me. I am a greedy pig. I touch Tammy's shoulders gently. Rub her head, something I've done before upon invitation. A flake of dry skin comes off her head in the palm of my hand. I want to keep it. But there are no pockets in my pj bottoms. I'm frantic to find a place for this piece of Tammy. I'm certain I will never see her again.

We both hear Nurse Emma politely tap against the door. Nurse Emma is a Winter, in more ways than one. Winter colours, bright and clear. Black tailored women's dress pants with a crisp pleat ironed down the front. Nurse Emma is an A-cup. A thin, trim waist that makes a mockery of all of us sluggishly riding side effects of our medication. Nurse Emma is a distanced, *How can I help you?* when her eyes are saying, *Please get as far away from me as possible and leave me alone.* Nurse Emma wears her professionalism as a shield. A force-field keeping her separate that reminds us who is well and working a job and who is the job she's working. I look down at my slippers as I hear Nurse Emma's sensible, yet stylish shoes click on the floor of the hall outside the smoke room. I know Tammy can hear it, too.

"I'm not taking any of my stuff," Tammy says.

A last protest. Part of her still gets to stay. I admire her guts. Even though I know she doesn't actually have much stuff to take or leave. What Tammy has, is style. And then she's going. And I'm stuck to my cigarette. I watch her leave in the reflection from the window. Holding her teddy bear. The one named Patsy.

Through the window of the smoke room door I see Nurse Emma holding a green trash bag. Ralph the psych assistant holds two other bags. Tammy's clothes. Almost all too small for her anyway because of the weight she's put on since she's been here. Then everyone's gone. I light another cigarette I don't want.

On the way to my room to hide, I pass her room. Tammy's bed is stripped. Nothing left of her in the room except a sad plastic pillow. The hospital's, not hers. And the vase of flowers Christina sent her yesterday. Flowers meant to get Tammy better. I remember her telling me how that fucking nurse had to come and fuck it up. How afraid I was for her, that in the five minutes in between checks Tammy could have stopped existing. There would be no more Tammy ever.

"The nurse was ten minutes too long. I wish you wouldn't feel this way. Wouldn't do these things to yourself," I'd said. How do you tell someone you wish they wanted to be alive, that their life meant something, without sounding trite? Everything out of my mouth was a cliché. A fortune cookie. My words got smaller and staler. I didn't really know what to say. How to fill the holes. And I don't really know how she feels. I'm not Tammy. Why do I have a right to say anything?

I don't really know who Tammy is beyond burns and scars, pus, scabs and Band-Aids. Covered everywhere in gauze-like White Out, trying to erase what can't be healed. All I know is the sight and sound of her crying. That ragged liquid gasp before she left the smoke room, "ACU is hell. And last time I was there some guy tried to make a pass at me. He came into my room in the middle of the night and climbed on top of me. Tried to pull down my pj pants."

Goodbye, Tammy.

September 22, 1999

I went into the main bathroom after lunch, into the stall closest to the sink. I hate going into the middle stall because people could come in either side and sandwich me. As I hover and try not to piss on the seat, I notice someone's written graffiti on the wall, just to the side of the toilet paper. None of the walls on the ward have a single bit of graffiti on them. Ever. I wonder how long this piece of graffiti has managed to stay unnoticed by any staff. In tiny dark letters, *Desire is the root of all suffering.*

I wipe with a wad of one-ply tissue. Pull up my pj bottoms.

Check my sandals for toilet paper strays from the floor. Trace the sentence with the tip of my finger.

September 22, 1999

    It's hard to cuddle with someone you never technically even went on a first date with when you're both locked up in a mental hospital. The nurses and the psych assistants keep looking in disbelief, as if what they think might be happening, can't be happening, because we are two girls. Like they think everyone knows two girls don't do those kinds of things even though there we are, doing just those kinds of things, right in front of them.

    The psych assistants anxiously distract us. When that doesn't work they encourage us to sit further apart. It's all a big joke, because we are already sitting on this cubed thing in the lounge that's sort of a couch, but isn't. It's a couch for mental patients with personal space issues. Designed as one separate block after another. Each armrest creates a separate, mini-barrier, so no one can stretch past the parameters of their cube. It's impossible to take up more than your one block of space at a time.

    The uncompromising arm-separators between each person create an almost-sterile box. Almost sterile, because Terry managed to piss on two seats today through her pants. Pissed in her pants on one seat, got up, and sat down in another seat for a while until the nurse came and took her away. This is the fifth day I've seen Terry do this. How often does Terry pee onto the seat when I am not there? What's the probability that her dried pee is tainting the seat I'm sitting on right now? I can't think about it. It's too disgusting. And there's nowhere else to go sit together.

debra anderson

Since dinner we've been trying to get cozy, but Jean keeps bothering us. First, she was hungry like always, so Jamie gave her two Tic-Tacs. Then she kept saluting us. After that, it was an impromptu *Ave Maria* concert, after which, she ran out of the room. Ralph, the psych assistant, looked very worried because it meant Jamie and I were alone. Except for Ralph watching us.

From down the hallway we could hear Jean break into, *Morning Has Broken*. She likes to play it every morning on the piano in the activity room. The activity room doesn't actually see any activity other than TV and a stale shelf of dusty Harlequins from the seventies no one touches. In her own way, Jean was trying to provide some ambiance for us.

Sitting in the lounge with the TV off made Ralph uncomfortable. He disliked that we actually had something to say to one another rather than just slumping in our cubes. Awash in the blue glow in silence. Warbled strains of *Morning Has Broken* trailed down the hallway.

"Okay girls, it's time to go to your rooms," Ralph the Official Third Wheel said. We were both really mad, but there wasn't anything we could do.

"I'll try to sneak into your room later to say, *Hi*," Jamie whispered when Ralph wasn't looking and winked at me. I didn't have roommates and she did. The offer reminded me of teen movies where boys crash the girls' sleepovers when the girls are waltzing around in lingerie, entering the house via a clumsy ladder or eavestrough about to rip off the side of the building. While this concept was sexy as fuck, it panicked me so much I couldn't feel my feet or hands. This wasn't a sleepover party. This was a mental hospital.

I didn't want to get in trouble for having a girl in my room in the middle of the night. Especially since it was well-known I was a dyke. I had the hots for Jamie, but I also wanted to stay away from trouble while on the ward. Even totally out there, on the edge in a fucking nuthouse, I still couldn't be the bad girl I'd always dreamed of being. It really was pathetic.

Despite myself, as I got ready for bed all I could think about was Jamie. My room would be dark like always, the pale yellow light of the hall spilling in the partly open door. Lights from the street, from nearby buildings, would glow through my windows around the get well cards I'd taped there. I always kept the curtains open, even at night. There'd be enough soft light to see and darkness to hide. Her eyes, wet shining stones reflecting back at me. I'd be too shy to look at the light rippling off her. Or so daring I'd burn those eyes of stone into stars. Open her until she felt safe enough to show her gleam, while the night nurse softly treads past my door in her white, crepe rubber-soled shoes, never suspecting. I pictured Jamie's energy careening off the walls. Windows steaming from her two stars beaming bright at me. Sinking to the floor as she held me.

I kept fixing my hair in the mirror even though I knew I was just going to lie down and mess it all up in the darkness on the plastic pillow. I decided not to take off my makeup or wash my face. I put on fresh lipstick. A dark and dramatic shade. I pursed my lips and wished I knew how to make them look cupid-like. With my lips highlighted I felt like I was waiting for a lover in the cheap motel we'd rented. I knew I was only in my crappy room on the ward, with narrow bed and sad plastic mattress. Not motel-like at all. It was more likely that the night nurse was going to stick her flashlight in at any minute than Jamie would arrive.

But still. I couldn't stop doing lame things in the mirror, like sticking out my tits every which way to see which ways they looked best. Turned on, like a bee buzzing around the room. I wished I had a pair of high heels with me so I could strap myself into them and move my ass and hips as I walked. Sounds punctuating the floor. I lay in bed and fell asleep waiting for Jamie, wearing my T-shirt and no bottoms. The blanket pulled up so the night nurse wouldn't know any better. Definite leakage between my legs.

I woke to yellow disappointment spilling through the dusty window. Every opaque get well card hung on the glass like a punch in the face. The sun was in my eyes, just like every day. Jamie hadn't come. I felt my bareness in all its' ridiculous glory. The air kissed my pussy a loud mistake. Why had I gone to sleep like this? What if Jamie had come and seen me? My eyes were crusted together. When I turned, the mattress made its usual awful squeaky fart sound. I saw black mascara stains on my pillow. Reminders of expectation only made me feel more humiliated.

I got up quickly to find some panties and pj bottoms before a nurse or psych assistant opened the door. Screw breakfast. Always sucked anyways. I didn't want to run into Jamie. I guess the old adage, *Don't date someone you work with* adage held true as *Don't date someone you're in a mental ward with*. Even someone really hot. I took a deep breath. *Time to be a big girl, Alex.* I slid some panties on and a pair of pj bottoms. Nothing fancy. Didn't want to look like I was trying.

As I approached the door, I noticed a paper someone must have slid underneath. A drawing of a mermaid in pastel crayons in rich reds and oranges. She didn't look like a typical mermaid. She wasn't thin or wearing coconut shells. She didn't have wavy long hair. But, she was so clearly beautiful against a sea of red. Jamie's signature was on the bottom. She had framed it with a thick boundary of masking tape around each edge. Mental hospital supplies. Art for me. Slipped under my door in secret as I slept.

I taped it right over my bed, in the centre of the nothing-coloured wall, just above where my head lay on the crunchy hospital pillow. I took down some older get well cards. Moved them around to make space for Jamie's piece that had slipped right into my red, messy heart. I sat on my bed, held my knees to my chest and cried. Tried not to make too much noise. Wished I could hear the waves. Wondered tonight, before my sleeping pill kicked in, if I kept my ears open enough, still enough, like wide, hungry shells on a beach, quiet and waiting, maybe, maybe I would.

September 23, 1999

Mary – coffee $2 double double
Diet Coke $2 for Kate
$10 for gel – Dep Xtra Hold for Jamie

September 23, 1999

    I found out today from Mary that Tammy is 34 years old and instead of making me take that awful liquid called Loxapine they're making me take Olanzapine/Zyprexa every night. That might be the Lily pill, but I'm not totally sure. If I'm better enough to be taken off Loxapine, why not just keep me off of it? Why add another drug? They aren't really reducing the amount of drugs I'm on at all. They just keep stacking them up like that game *Jenga*.

debra anderson

September 23, 1999

When I was manic I felt sharper than I'd felt in my entire life. All of a sudden I completely understood everything. I knew what I was meant to do. What I was capable of. As time goes by on the ward, I'm losing that focus. Soap shrinking under a shower spray, I'm on slow dissolve. On the ward, the nurses and psych assistants maintain sameness. Difference is a loud, disruptive crackle in the dull hum of homogeny on the floor.

The walls inside our rooms are white. Everything bland and calm. The women only get excited when the kitchen serves ice cream for dessert. No wild flavours like pistachio or rum and raisin. Chocolate, strawberry or vanilla. No second helpings. Everyone grabs their own pre-packaged cup of decadence.

Dinner is served at the same time every day. So are all the meals. I still haven't managed to figure out when that is. I can't keep track of anything. Not the time, the day of the week, or any of the dumbing down routines. I want to eat when I'm hungry. I want to live where ice cream doesn't come in a tiny paper cup with a waxed paper lid. Where someone else, desperate, won't take my share. Not in this place that wears you down with sameness.

Despite the routines and their determination to eradicate difference, there's no comfort. For any of us living here. I don't feel safe, locked on a ward, living inside a room that isn't mine. I don't need to be imprisoned in a place where vanilla ice cream is the only cause for celebration. That only makes me sadder. And angry.

CODE WHITE

September 24, 1999

I can't believe what an ass I've made of myself. Over the last few days I've left at least four messages for Max on that pager number she left me. I wasn't trying to seem like a stalker. I just wanted to say, *Hi* and to see what was going on. Why she hasn't been around. When she was coming back. I hope I didn't sound desperate. I kept thinking she was going to call me back. Like she always does. Until now. I don't think she is. Because if she was going to, she would've by now. And I'm finally just getting it. That she isn't going to come back.

I just don't get it. Out of all the fucked up, crazy shit I've done since I've been here, I would have put my money on me scaring people away when I first got here. When I was completely out of it and had no clue that I was. Not on making people want to stop being around me now. When I'm trying to get my shit together. When it seems like I could be this close to getting the fuck out of here.

If only I hadn't made so many calls to her. If only I hadn't called at all. Not that I said anything all that major, but still. All those unreturned calls are humiliating. I'm cringing at the thought of Max listening to my messages. Whatever it is she's thinking about me. Knowing she's decided already not to come back. That she's not going to call, either.

Sometimes I hate the fact that there are those stupid payphones here on the ward for any one of us who has a quarter or a calling card to use. I'm so embarrassed by all the awful phone calls I've made since I've been here that I totally shouldn't have. Including all those calls to Max. One huge mistake. If I'm going to be locked up in a prison, it might as well be a prison. No luxuries like outside phone calls giving me the opportunity to make a fool of myself with my shitty judgment. Sitting around moping in my room, wishing there was a way to erase it. Except there isn't.

I just have to move on. Just like with all the rest of the stupid phone calls I've made. Hope that Max isn't sitting in her apartment thinking I'm a total idiot. Which she might already be thinking since she doesn't want to come back and visit me. Just try to forget I even made the calls. Like they don't even exist. Like Max doesn't exist. Except she does. And she doesn't want to visit me. There's no way I can forget that.

September 24, 1999

Snapshots

Alice speed talks of lacquered
    Bat Mitzvah party
    dancing awards.

without a break for air
she details athletic
past accomplishments.
    Teen Stardom.

    synthetic memories
like rubber runners
protecting carpets
and sheathed furniture.
plasticized covers hiding
what's underneath.

CODE WHITE

acrylic nails,
coated proud daggers
her crystallized beauty,
   sharp
     and not quite her own.

September 24, 1999

    Martha glides down the halls in a silent black housecoat of depression. Matching black slippers with a sheepskin trim. Her frizzy, fuzzy hair is so thick it stands as high as it is long. White roots as long as the tip of my finger. Her cigarette burning is the only noise she makes in the smoke room. *Crackle, crackle.* When she talks in that low voice of hers, very occasionally, and when you least expect it, she makes me laugh out loud. Smile for hours afterward.

September 24, 1999

    Jean – small, one milk, bring packet of sugar $2 bucks
    Christina – small, black.
    Sunshine – zucchini nut muffin .75 cents

September 24, 1999

    Jamie's a safe distance away from me, perched on the end of my bed. We've left my door wide open so none of the staff can say anything. Jamie always looks so polished. Never in her pyjamas. Jeans always clean, with no rips. Men's dress shoes perfectly shined. I try not to feel weird that I am the dirtiest, the skankiest that I have ever looked. Wearing the same thing every day. No bra. Gross pyjamas and T-shirts from home I wouldn't even want my best friend to see, never mind someone I have the hots for. Dry skin peeling across my ugly feet. Makeup pooling under my eyes.

I know Jamie isn't seeing any of that when she looks at me, eyes shining. Following me around the ward, keeping back just enough so the nurses don't always get what she's doing. And when they figure it out, they can't stop her. Because she's not really doing anything. Except they know we are. Up to something. None of them likes it. But I don't care.

I think about what my life would be like if I never got sick. If I was out there, right now. Back in touch with Max. Would she have me? So weird, like I have separate handfuls of the same life. Every piece heading somewhere else, even though it's all mine. I can't think about Max. She's not here. And she won't be. Right now, life has brought me Jamie. I can see where that goes or not. At some point, later on, Max may be there. Or she won't. Probably won't, as she stopped visiting me. She probably hates me. But I won't know until I get there. In the meantime, I'm not going to pass up what comes my way. I want to experience things. Even in here.

There's a low barking sound from the end of my bed. Jamie's waving this little stuffed dog that my parents brought me. Someone had given it as a get well gift and asked them to bring it to me. I'm not really a fan of stuffed animals, so I left the dog, unnamed, in a corner of my room. Jamie's rescued the animal.

"Cut it out," I say, laughing.

"My mommy doesn't love me. She leaves me on the floor – "

" – Knock it off, Sparky," I tell her. Jamie bounces the dog across the bed and into my lap.

"You need to take me for a walk," she says in a baby voice. "Go ask for a pass and then your handsome friend will get a pass, too. Then you'll be able to leave this place with me and go on a date with your dashing companion, all at the same time. The nurses will never know."

"Who knew I had such a dog of subterfuge living in my room with me this whole time?"

Jamie kisses my face with the dog. It's sort of cute, but sort of creepy, too. I wrench it out of her hands and throw the dog back in its corner. We burst out laughing.

"C'mon," Jamie pleads in the doggie-voice.

"NO. And stop talking like that," I say.

"Woof?"

Holding my stomach I collapse over, laughing. I don't know why. It isn't that funny. But somehow it is. We're trapped. And we're not. Jamie is a door. A window. A sliver of some way to normal, to get a piece of it, even when I'm still not. Not by being here, at least. I miss the way things used to be.

"Does the dog need its own special pass to get off the ward? Or does it just piggyback automatically on mine?" I ask.

We can't stop laughing. Suddenly, Nurse Susan is at my door. Lurking in the hallway. Eyeing us.

"Can you girls please keep it down? Jamie, you're not supposed to be in here." She waits in the hallway to make sure Jamie leaves. I stare at the one square of floor tile that the plush dog has managed to secure as its own.

Out of the corner of my eye, a shadow stands up and leaves the room. Jamie.

September 25, 1999

Today we had group. I hate to go, but we're forced. The topic was *Self-Care*. We were discussing, "What Can You Do For Yourself?" The rule was it had to be THINGS FOR YOURSELF. Not for anyone else. At first, most of the suggestions were stuff for other people. But the idea was to focus the giving energy on ourselves. The facilitator, this social worker, Priscilla, decided to take a mini-vacation. She refused to pitch in any suggestions. She forced us to make up stuff for her to write on her big pad of paper. She wasn't on strike for the note-taking part.

The brainstorm wasn't much of a storm. More a pathetic drizzle. Everyone wishing it was over. We sat around in silence. The longer it went on, the more it felt like no one could move. Like no one could move anything. Not raise their hands or open their mouths to speak.

I thought of some ideas. I may be stuck on a mental ward, but that doesn't make me stupid. But, in solidarity with our group silence, I didn't say anything. I also hated brainstorming and our "Support Group." But it was even harder to see the concepts the group finally came up with. Priscilla exclaimed over each idea as if she'd been handed a freshly scrubbed, burbling baby or a beautifully wrapped present with lovely curling ribbons hanging over the edges. Scalloped with sharp scissors none of us were allowed to hold by ourselves.

The group came up with a lean list. Priscilla pointed out we should endeavor to do them wherever we were, on the ward or at home.

- Stay up
- Watch a soap opera
- Go to sleep (nap)
- Spending time with someone
- Walk
- Get dressed and stay awake

(I noted we were all in our pjs, except for the social worker.

Priscilla was wearing a pantsuit. A purple one with big, gold buttons that looked like it was from Zellers.)

- Paint toenails
- Pet cat
- Take a bath
- Change bed linens

After Priscilla congratulated the group on their brainstorming skills and scowled at me for keeping my mouth shut, we were done. The only place I felt like going was to bed, for a nap. Which, to be fair, was on the list. My whole body was weighted down. Caught in a heavy mesh rope trap the army drops. I could barely drag myself around. I needed sleep. Rub away the last hour.

September 25, 1999

When she isn't singing, Jean putters up and down the halls all day. Makes her own soft shuffle in her worn, fake dollar-store Keds. Muttering. I heard her through the door to my room today when I had sex with Jamie for the first time. I couldn't believe we were actually doing it. Here on the ward. It felt like something we were supposed to do. Regardless of where we were. Like a map unfolding and there we were, this well-placed dot on a spot that was meant to be. Whether we wanted to be there or not. Even if that sounds dumb. I didn't feel like waiting until I get out of here. Whenever that is. Neither did she. We just prayed we wouldn't get caught. I tried not to think about what might happen to us if we did.

We were on the floor. Hidden on the side of my bed furthest from the door. But anyone who came in would see us anyways. Crouching behind my bed made us feel an imaginary safe. We tried to be really quiet. It was all so fast.

I had a mantra inside. Sentences unfurling like party streamers rippling and curling in the air. Bright colours. *Feel this. Remember you have a body. Nothing for granted.* And desperate prayers. *Please let us finish. Let us decide we're done. Don't let them notice we're both gone.*

All I could hear was the pounding of my heart. Each of us breathing hard and trying not to. The noises Jean made as she shuffled past my door in the hallway. Footsteps like time markers. Each shuffle knocking at the back of my mind letting me know how much time we'd swallowed inside my room. Ward time. With each pat of Jean's shoe I budgeted how much more time we might dare to steal without being caught. Her paces a quiet warning. If we took too long, the next shuffle could bring someone down the hall with Jean. Someone who would quickly knock at my door and open it even faster. Catch me on top of Jamie, shirt yanked up, pj bottoms pulled down, stretch of pale skin glaring like an eclipse. All without ever waiting for me to give them permission to come inside.

After, we quickly cleaned ourselves up. Opened the door to my room again. Jamie flopped on the end of my bed like she'd been deboned. My slipper bounced on the end of my foot. I could see every single one of her eyelashes. The light in the room seemed brighter. A shy smile tucked on her face like a silk handkerchief blooming in her breast pocket. We couldn't stop grinning. Jamie reached for my hand through a small tunnel in the thin blanket. I thought of groundhogs and every other thing that burrowed and hid underground until it was the right time to come up for air. A couple minutes later, Nurse Emma strode by in the hallway and stopped.

"You girls shouldn't be in here. You need to go in the lounge. Why don't you see what's on TV?" she said in a tight voice, even though I didn't ever watch TV.

We didn't care that no one else ever got kicked out while visiting together in their rooms. It didn't matter anymore.

September 26, 1999

Everyone wants a little piece of something to call their own in this place. Something that's not the ward's, only theirs. Something that resembles a home. Except, this is a public ward shared by at least twelve women at a time. So it doesn't work. It becomes an over-drugged turf war. If you can't solve it yourself, the nurses get involved. And, it is truly every woman for herself. No one stands up for another against the nurses. Especially not when you hate the other patient. Like Shira. Shira has no friends. Even the nurses dislike her. They can't admit that, but I can tell. Shira's been here forever. Knows all the staff. Shira has tons of privileges. She seems to be allowed to go off the ward whenever she wants. Always has places to go. Dates with friends, boys, doctor's appointments. I don't even know why she's here.

If Shira doesn't get what she wants, she'll throw a temper tantrum. The nurses give in so they don't have to hear her whiny voice anymore. Either that or she has a really rich parent who the staff is nervous to piss off. I try to be nice to everyone. It's hard to find something nice about everyone here, but I try. We all have to share this space whether we like each other or not. I'm all about trying to create positive energy, especially since I got here and found there was none. But even with my sunny rainbow philosophy, I really can't stand Shira. Just like everyone else. She completely grates on my nerves.

debra anderson

Leah is this addict in her forties who looks hardcore even in desert boots. I noticed her pinky nail was super long, but waited for her to tell me she had a big drug problem. She also told me she's a dyke. I wasn't completely sure, but had sort of guessed. Leah said the most perfect thing about Shira.

"Princess Shira," Leah said, "uses this place like a hotel. The nurses are her fucking maids and answering service. She waltzes in and out of this place so much I don't know what the fuck is wrong with her or why she's here. She'd rather live in this stinking hole than in her own apartment with no one to order around."

There are three payphones for the ward. They take incoming calls and do outgoing, too. No one much uses the one on the other side of the horseshoe-shaped hallway near some patient rooms. Some people use the phone across from my room, which is annoying when they're loud. Or sobbing. Which is most of the time. As soon as I close my door to give them privacy and get some, a psych assistant will come on their fifteen-minute check. Open my door again. Let their voices come running in and stain me.

All the real phone action takes place by the locked ward door in the lounge and kitchen area. There's a chalkboard there for messages. The phone is always ringing for someone. Or else someone is on the phone crying. Begging someone for something. The patients answer incoming calls, not nurses. And most of the patients are completely out of it on meds. They forget to write down who called for you. Or, partway through writing the name, they forget. They just make up a name and write that down. You look at the board and see that "Sherrie" called for you, no phone number noted. You don't even know a Sherrie. The only person whose name you know that starts with an "s" is your friend, Sadie. You don't want to waste a quarter to call and find out if she called you. And you don't want to look unnecessarily needy. So you don't call. Maybe you're not returning her phone call. Or maybe it's not an issue, she never even called. There's no such thing as a casual call when you're in a mental institution. The shitty message taking here has really fucked up my life.

The neat freaks and obsessive compulsives on the ward like to wipe down the chalkboard before you get your message. After every call gets posted, they wipe it off. The person who called thinks you got the message, because someone in the ward answered and took down their name. They wonder why you never call back. They think maybe you're too sick to talk. Or busy with company. And they stop calling.

The day I fought with Shira, my friend Ruth called. I managed to intercept the call to speak with her. No annoying non-messages. An actual conversation. During which Shira hovered close. Unbelievably close. I glared at her, but she wouldn't leave. I turned my chair to get privacy. And then, a tap on my shoulder.

"I'm expecting a very important phone call. You need to get off the phone," she ordered.

The conversation I was having was important. Like when you're flailing underwater and think your lungs are about to burst and you somehow find your way up to the surface to take a huge gulp of air before you sink down again kind of important. Talking to people from my old life, the life I had before I landed here, is really important. Makes me feel more normal. Like people remember me even though I'm here and think no one does.

"You have to get off the phone," she whined. "I'm expecting an extremely urgent call."

It wasn't as though I was some pesky kid tying up her line when potential prom dates were trying to get through to ask her out. There's an official rule on the ward about the phones. TEN MINUTES AT A TIME. No one's allowed to talk on the phone for more. That way you don't tie up the line for the other women expecting a call. Or for anyone who wants to make one. I hadn't been on the phone for longer than three minutes. Ruth and I had things to say. There was no way I was going to stop at only three minutes when I had seven more. Maybe for a patient I liked, who truly needed the phone. No way for Shira.

Who knows what I said to set her off. Whatever anyone says to her always resulted in a scene. I probably simply explained I still had time left on my important phone call. And I'd get off when I was done. That if her call was important, the person would keep trying to get through.

"Get off the fucking phone! That's my phone! I need the line open to get my call. If you don't get off the phone I'm gonna make you get off of it," she screamed.

It would have been more dramatic if she got violent. Wrestled me for the receiver. But Shira was smart. She knew how to play on the ward. Always pushing for more for herself, bending the rules without ever totally breaking anything. She knew how to get her way without having a Code White called. So instead of violence, she pulled out her other card. Tears. The whole thing felt so pathetic, watching it spill down her blotchy face. Snot threatening to drip out her nose. We were fighting over a few lousy telephone minutes. I was better than this. Better than Shira. And better than this place that was reducing me to this scene. I decided to hang up. I was saying goodbye to Ruth, completely embarrassed she'd heard the kind of place I lived in and the people I had to deal with. And then a nurse came over.

After hearing Shira's story delivered in-between sobs, the nurse was all sympathy. For Shira. She'd made herself out to be some street urchin out of a Dickens novel. Everything, according to Shira, was an evil plot against her. And that included me.

"Alex, you need to hang up the phone now," the nurse ordered. "If your call is important you can call your friend back. Don't you think that's equitable?" she said with zero irony.

Of course I didn't. Just because the nurse stuck a two-cent social worker word into the mix didn't actually make the injustice she was orchestrating easier to stomach in any way. Did she think I was an idiot? I knew the rules of the ward. And I knew when they were being broken. For a swollen-eyed, red-faced snotty bitch standing in front of me. Who had now stopped crying as suddenly as she had started. Now that she had what she wanted. I didn't want to hang up the phone.

But I also didn't want any privileges taken away. The nurse stood there, waiting for me to do what she said. And I'm embarrassed to admit my principles went elsewhere when I thought about the tiny bit I'd managed to acquire here. I didn't want a Code White called. Even though at that moment I felt like taking the receiver and smashing a double blow to Shira and the nurse.

I said goodbye. Hung up. And let the phone that was supposed to belong to all of us belong to Shira. In retrospect, if that was what it took to give her a little piece of home on the ward, even though I didn't like her, how could I begrudge that?

I stuck around. To see what would happen. When the phone rang the next few times it wasn't for Shira. She stuttered and paced the common area. And then she bumped off those callers, too. Eventually the phone was for her. She talked for forty-five minutes. The nurse who kicked me off the phone was nowhere in sight during this marathon call. I watched Shira through every minute of her precious call from across the room to give her privacy. Counted the contraband minutes through a red-hazed rage.

September 26, 1999

I was coming out of the smoke room. Sunshine was sitting with a visitor. Some guy in Birks and a tie-dye T-shirt. Dirty hair. When she saw me, Sunshine ran up squealing. Grabbed my arm. Her teeth cute little peaches and cream niblets.

"C'mon, Alex, come and sit with us!" she tinkled.

I wanted to go to my room. There was a mean edge floating inside me today. A taste of something bad in my mouth.

"No, I don't think so, Sunshine."

Sunshine didn't take *No* for an answer ever. So I was dragged through the lounge and plopped into a chair across from Scruffy. I listened to them talk, but couldn't really understand what they were saying. A lot of stuff about the beautiful universe. Raves. Organic produce. Partying.

"Do you go to raves?" Scruffy asked.

"No," I told him. It didn't push the conversation along. He didn't seem to care.

I kept pulling out my notebook. Scrawling all the things that barreled through my head. A subway car hurtling.

"Can I write on a page, too?" he asked. Sunshine looked on, smiling. It was one of those moments I still felt like I couldn't say, *No*. Even in my newfound freedom as a crazy bitch. I didn't have to be a bitch to want every page in my personal notebook to be all mine, but I could tell they felt otherwise. So I slid my notebook over to him with a clean page. Watched so he didn't browse through anything else. After a bit of doodling, he handed it back.

"Thanks," I said and took it without looking. Enough time had passed that I could safely escape for another smoke. "See you," I said to them.

"Catch you later, dude," Scruffy said and I winced, but he couldn't see because by this time he was already talking to my back. I hate when people call me *Dude*.

I examined my notebook. He had been busy. Scruffy had meticulously drawn doodles of a mushroom, a cartoon face of a dog, a labyrinth, his horoscope symbol (Cancer), and the Grateful Dead insignia. He also wrote the words, *Ohm Mantra*, and left me his phone number. I realized Scruffy's name was actually Bartholomew, the name written next to his number. We hadn't technically been introduced. Next to his real name, he had also written *Shaman Rogue Knight*. I guess meeting anyone was possible where I was living now. Since when was being in a mental ward such a pickup magnet? I didn't view it as an attractive selling feature. Yet, I couldn't remember the last time I'd received so many unsolicited phone numbers in such a short time.

September 27, 1999

Listening to Kristin Hersh's CD, *Strange Angels*, in the smoke room on my Walkman. This CD is so intense. Like it was written just for me. So much music seems that way lately, but this CD in particular. Her voice cuts under all the layers that keep everything else out. I smoke hard. Listen to her song, "Hope." The smoke goes down, rough sandpaper rasp against my throat, into lungs tight and small. I feel every inch of expansion and contraction as my body grows and shrinks. My hand brings the shrinking cigarette to my mouth to inhale, then to the over-sized juice can covered in flecks to tap off the ash, and back again to my waiting lips. A perfect circle.

I can't stop pressing repeat. Something will happen if I stop. Or the something I need to happen won't, if I don't keep my audio watch. I continue my vigil. *Tap, tap.* Put out my cigarette. Pull out another one. Light it. Inhale deeply. Kristen Hersh sings, *Nobody told me this would be so hard.* The sound of her voice, of each word, hits every part of my body just the right way. Falls into the whorls of every fingertip. Collects in the two spaces in my collarbone.

This sounds melodramatic when I write it in my diary, but I don't care. It's my truth. It's all I have. It seems like she wrote that line just for me. That isn't true. Yet, it feels that way. She wrote this song for me, sitting in this mental ward feeling like I might not make it. Like I'm never going to get out. I just keep listening to this song. Like a fresh coat of lip balm. Filling in my cracks.

I've felt this before. But tonight, it's unbearable. I wish Max hadn't stopped visiting. I must've exceeded okay behaviour the last few times she visited. Even for someone who was crazy. Pushed her too far. Asked for too much. She must be repulsed by me. I am.

I miss her so much. I wish I could call her.

September 28, 1999

Sadie came to visit again. She helped me write out a list of

advice in my journal so I'd remember it for later. Here's what we wrote:
1. Don't over-stimulate yourself.
2. Do things one at a time.
3. Start something and finish it.
4. Saying you feel "scattered" is negative. Start saying you feel *focused*.

"But the last thing I feel is focused," I told her.

"Never underestimate the power of positive thinking. Self-affirmations," she laughed. It wasn't actually funny, but I didn't feel like getting into it with her. I know she means well. She just doesn't understand what it's like. To be so depressed you can't get out of bed no matter how hard you try. Sadie can't comprehend not being able to change out of smelly pjs no matter how often the nurses threaten you. Even if you know you're gross. She doesn't understand what it's like to be locked up on this ward. That the "power" of her positive thinking doesn't have an effect here. Positive thinking doesn't unlock a locked door. It won't bring my release date any sooner. Won't bring me more visitors. It won't change shit. I'm still stuck here listening to Jean play *Morning Has Broken* fifty stupid times a day on the piano in the activity room. Singing in her warbly, childlike voice. Stuck.

I felt like telling Sadie to go stuff her positive fucking thinking. See if that would get me a goddamn day pass. But I kept my mouth shut. I'm so lonely for visitors I really want her to keep coming. Most people are so freaked out by me being a scary mental case on a fucked up mental ward they won't come. At least Sadie comes.

Sadie drops by the ward after her job. But I'm always locked behind this ward door. Try to watch the seasons change behind windows that don't open. I can't just stroll leisurely around the city. Rent a video. Go to a bar to cruise girls. Bake cookies. Take a bath. It's nice of Sadie to want to come here and try to help me. But she doesn't understand. It's not just a matter of thinking positively. It's a whole other thing. And being *focused* is not necessarily going to patch things up nice and easy for me.

Sadie leaves to go to the market, pick up groceries and make a wonderful dinner. Fancy cheese, olives, bread from that nice bakery and fresh vegetables to go for pasta that won't sit in a steam tray for hours before she has to eat it. I'll watch patients sit in front of the blue glow of the TV watching *ER*, bodies so slack they don't look conscious. I'll hear the nurses coerce Alice loudly into taking more medication. To go lie down in her room after yet another one of her temper tantrums because she misses her husband. Needs more attention. These fits that somehow always escape being called a Code White, but result in her being so overly medicated she's a zombie for days, walking among the rest of us. Barely.

September 28, 1999

"Sorry I was cross with you before," Jean said, "but they pumped me full of drugs and I was so full of energy to do the Lord's work. It is Sunday, after all."

Later it was snack. All of us unlucky enough not to have a pass or somewhere else to go are stuck on the ward. We choose an apple or an orange or a Saltine cracker to eat. Jean touches all of it, picks up a cracker and shoves it in her mouth.

"Munch, munch, munch," Jean says and sprays the air with cracker bits. I subtly try to move to avoid getting any on me. I don't want to be contaminated, but I don't want to offend her. "Hey, why not eat?" she says.

CODE WHITE

And I think, *Why not? What else is there to do in here, anyway?*

September 28, 1999

During her visit Sadie had some more advice. Sadie thinks Jamie's not a good person for me.

"Jamie's dangerous. She's sick and that's why she's in here. You need to remember that," Sadie told me. "I've heard things in the community over the years. Bad things. Like Jamie is an abuser."

"Where'd you hear that from?" I asked.

"More than one woman. It's true, Alex."

Makes me wonder what's going to be said about me whenever I manage to get out of here. Maybe it's all being said already. I'm pretty sure there's a lot of gossip floating around about me. Or gossip waiting to happen the second I poke my head out in the community. And I know things will be said by more than one "well-meaning" woman. Probably actually a bunch of bitches who can't keep their sharp little tongues in their mouths. Women with some kind of grudge. Petty reasons. Now that I'm in here, it's their chance.

Admittedly, they'll capitalize on the bizarre shit I did while I've been sick. Frame my craziness in flashing, marquee lights like I'm some kind of freak show. Gossip – a quick fix as hot as flicking a Hitachi Magic Wand. Instant relief for that itch that needs to get scratched. Fills that hole. They'll grab my story. Twist it. Pass it along their broken telephone. Fondle the cords. *Oh, did you hear! Well, I heard she actually did!*

When it isn't satisfying anymore, when it doesn't quite reach the fever pitch necessary to take them far enough from their own lives, they'll flick the switch higher. Create a collective hum so loud it drones out anything anyone possibly might remember about me before. Before I was reduced to *Alex, that crazy dyke who cracked up!*

Does that make their stories true? Maybe it's different when people in the community try to warn each other about a perpetrator of abuse. I know Sadie means well. And Ruth has also heard the same rumours about Jamie. Warned me when she visited. Still, I don't know. I don't want to believe those things. I really care about Jamie. She's always so nice to me. It sounds stupid, but she's just too sweet for what they're saying to be true. I know that's dumb. And shallow. It's just she's so utterly hot. In the dyke community, almost all the shit that goes around is just gossip. That's why it's called dyke drama. Because it's bullshit. I try to stay away from all that. Just because Sadie's heard more than one woman say Jamie's an abuser doesn't make it true. It could be mean-spirited rumours out to destroy someone's reputation.

Sadie made another list:

1. Defer sex until it is less dangerous.
2. No matter how much you want it. **DEFER!**
3. Someone can be beautiful and artistic. You can love the good side of them, but if they also have a violent, psychotic side you shouldn't date them.
4. **BE CAREFUL OF JAMIE!**

Sometimes, Sadie talks like some parts of what she's saying have been highlighted in bold to capture my attention. "It takes a lot of energy to mix your energy with someone else's. To be in love. Right now is your **HEALING TIME**. You're in here to heal. You **MUST CONSERVE YOUR ENERGY**," Sadie said.

"You need to keep your perspective. You're losing it in

here. You think you're in love with Jamie, but **THINGS LOOK DIFFERENT IN THE WARD THAN THEY DO IN THE WORLD OUTSIDE.** You need to focus on **GETTING BETTER** and on **YOURSELF.** Then you can get out of here ASAP," she added.

I try to argue, but Sadie seems so sure of herself. It's hard to go against her. She is a house of bricks, and I'm a makeshift shanty of branches, collapsing in the wind of her hot, impassioned breath. Sometimes, I'd like less lecture, and more of something else when Sadie comes to visit. I don't know what, exactly.

For what it's worth, Sadie's still coming when almost everyone else has stopped. They don't call and they don't visit. Sadie gives up her time to see me in this shithole. Most days, part of me knows what she's saying makes sense. Even though I'm not so sure of myself. Not really so sure of anything. I know I need to get better. I need to focus on myself. But I also don't think that means I have to become a nun. I wonder if Sadie is jealous. Before I got sick I always worried she had a tiny crush on me. The kind I pretended didn't exist. Maybe she's jealous of Jamie. That's why she's so adamant I stop seeing her. *Too bad for you, Sadie,* I think.

"Things will look different to you in a month because *you* will be different in a month," Sadie said, brows knitting together on a point. I can't argue with that. Except wouldn't I be different in a month regardless of whether I was living here or on the outside again? And right now, the truth is that I love Jamie. I can try to get myself better and watch our romance bloom all at the same time. One of those experiments in kindergarten planting a bean in a styrofoam cup. The sprout came up. Reaching for the sun. I can handle this. One day, me and

Jamie will have our freedom back, too. *One day, we will be out of here and together*, I think.

"You need to take a **CONSCIOUS SELF-CARE APPROACH.** That takes energy. But it will ultimately make you well," Sadie told me.

I am not entirely sure what a "conscious self-care approach" means. What that would entail. I was too busy fantasizing about the time Jamie and I had hot sex on the floor beside my bed between nurse's checks leading into some la la future filled with lace and flowers and meaningful looks, and of course, more really hot sex, off the ward. Me and Jamie hand in hand. We'd be free at last. Completely well. Flush meds we wouldn't need anymore down the toilet. The only locks on the doors would be ones we would have the keys to.

Just the opposite of what Sadie's advice had intended. I want to love Jamie AND get well, too.

Every time she visits, I make Sadie write down what she tells me because I know somewhere inside she's right. Or partly right. More right than I feel lately. And I can't remember what people say anymore unless they write it down. This way, I can re-read it later once I've forgotten. She wrote this in my journal for me: *Alex is smart. No one can take that away from her, including this place or her illness. Don't dwell on the stuff that's not true.*

I forgot it was there. I miss my memory.

four

September 29, 1999

I remember when I first got here. Not showering for two weeks solid. The pride in resisting. Resisting whatever was in my small power to withhold. Deathly fear of the water. Insisting water would wash away the layer of power riding on my skin. A layer of protection. As much as I'm embarrassed now at how long I went without washing, part of me's still afraid. Water is still the enemy. Even though that's crazy. I still hate going to the washrooms here. Washrooms every other woman on the ward goes into. Leaves her germs behind.

September 29, 1999

All the kitchen tables are covered in piles of old newspapers and magazines that Colleen brought in for us to make collage picture frames with. Kate is busy cutting out glossy pictures of kittens small enough to glue around the cardboard frame, which serves as a base for each of our projects. Jean is having difficulty making her pair of children's scissors work. Her hands are tacky with paste. Sunshine is all about snipping pictures of the rainforest she's managed to dig up out of an old *National Geographic*, curling at the corners.

"Check out this magic little toucan," she squeals as she sticks a brightly coloured bird on one side of her frame and then won't shut up about it for the rest of Arts & Crafts.

My hands are grey from sifting through old newspapers. Nothing seems worth cutting out. And having to use old children's scissors, blunt points and dull edges, thick with dried glue is depressing me. What's worse, is I know Colleen will count them all when the session is over. Make sure no one's trying to steal the lamest excuse for sharps I've ever seen.

I want to go to my room, but Colleen's enthusiasm is one of those big red magnets, pulling each one of us there whether we want to go or not. Once we show up for Arts & Crafts, we're hooked for the whole shebang until she says it's over and it's time to clean up.

Jamie is sitting alone at a table by the window. Hunched over a pile of newspapers whose pages she keeps whipping through, frantic. Trying to find that necessary thing for whatever it is she's making. In her hands, the scissors flash, dip in and out, cut circles around the rest of us. Colleen is used to Jamie's "artistic temperament" and, for some reason, spares her the chipper badgering the rest of us get. Jamie is allowed to sit by herself. Do what she wants, like an errant camper sitting on the edge of the dock while the rest of us have to follow along.

There's only a few more minutes left in Arts & Crafts.

"And how have we been doing?" Colleen asks, pushing aside the pile of papers in front of me to find a bare, cardboard frame. "Oh," she says, averting her eyes in embarrassment from my artistic nakedness and incompetemce. She goes to help Jean detach her scissors from both her hands and the loose pile of scrap paper she has managed to get stuck to.

I hear Jamie scrape her chair back from across the room. Stands up with something in her hand. I pretend not to notice. She strides over to our group table, dropping off the hacked up pile of newspapers and magazines she's been using.

"Thanks, Jamie," Colleen crows, "We hope you'll be back to join us next time!"

Jamie drops what was in her hand in front of me before leaving down the hallway.

"For you," she whispers.

A picture frame decorated all in newspaper personals. It's genius. In the middle of the frame, Jamie has created a collage from magazines. A bird constructed out of shades of different blue papers, cut and ribboned together. The glossy bird is trying to fly out of a half-opened, newsprinted window. The look on its pieced-together face.

September 29, 1999

Terry's floating in the hallway.

"I want to go home," she tells me.

"Why?" I ask, thinking I'll get serious insight deep into the core that is Terry.

"Why'd I wanna stay here?"

Why indeed. Who the fuck would want to stay in this place? Terry has the right idea. But neither of us is going anywhere.

"What are you in for?" Terry asks.

This is the part of the movie where the prison inmate roommates spill their guts about all the evil things they did on the outside. Every crime they ever committed toughly exchanged. Except we're not criminals. In here, we have other badges of distinction. Scars that set us apart from people.

"Manic depression," I confess, like it's all my fault. Like it most definitely makes me less than. I wish I could have whispered. Or not answered at all. It feels too private to share, which is ridiculous. We live on this hugely public ward. Nothing is kept even remotely private. Everyone knows the second you take a dump. Or if you're thinking of crying. But I still look over my shoulder. To see if anyone heard.

"Me too," she says quietly. Looks past my eyes. Somewhere I can't see. Her eyes look like little, flat hockey pucks. Terry rubs under her arm. "They've been giving me the ECTs. I hate the way they make me feel. Cloudy."

Terry gestures to her huge body, spilling out of two hospital gowns. She's wearing one on her front and one on her back, tied at the sides to fit the bulk of her. "Hospital Property" speckled all over Terry's body like ants taking over a picnic gone wrong.

"How many have you had?" I say, scared to ask. Feeling like I need to know. In case my doctor and nurse end up making me get electroshock therapy, too. Like so many of the women on this ward.

"Eight."

"How many more are they going to give you?" I ask, thinking Terry's going to tell me to screw off with my nosy questions. In her hospital gowns, she already looks pried open. Her sides leaking out.

"I hope it's the last one. Are you on meds… too?" Terry asks slowly, with some difficulty. She speaks as though there is a big, heavy magnet pulling at her tongue, weighing down things inside her mouth.

I don't want to answer, but that hardly seems fair, given all that Terry has just shared.

"A little," I answer vaguely. Feel like a snob for not just saying outright how things are for me around here. As if I belong to some country club. Not like the "real" patients who have to take medication or get ECT. I'm here by accident. *Don't mind me. I'm just waiting for the waiter to bring me my martini.*

"I'm on Epival," Terry volunteers around the magnet in her mouth.

"Me too," I offer. We smile.

"I just want to go home." We hang on that for a while. Our

bodies still stuck here. Our heads anywhere but. And then Terry asks, "Gotta light?"

We aren't in the smoke room. Terry can't smoke out here in the hallway. Has she forgotten? The nurses keep Terry's lighter behind the nursing station. Terry is supposed to ask one of them for her lighter when she goes into the smoke room. Then a nurse takes it back from her when Terry leaves the smoke room. I'm not sure of the rationale behind this even though they did the same thing to me at one point. Maybe they don't trust Terry to have a lighter. Maybe she sets fires. Maybe she burns herself. Maybe she'd burn someone else. I picture Terry burning a nurse with a little, plastic gem-coloured Bic lighter. Trying to burn down the ward. Code Red. We'd all be trapped. Locked in the flames as they flickered higher. Would the nurses cower in their station, or let themselves out through the locked door, leaving us behind?

I know it is the pettiest, meanest thing, but I don't want to give Terry my lighter. To give her a light would mean I would have to actually give her my lighter. Not just light her smoke. She'd have to take my lighter to go use it in the smoke room. And something tells me Terry isn't the kind of crazy who would give it back. Even though my name is taped right onto it. Maybe it's the ECT that has erased that kind of consideration. Or maybe it just isn't in Terry's nature. Terry, after all, is the woman who pees on all the chairs in the lounge. I know if I give my lighter to Terry I won't get it back. That may seem like a small thing. But that lighter is mine. And, I don't have that many things around here that belong to me. I've become that petty that I actually don't want to give someone my own stupid, cheap, disposable lighter.

"Gotta light?" Terry asks. Her hockey pucks look me right

in the eye. They don't slide past. Don't lower. They stay right there, with me. Widen into normal, regular eyes. Nice ones. That hold me. I don't want to go anywhere for that moment. I don't want to look over my shoulder to check for spies. I don't want to hold anything back. I don't feel dirty about anything for a second. Not for why I'm here or the meds I take or how often I cry in my room or the fact that I don't want to give Terry my lighter.

I reach into my pocket. Hand Terry my lighter. As I touch it for the last time, I run my thumb and finger over the worn, beige masking tape a nurse had stuck on there a long time ago. I had watched her rip off a strip. Wondered what she was going to do with it. She pressed it against my lighter. Wrote my name on it in her kindergarten teacher handwriting. I don't make up the rules here. I make my own choices. And I'm trying to decide something else. Not let this place decide for me.

Terry lets her clammy hand, the pudgy one that was rooting around in her underarm moments earlier, touch my hand for a few extra seconds as she slowly takes my lighter from me.

"Much obliged, ma'am," she says. I swear I see Terry wink at me.

September 30, 1999

Jamie watches me grind the cherry on my smoke out in the cheap, foil ashtray. It's so quiet in the room the hot crunching sound is all we can hear. For once, no one else is in the smoke room. Except me and Jamie. Staff passing the tiny window in the door on their way to check on something are little blurs. Shadows like sharks circling. I'm abruptly aware of my mouth. Jamie won't stop staring at me.

"Stop it," I say. Nervous. "Someone's going to come in any second."

"No one's coming," Jamie says. Confident. Assured. Suddenly, there's no reason to point out the obvious. This isn't our room. There are no locks. We don't own this place. And yet somehow, the more she keeps looking at me, the more I stop worrying. Believe her. Even though it's stupid. I know no one's coming, either.

I touch her knee. Soft and quick. Move my hand up her thigh and squeeze. Take it away before any of the shadows through the window see. Even if below the waist is a poor sightline from outside that window, looking in. Our advantage. I don't want to take any more chances. Do I?

She grabs my hand. Keeps it low. Stares right at me. And somehow it seems, with this other set of eyes, she is also staring through the side of her head. At the window. Making sure we are okay.

Then Jamie is standing in the corner. Her cigarette left burning in the ashtray. Smoke streaming into the air. She's standing in the corner behind the door. The corner where no one can see much of anything from outside the smoke room. Not even through the window. Not if we time things right.

"Are you coming?" she smiles.

I don't know how not to.

I've jammed Jamie into the corner, holding myself up against her, my hands pressed against each wall where they meet. The hinges of the door bite into us. There is not much time. I've never done something like this. I tug at her hair. Something in me catches. I wipe my lipstick off of her in a blind rush.

"You have to go," I tell her, hurrying back to the other side

CODE WHITE

of the room. Safe. I put out her cigarette. "Go, before we get in trouble."

Just as she leaves, Kate comes in the room. Jamie grins easy and waves at us both.

"See you guys later," she says and kicks her foot at the floor like there's something there.

"Bye, Jamie," Kate says.

My heart is beating too loudly to hear what Kate says next.

September 30, 1999

On my passes I walk around the neighborhood. At first, I wasn't allowed to go by myself. My mom would come and keep me company. I felt like a total idiot needing a babysitter to walk around for an hour with me. Make sure I didn't get into trouble and went back when the time was up. But I didn't have a choice if I wanted to go out. And I wanted that more than anything. We'd just walk around. See all the garbage on the street. Whatever. As long as I was outside, I was happy. Air on my face. Sky over my head. I never had much to say. I'm sure my mom was bored. But it was much better then all of the times her and my dad came to visit me on the ward.

Now, I can go out once a day on my own for an hour. I don't really have a route. I walk down College Street and then weave up and down the side streets. Sometimes I walk through Kensington Market, but since I don't have money to buy any treats it's partly torture. I'm not complaining about being able to leave the ward. I LOVE that I get one hour to walk anywhere I want. It's total bliss. But I can't walk too far from the hospital. Not in an hour. I take my Walkman. Sometimes, I even sing out loud and let my voice carry in the fresh air. No walls to stop me. I wrap my scarf around my neck and try to appreciate that

debra anderson

I'm outside. Feel the air on my skin. Cool and crisp like the fake mirror in my room when I press the length of myself against it. While I've been locked inside, the seasons have changed without me. Summer's over now. I missed an entire season. Witnessed behind glass. I try not to let my bitterness rankle me as I walk outside. I don't want to ruin the feeling of my feet moving forward, even if they have to turn right back to where they came from after an hour.

On the ward is slipper terrain. Sock country. You only have to deal with white speckled floor tiles. Clean and smooth. Nothing jagged to hurt your feet. No trash except in the appropriate receptacles. Outside, everything is different. Rough and dirty. The wind whips against my face. Stirs my hair all over. Makes me messy. Everything looks so unclean. The sidewalks are a dirty colour. Even after it rains. Dirty grey. And always covered with litter. On the ward, almost all the women walk with their heads down. They watch the ground because there's really nothing to look at on the ward. They've already memorized everything there. There are no pictures on the walls. No interesting shop windows to peek into as you pass by. Nothing. Just mental ward chic.

On my walks outside, I remember there's another, more practical reason for walking with your head down. Outside, people stare at the ground to deal with all the dog shit. Like trying to avoid mines. Yesterday, I was about to step in dog shit three times. I can't remember the last time I was happy almost stepping in dog shit. I wasn't one bit pissed. I looked above my head. Saw the wide open blueness of the sky. Felt the rough concrete under the soles of my shoes. Thought, *I'm wearing shoes, not slippers!! I'm outside! There's cold air on my cheeks! And I'm all by myself.* No babysitter psych attendant in sight.

Not my mother, either. It felt so good to be off the ward. To have everything so different. My feet never felt so good on the ground, two centimeters away from the grossest pile of dog shit I'd seen in a long time. If I closed my eyes I could almost feel my soles tingle. And I knew I'd made it. Soon, this would be regular for me. Being on the outside would be the twenty-four seven. And the ward would be no more. I had graduated. Now I was dealing with dog shit. Again.

September 30, 1999

Jamie's being a pig tonight. I'm so angry. I'm not sure where to keep it all. I acted like such a bitch. I needed to retaliate after her little performance with Alice. But when I remember her and Alice in the smoke room, I don't feel sad at all. Just glowing hot coals in the palms of each of my hands. Smoldering. That goddamn Alice. She doesn't even smoke. She shouldn't even be in the smoke room. She was only there because she has a total crush on Jamie. It is so obvious, it's embarrassing.

Alice refuses to admit she could have a thing for another woman because she's married. And she's this big, newly-converted Orthodox Jew. Alice doesn't believe in homosexuality. Before Jamie came Alice was always following me around. Trying to save my wayward Jewish lesbionic self. Bring me back into the fold. It got annoying fairly fast, but sometimes it was sort of cute. Alice was extremely earnest, yet completely sly in her conversion tactics. Constantly quoting the Torah as if that would make me realize I wanted to become Orthodox like her and grab myself a husband. She'd sing these Jewish songs to get me all nostalgic and talk about different Jewish holidays. Promise me latkes and matzah ball soup when she got better and had access to her kitchen. I knew she never cooked anything. Her nanny fed everyone in her family. On top of everything, she'd ply me with presents. Sparkly hairclips she bought on a pass or a few flowers out of a bouquet someone brought to her. To show me the kindness she felt in her heart. And how great practicing *tzedakah* made people feel. Charity begins from the home and all that.

But she refused to ever sit beside me or get too close. Always kept a healthy distance from the perverted lesbian she was trying to save. Now that Jamie's here, Alice seems to have forgotten her feelings about homosexuality and abomination. And her marriage. She has a major crush on Jamie. It's so fucked up. Tonight the two of them were so drugged. Each on their separate meds. Alice was wearing her latest wig acquisition to cover her hair in good modest fashion, in keeping with the tenets of her new religion. A lame cheap Tina Turner rip-off, crooked on her head. She was too out of it to realize. Jamie wore her little black cap, the one I'd adored when she was first admitted.

"It's singing time," Alice suddenly announced. "I know the EXACT song we are going to sing. Okay, Jamie? Okay, Jamie? *Islands In The Stream*," she barked.

I was cursing at Alice because I LOVE that song. Now they were going to crush any good memory I ever had of it. I tried to breathe away the hate I was feeling, but it wouldn't go anywhere. Stayed in my stomach, curdling. The two of them attempted to stand in the middle of the smoke room. Weaving unconsciously back and forth to do their inpatient unit karaoke duet.

And then the worst. They started to sing. Both their mouths were too slack from meds to form the words properly. They just sounded drunk. I guess it made the karaoke experience more authentic. Alice kept putting her arm "innocently" around Jamie, while winking at me as she did it so I'd be sure to catch what she did. She was wearing her electric fuchsia silky housecoat and matching nightgown. Even her stupid flip-flop slippers were that ugly eyesore pink. They kept falling off her feet as she shuffled along. Alice kept pointing her toe and kicking her leg out as if it were sexy. It was just sad watching her hike up her nightgown to show off her leg. Extending it as if she was a showgirl doing the cancan. Thematically it didn't even match the Dolly Parton song.

    Alice took Dolly's part, except she didn't know the words. Jamie, of course, was Kenny Rogers. I knew all the words, but no one had asked me. Alice and Jamie's thing. Even though I thought Jamie and I were a thing. Even though I thought Jamie really felt something for me with all those fucking love notes she kept slipping constantly under my door. And the paintings she kept making for me in Arts & Crafts. Not to mention the myriad of scratch lottery cards she'd bring me back from the store on her passes, unbidden. How she liked to plant herself wherever I was on the ward and watch me just enough so I knew she was paying attention, but not too much so that all the nurses and psych assistants would separate us and make her go sit somewhere else. The sex we'd sneaked in my room was seeming like a dream and a mistake. And here I was watching Alice, the married Orthodox lesbophobic bigot drape her silky fuchsia arm over Jamie as if it had always belonged there. Like it had always belonged over the shoulder of my handsome butch. Jamie's argyle sweater vest had started to ride up, disheveled. She was too sloppy to notice, her skin numb. Jamie who always kept herself together NOT EVEN NOTICING herself looking like a STUPID, GODDAMN SLOB.

Alice pulled Jamie closer to her with the hand draped over Jamie's shoulder. The hand that must jerk off her husband. That very hand was possessively clinging to Jamie as if Alice owned her. And Alice's tacky fuchsia acrylic nails shot out from her fingers like daggers, highlighted against the navy of Jamie's sweater vest. Alice dug in as she smiled at me as if to say, *I'm still the prettiest girl. All the boys love me, Alex.*

Jamie staggered from the force of Alice yanking, but didn't notice her footing was lost. And I thought, *Alice can have her. I don't want any part of this.*

And then they sang together again, louder this time:

Islands in the stream
That is but so far
No one is seen
How can we be strong
Flail away with me
To another girl
Where we'll lie on each other, oh year
From a lover to a lover, uh-huh.

The words were jumbled. Not even the right words. I didn't want to seem like a spoilsport and leave in the middle of their performance. I didn't want to let Alice think she'd won anything. That this was a big deal in any way. And besides, I was trying to have my cigarette. They were both so wasted on their night meds and attention from each other that they looked about ready to plow into the floor, or into each other. Their arms were propped around each other holding the other up, about to give way any second.

Jamie's bad boy unfurled as she flirted with Alice, looking

at me quickly now and again like a kid not getting enough attention, making sure I was watching. Trying to make me jealous. Alice's affection for Jamie increasing solely because she was now an object of desire. Pride strokes. And me getting jealous, despite trying not to. Them watching me get jealous. Getting off on it.

I demand an apology from Jamie afterwards. Once we are alone. The boy in her humbly admits she's getting her period.

"I really don't know what came over me, Alex," she says softly, her eyes quickly flicking up to my face and then sticking to the floor. "I plead temporary insanity. Please forgive me. I don't know what I was doing."

I know she has debased herself by sharing this. Admitting she bleeds just like me. Opened herself to me to be viewed as a woman. Not the way she likes to be seen. And not a way I generally frame her. Hard to explain, because we know that's what she is.

I hand her three long maxi pads from the corner of my room. If I were an artist, I'd draw a picture of tonight. Three long pads with wings floating across the page on an inky blue sky. On each pad I would draw a face. Me. Alice. Jamie. Superimposed against the whiteness of the pad. And Alice's wig floating out of context on the edges of the paper.

"You need to give me a written apology if you think I'm going to forgive you," I demand. My meds make my memory foggy. I want her apology in writing so I can reread it to make it real.

I hand her the note I wrote after I left them there, staggering in the smoke room. "Read this every day. To remind yourself of what a fuck up you are."

"I will. I'll laminate it," she says and is so earnest I know she isn't joking. "I'll polish your boots in contrition. If you'll let me."

My boots need a good polish and I don't like to do it. But I know she'll like doing it too much. I don't want her to do anything that makes her happy. I don't know why I am talking to her.

We're in my room with the door open in case a nurse walks by. I don't want to get in trouble for her. At least not tonight. I casually pick up my belt; it's lying over my chair. I wrap it around my hands tightly. Her eyes follow me. Once my movements stop in measured tension, her eyes gleam. I look into them and see she's still very high. I don't know why I'm bothering to tease her. It's too easy. She wants attention from me. It's flattering, but tonight she has demonstrated she's a vacuum. Not discerning about what she picks up.

"I want to take you to a hotel. I've been saving my money for us. It's the money I've been making on some of my passes when I go out," Jamie stammers.

Jamie lies to the nurses to get emergency passes. She isn't "formed," like me, I think she's allowed to leave the ward. I'm not totally sure of all the details. I know she goes to Chinatown to gamble. At least that's what Jamie tells me. When she comes back from her passes she always has a big wad of cash that she sometimes shyly, sometimes eagerly, pulls out of her pants to show me. Fans out bills and I try not to care. I try not to be envious while I think of my confiscated bankcard the nurses are sitting on in their station. The empty wallet they gave back to me, useless. All my time stretching out here. Absolutely no possibilities. In Chinatown, Jamie tells me, they think she's a boy. She passes for a boy, bets and often wins. Sometimes, she tells me she goes to some racetrack somewhere else in the city and bets on horses. Gambling makes me uneasy. Jamie keeps saying she wants to take me somewhere. Escape our problems. Jamie wants us to go away, even for a few hours, each on a pass if we can arrange it and trick the nurses.

I know that won't solve anything. It won't solve why we are here. I look into her eyes, but can't tell her that. Even though I don't want her money and I want this conversation to be over, I tell her to save her money.

"Buy me something instead," I say, even though as I say it I am hoping she won't. Because then I will have to give it back to her.

And then a nurse comes by in the hallway and sees Jamie.

"Leave Alex's room," she says. For once I'm glad at the intrusion.

When I try to sleep that night I can't. All I can see is Alice. The way she kept kicking her leg. Tripping over her ugly flip-flops. Her arm around my Jamie. Alice gleaming triumphantly at me. Lipstick on her teeth. Jamie's unfocused eyes. Her desperate apology, which I'm not even sure rings true. Their horrible voices singing one of my favourite songs. Words that won't let go even in the darkness. Electric fuchsia.

October 1, 1999

In the smoke room before bedtime Christina told me that between nurse's checks last night Jean snuck into the room Christina shares with two other patients. Everyone was asleep, including her. Christina sat huddled on a bench, hugging her knees and rocking herself, as if the words tumbling out of her mouth were putting her in the same place Jean put her last night.

Jean slinked in and stroked Christina lightly all over until she woke up to the feeling of little spider hands tingling everywhere. Creepy body kisses from the palms of Jean's hands and the tips of her fingers, sticky from the oranges she always eats. Hands with quick med tremors. Christina didn't know who was filling her room with an awful screeching noise, layered over the calm sound of Jean crooning, "Daddy's here, it'll be okay now."

The night nurse, Rhoda, had to carry Christina to the washroom. The psych assistant on duty, Ralph, dragged Jean out and gave her a sedative. Christina took one, too, and went back to bed. Then, at about two-thirty, Christina woke up to pounding on the door to her room. Disoriented from the sedative, she thought maybe there was a fire. A Code Red. She got out of bed and opened her door. There stood Jean, smiling and waving at Christina.

I wish we could put a secret cot in my room. A hide-away bed for Christina that Jean wouldn't know about. The nurses would never go for this plan. They'd never let Christina sleep in a room to which she wasn't officially assigned. For sure not a room allotted to one crazy dyke. So I don't discuss stowaways with Christina. Or how Christina will have to sleep in her own room. The room where Jean will know where to find her, down a dark hallway in the middle of the night. Far away from the nursing station.

Christina's hand is twitching. She hasn't had a smoke in a bit. I hand her one of my cigarettes. Wish I could lay my hand over hers, but I don't. She's been touched enough in this lifetime. Christina takes the cigarette.

"Thanks," she says.

I lean forward, not too close, light it for her and watch her inhale deep.

CODE WHITE

October 2, 1999

Jean did it again last night. Christina is falling apart just as fast as she was getting better. I don't understand why the nurses can't stop it. Jean stole into her room again last night while Christina was sleeping. Crept up beside her bed in her stained nightgown. Caressed the side of her face and murmured, "Daddy doesn't love me."

Christina didn't have to tell me she has some kind of abuse in her past. It's pretty obvious. She did tell me she told Jean, "Fuck off, you're triggering me," which didn't faze Jean at all. She's not big on the concept of personal boundaries. Jean wouldn't leave. She was in some kind of trance. The nurse had to be called to get her out. Then it was happy hour again with the sedatives. I don't understand why Jean doesn't trip over those slip-on sneaker imitation Keds she always wears. She's so heavily doped up. Christina said Jean apologized today, but later started that daddy stuff again. I'm so pissed, like my face is burning red. Like it could melt off my head in a pool of wax.

But it's obvious Jean is going through a lot herself. This level of acting out has to be a cry for help around some serious unresolved issues. Jean needs therapy to heal and move forward. Except, on the ward they don't let you get any therapy. They just medicate you. They want you to be "stabilized." Only when they feel you are "better" will they release you. Only then can you go get therapy. Jean isn't stabilized. So, she doesn't get discharged, she doesn't get any therapy. In the meantime, she's going to terrorize each one of us every night on the ward. We're the helpless, over-medicated victims in the kind of horror movie that everyone's seen, yelling warnings at the actors who wait to get slaughtered on screen. Christina's fingertips are pink and raw from her chewing on them. I saw them when she was smoking and tried not to stare.

"Don't tell anyone, but I think Jean should be put in restraints," Christina said. "Except, then she'd just sing *Ave Maria* and drive us all bonkers," she joked, still rocking herself in the smoke room. Rocking everywhere she sits now. Permanently hunched shoulders. Wearing five layers of clothes over her thin frame.

I picture having to listen to Jean sing. The nurses hushing us. Sending us all into our rooms. Shutting the doors. How they always try to shame us when a Code White is called. We linger in the hallway, trying to see what's happening. Each fearful it could be us next time. The nurses act like we are all nosy. Out of control gossips. I want to watch so that I can document what happens. When I get out of here I want to give an accurate report of what actually goes on inside. So that maybe someone other than me will be outraged, too. That worse than the actual procedures is that there is official go-ahead from way up high. How am I supposed to give my report if they kick me out of the hall so I can't actually see the details of what's happening?

The nurses say, *The woman who is having the Code White would really appreciate her privacy right now.* And I am sure she would really like her dignity. Unfortunately, I'm not the one who is able to give it back to her. So, we all sit in our rooms. Listen to her scream and howl, wrestled down by the psych assistants. Listen until she's so limp from pushing and from the sedating, there's nothing to hear except the boisterous voices of the staff. Shuffling through her room, while she lies wooden across her bed, like another piece of the furniture, frozen and silent. A model patient.

CODE WHITE

Even though I hate what Jean's doing to Christina, I don't want to hear. Jean screaming at the top of her lungs that goddamn *Ave Maria*. Thrashing in panic in her restraints. Hearing it from down the hallway as her notes seep through the crack in my doorway into my room. Tears running down my cheeks as her singing gets lower and lower. Words fumbled. Mumbling as the meds in the injection take hold. The needle they gave her quiets her voice and stills her body. Makes her drop the only thing that had helped her in that moment, the only thing that gave her a piece of herself. Silent, tied up and lost. Code White.

October 3, 1999

I told Sadie how embarrassed I was at all the crazy things I did when I was manic. All the weird phone calls I made. The things I said. What scares me even more are all the calls I made that I don't remember. As if I drank a big bottle of whiskey in my room, walked to the phone, pumped it full of quarters like a pinball machine, picked some numbers and made my fingers push.

It'd be easier if I had been drunk when I had called all those people, whoever they were. I don't know who I called. Or what I said. What they said back. It's probably a blessing, this blackout. Except, I know there are rumours. People talking about me and there's not much I can do to stop it.

"Alex, breathe," Sadie said. "What's done is done. You did what you did when you were sick. It's over now. You have to move on. You move on, others will too."

I know she's right. Only I still feel so embarrassed. It's easy to talk about moving on, but I'm the one locked with nowhere to go but my head, fingering each phone call I can remember. I can't stop concocting all the degrading conversations I must have had.

I approach a shiny slot machine. My hand trembles as I reach for the giant arm, atop which is a golden telephone receiver. I wrap my hand around it, pull the lever down. The slots go round, the machine clicks and whirs. The first slot rests. A payphone. The second slot stops. A payphone. The third slot rolls to a stop. The machine goes wild. Three payphones. The slot machine rings like a phone, lights flashing. Spews quarters at me until I'm drowning. Tosses bowlfuls of quarters at my head. It hurts. I'm scared the quarters will leave bruises. I struggle, but my feet are trapped in quarters. The pile grows. My winning slot machine shows no sign of stopping.

Somehow, for each coin I'm getting, I know I've used that quarter at some point, with someone, to start a conversation that I may or may not remember. I finger the quarters nearest me nervously, my sweat mixing with the metal until we are a slick mess. *Where have we been?*

"Move on," Sadie told me. "Let it go."

I really wish I could.

October 4, 1999

Lee's always either in the smoke room or pacing in the hallway. The hallway doesn't lead anywhere, just forms a small horseshoe around the ward. That doesn't stop Lee. In the smoke room she sits on the bench and hunches over her cigarette, skinny legs wrapped in shiny black spandex pants that sag. Her legs poke out from the bottom of oversize sweatshirts. A little brown tweedy hat with a brim covers her hair, which I know is greasy and hasn't been washed in a long time. Lee has to get one of the nurses to help her shampoo. I know because she asked me to do it once for her in the laundry room sink.

"Oh boy," she groans beside me.

I wonder if she'll ever not be depressed. If she could go to the future and hear how she sounds now, would she get better any faster? Would any of us?

October 4, 1999

Being in this place is making me feel like the biggest monster. Like I've transformed into this thing that no one else is ever going to want to be near again. Exiled from everyone, locked on a ward. I'm stuck here. Almost everyone I know is either too scared or weirded out to visit. Even Max. Who seemed immune to the repellant nature of this place. Now, she won't ever come back. No matter how much I want her to.

I wish I knew what it was that I did to make her stop coming. To not even explain why. I want to refuse to let this cancel out my memory of that smile she gets when she's around me. Shy eyes turned down. Blush staining her skin. I want to believe she likes me back. And that once I get out of here, we'll have a chance. That I didn't wreck everything somehow by being me, locked in here, driving every possible good thing as far away as it could get. Except it's kind of difficult to hold onto any of that.

She didn't even say goodbye. Not even a, *Sorry, I'm really busy*. Or, *It's just too hard to come to this scary mental hospital anymore*. I would even have understood, *I can't see you like this anymore, it hurts too much*. Instead, I got nothing. She wouldn't even return my calls. I cringe now at the stupid messages I left. At the time, I actually thought she'd be coming back to visit any day. That she'd just gotten a bit busy. I wish I could take every word back off her machine. But I can't take any of it back. It's all me. All mine. And I know I'm what drove her off with nothing to say. Not this place.

October 5, 1999

At breakfast, Christina looks even paler then usual. Lilac half-moons under her eyes. Darker than I've ever seen them. Sunken, like marks from a coffee cup sitting on a piece of paper. I want to touch the stains under her eyes. Gently coax the thin skin there to fly away.

"Last night I dreamt of little white spiders crawling on my walls. There were thousands of them skittling up the walls," she said dully over her bowl of popping Rice Krispies. "Their writhing bodies glowed in the moonlight. Iridescent. It was as if the walls were moving. Breathing all around me."

I could see it exactly. Pushed my toast away. I wanted to take her small head into my arms. Brush her long, tangled hair. Instead, I listened to the hiss of her cereal. Asked her about the guy she was seeing on her passes.

October 5, 1999

When Mary's dad comes to visit they don't talk about Mary.

"What do you talk about?" I ask Mary in the smoke room. She's just finished a visit with her dad and her stepmother. She looks younger and like she's about to cry. Mary shrugs.

"Stuff like the weather. Nothing really," she answers. "And there's this huge thing we can't talk about. Me. Why I'm here. What's wrong with me."

We sit in silence. Mary, me and Christina. Then Mary breaks it like a tidal wave gushing from her mouth.

"I asked his wife to bring me razors, you know? So I could

shave my legs. She said, *Absolutely not*. I told her she would have to turn them in right away to the nursing station. That it'd be fine."

"Won't they let you use one of my new ones I just bought? I'd give you one of mine, Mary," Christina says.

Mary shrugs. "Policy."

"Policy."

We don't talk about Mary's multiple suicide attempts on and off the ward. That that's why her stepmother won't give her razors. We don't talk about how humiliating it is for Mary not to have her own razor to shave her legs. How degrading it is to ask a nurse each time. To be supervised while shaving. We don't talk about these things because we know them already. But, we also don't talk about the weather.

Instead we all smoke. Someone puts out a butt. I light another. We sit. Together.

October 6, 1999

I'm afraid to go to sleep. I'm stuck in the bed. My entire body is the tip of my tongue and the mattress is a block of ice. I keep hearing people outside my door. It's probably just the night nurse and the psych assistants checking on things. Sometimes, they open my door and shine their flashlights in. It hurts my eyes. I've never gotten used to it. Strangers randomly opening my door in the middle of the night. The pitter-patter sounds like rats scurrying. I don't know when they'll choose their moment to strike. There's nowhere to hide. Besides, I'm immobile. Pinned to the bed by this sack I've been lugging all day. Like a fisherman's net. The sack sits every night on my chest, huge and heavy. I can feel the wooden bedframe underneath aching through the thin mattress. All that weight makes it hard to breathe.

The psych assistants don't see the sack. Or else they don't care. They see my eyes, open. Glittering in the dark. Shells broken on the beach ready to cut their feet if they get too close. They tell me to go to sleep. *Alex*, they say, *it is very, very late. Alex, it is time for bed*, they chide.

Suddenly I am eight years old and the psych assistant isn't actually my psych assistant, but my babysitter who pleads with me to go to sleep before my parents come home. I'm eight years old again and I don't get to say when I go to sleep. I have to ask permission to stay up just a tiny bit later. *Please? Just for one more TV show?* I have to barter for what I think is best for me. Even though I've been putting myself to bed for eons with much success. I go when I'm ready. Now suddenly, some other person, a stranger, gets to decide all that for me. *Go to sleep, Alex. Stop making trouble for me, Alex.*

The psych assistant leaves my room. The door is left halfway open. Yellow light from the hall tumbles in. Something flickers red inside me. I let myself feel enough to locate where the spark is coming from. So I will remember next time what this feels like. So next time, I will know where to find that red. Hold onto it instead of stashing it somewhere no one can see.

October 7, 1999

Terry's wearing one of those large, loose knit acrylic sweaters from the eighties. Green like a tart apple. The kind of apple they don't serve here. The print design looks like it's out of a dot matrix printer. Cranking out words real slow.

"I hate this place, I want to go home," Terry yells at a nurse before she slips into the smoke room. Terry doesn't seem to care if she gets in trouble. She just keeps yelling. Says everything she feels with no remorse. A ream of paper constantly spewing. Terry doesn't care about a Code White being called on her. Not today.

I wish I could be more like Terry. It seems a much better way to be than too scared to say even half of what crosses through my head. I hate this place, too. I want to go home, too. I want to yell and scream things. Really let go and holler. Just like Terry. But I don't want to get in trouble. I don't want to have ECT. I don't want a Code White. And I don't want to end up having to stay here longer. I can be good. I can wait out my punishment in the corner. Can't I?

Inside the smoke room, Tammy tells me about the most recent time she was in the middle of hanging herself, when she was still on ACU. Before they sent her back up here.

"I was thinking blue. Cold. I couldn't remember anything. Not a single thing. My whole life didn't flash before my eyes like they say it does. That's bullshit. It was just cold and blue. And then the fucking nurse comes in and goes, *Mind if I check on you?*"

Kate's there, too, sprawled on the floor in a long, white cotton nightgown with two kittens on the front playing with a ball of yarn. At the bottom of the nightgown, there's a smaller ball of yarn that's also pink. Some unraveled strings printed around the bottom. It's cute and matches Kate's pink, flat-footed gymnastic slippers that remind me of ballerina slippers. When I was younger I always wanted a pair. I thought they'd make me graceful. That I'd flutter down the street with neat hair in a bun. A beautiful swan. Kate's slippers have a delicate strap across the top of her foot with a bow on them. Whenever Kate sits on the floor in the smoke room, she spreads her legs and does all these flexing exercises with her feet inside her slippers to stretch her arches. Usually Kate wears stretchpants with her nightgowns. Today she's forgotten. It's just her bare legs flexing her arches really fast. First one and then the other fluttering like the wink of eyelashes out of control, some sort of nervous tic. Sometimes she does both at once like a hard blink.

"I'm feeling so good today," Kate says as she tries to put her cigarette into her mouth and misses, hitting the side of her cheek with the filter. Light shines out her face like someone has put a bright spotlight behind it. Kate puts one hand on the wall and pulls herself up drunkenly, palm slapping loudly against the slick paint. Standing, she keeps bumping into the wall even though ordinarily she has perfect balance. Now she is ready to do the rest of the ballet stretches she wants to show us. She turns her feet out at the toes. I worry she's going to topple over. She's still holding that lit cigarette, ashes spraying down to the floor.

"I'm glad you're feeling better now, Kate," I say, even though it's clear that she is perhaps feeling too much better.

"A refreshing change. I wish it'd stay like this, but everything that goes up must come down," Kate says and kicks her leg up and out to the side, her cigarette getting tangled in her hair as she raises her free arm for balance.

My eyes search for the cherry on the end of her smoke to make sure it isn't buried in her hair. Burning her somewhere. Everything seems safe enough.

Kate has one smoke going in the ashtray, one in her mouth, and is pulling another out to light it, all while doing her ballet exercises standing against the wall. I need to go somewhere else. I wonder how long it's going to take Kate to come down this time. Will she come down so hard she'll curl up in her room for days, unable to come out? Like last time. Just before this quick climb. How much it would suck on top of everything else to be a rapid cycler like Kate? Go through the up and the down like someone else was really bored, watching the television show that is your life and flipping through the channels fast. Never, ever giving you the remote control.

October 8, 1999

In the washroom today someone scrawled a new piece of graffiti in blue ballpoint. *If feeling is to grate take yr clothes off. Do it.*

It makes me smile. I wonder who wrote it. My hand itches to fix the spelling mistakes. Clean up the grammar. I instantly feel like my whole body fell in a big bucket of dirty water and I'm coated in the heavy, dark colours of garbage. Why can't I just enjoy things for what they are? Why do I always have to end up being the kind of person I want to step outside of and leave behind, embarrassed and ashamed of myself?

October 8, 1999

Leah's waiting to get into a rehab centre somewhere, pretty much anywhere that will admit her. Except nowhere will take her, because she's an addict with mental problems. In the rehab people's eyes, that seems to qualify her solely as a mental patient. Here on the ward, they won't give her certain drugs that she needs to get stable because they're addictive. Like all those 'pam drugs to smooth out the jitter when she's anxious. No Chlonazepam or Ativan or whatever for Leah because she's an ADDICT. Leah can't win. Even though she's voluntary.

Leah wears desert boots that she sleeps in so no one can steal them; she told me.

"You have way too much shit in your room, Alex," she said.

"You're just asking for trouble. Someone's definitely going to rip you off."

Leah has been in a lot of institutions before and is very wise to what happens in them. I didn't know they still made desert boots. Leah's tough and I like her a lot. I'm not even sure what she's addicted to. A mélange of things, I think. She is a lot older than me and spends a lot of her time in the smoke room or on the payphone making desperate calls to people for help. She asks in a low voice either for money or help getting into a rehab place. I know this because she always uses the payphone outside my room. Or else she is on the phone calling rehab places directly, which never amounts to anything. It makes me sad.

Leah summed up the ward cabin fever nicely one day in the smoke room. She'd finished crying after being rejected from rehab for the seventh time since she arrived. Leah's very butch. Doesn't hardly cry. I handed her some Kleenex from my room and she said, "You beg to get in here and then you want to run out as soon as they lock the door behind you. It's strange."

Yes, it is, Leah. It is very strange. "No one wants a door closed on them," I said.

"And how," Leah snorted into her tissue. Looked up at me and smiled. Tossed her dead butt across the room onto the floor. We giggled.

I love you, Leah. I wish you could get better.

October 9, 1999

Jamie hurled a plate across the kitchen earlier tonight. True, the kitchen has started using paper plates and plastic cutlery since they say the dishwasher's broken. So it wouldn't have hurt anyone. But Jamie hurled it at Nurse Dee's head. If it was a real plate it would have done some damage. I keep seeing it over and over. Jamie furious at something Nurse Dee said Jamie couldn't do. Jamie's body coiled like one of those snake-in-the-can gag things. Ready to explode. Face scrunched up. Eyes condensed into tiny slits. Jamie picked up her piece of cake and held it clenched in her hand. The plate curled around her fist. I didn't want to see what was coming.

"Put the cake down, Jamie," Nurse Dee warned.

I knew she shouldn't have said anything. Not when Jamie was like this.

"Okay, I'll put the fucking cake down. I'll put it wherever the fuck I want," Jamie said.

Jamie threw the plate. Like an indoor Frisbee. Cake crumbs spattered. I couldn't believe it. My ears buzzed. The plate rotating until there was nothing else.

The cake crashed to the floor. Pink and yellow flowers smushed against the floorboards. Seared onto my eyelids. Jamie looked at me. As if I would get her off the hook. Like we all hadn't just watched the same clichéd episode whose theme today was, "Abusive Behaviour," and "Anger Management Problems." Now we were at the part where we all wondered, would the offender admit she had a problem? Would an intervention be needed?

Jamie kept staring. Soft. Big wet eyes and pouty mouth. As if I could wipe her behaviour under the rug, away from the nurse's eyes. Clean it all up. Eyes burning, I looked up to meet Jamie's, who'd been watching me stare at the desecrated cake. I wasn't going to save her this time. No well-placed, casual joke about the whole thing to defuse the situation. Screw that.

"You're on your own," I told Jamie. Nurse Dee's face didn't

change, but it seemed like her eyes opened wider. Like she smiled inside or something.

"It's not a big deal," Jamie joked, all charm now that she wasn't angry. Now that she was afraid she might have her privileges revoked. "It was only a paper plate. I'll clean up the cake. I'm sorry."

What if it had been a real plate? What if that had been her fist aimed at someone's face? Jamie was dangerous. Not just to herself. I was really seeing that now. Even though I didn't want to.

"Throwing things isn't acceptable. You need to figure out how to talk about how you feel in a way that doesn't scare everyone around you," I said to Jamie in front of the nurse. Not exactly what she wanted me to say. Too bad. She couldn't meet my eyes. I couldn't tell if Jamie was ashamed or furious. I didn't care that I sounded like a two-bit therapist. Then I walked out the ward door on my pass.

I met Sadie for ice cream.

"Jamie's an abuser. You're not responsible for her. You don't have to be involved. You can be compassionate to her from a safe distance."

"I feel bad for her though. She's been through so much," I said.

"Write this down so you can read it later. Don't act on all of your impulses. Think through the consequences of your actions. STOP, LOOK AND LISTEN. Jamie's a bad choice for you."

"Even though a part of me says she'd never hurt me, and today had nothing to do with me anyways, I still can't get the way she looked when she whipped that plate out of my head," I mumbled.

CODE WHITE

"A person who cares about you isn't going to push you to do things you don't want to do. They'll respect your boundaries," Sadie said, softly smudged brackets of chocolate ginger ice cream riding at the edges of her mouth. I didn't offer her my napkin and I didn't know why.

It was time to walk back. I was scared to see Jamie. I'd almost decided to stop seeing her. All I could see was Jamie's paper plate hurtling past the nurse's face. Smushed cake against the floor. Icing crumpled everywhere. I had to focus on my own recovery. Jamie was obviously too sick for me to be with in a lot of ways.

When I got to my room there was a drawing there that Jamie had made and slid under my door. It was a picture of a merman wearing a tie swimming in a red sea. On the back, at the bottom in tiny, smudged letters it said, *I'm sorry*. Across the top in Jamie's clean handwriting she'd written, *When can I see you?* In the centre in big, bold black letters, *I want to fuck you*.

It just wasn't good enough. And it scared me. Jamie's eyes squinched shut in anger when I left the ward after refusing to help her. Polaroid snapshot of her clenched fist, the one sealed shut while the other was busy throwing that stupid paper plate. Short nails biting into her hand as she gripped that fist tighter. Imprints I didn't want to see. I didn't want to see any of it. I shoved the painting under the chair in a corner.

I wanted to be left alone. Now, I wasn't sure how.

five

October 10, 1999

On my wall is an old, wide elastic that I cut open and taped there. The one Max wrote on a long time ago. Before she stopped visiting. It says, "REMEMBER WHO YOU ARE" in big, blue, ballpoint capital letters. On some parts, the blue of the ink has faded a little where the tip of her pen had pressed firm against the elastic. Max concentrated when she wrote it. Formed each letter like it mattered. Like I mattered to her.

After I wore it constantly for a while, I got terrified the letters Max wrote would fade too much. Or that I would rip it. Something would happen to it and I wouldn't have it anymore. So I cut the bracelet in two. Taped one piece in a scrapbook and the other above my pillow on my wall in the star place amongst where I had put up all my get well cards for inspiration.

It seems like such a long time ago. I can barely remember who it is I am anymore. But seeing that rubber band gives me strength. I know there's an Alex who existed before I got sick. I know there are people who believe in me.

I miss Max. I wish she'd come back. I wish I could use this quarter in my hand that I can't stop fumbling with and call her. Find out exactly what I did to make her never want to come back. But I can't. Even I have limits again now as to how much of a fool I'm willing to make of myself. Is that a sign that I'm getting better?

Remember who you are.

CODE WHITE

October 11, 1999

"Does it hang right at the back?" Lee asks, modeling her clothes in the hall. There are a lot of visible threads and the hem is coming undone in three places. But that isn't what Lee is asking my opinion on.

"Lee, you look great!" I say, and try to put sparkly confetti in my voice to rain down on her. Lee hasn't been to a party in a long time, so I always try to give her one. Even something tiny. It's a good sign she's getting dressed up.

"I'm not going anywhere special, you know. You can go out to get coffee now? Oh, okay, well then, I won't keep you," she says. Her head sinks back into her shoulders, hunched like a defeated turtle.

Lee paces beside me. She's wearing these weird shoes that used to be dressy, except the heels are mostly worn down. She's wearing them with thick burgundy socks. The shoes are three different shades of taupe, and around the ankle is a dark brown lizard skin strap. A bunch of scales flake on it like bad dry skin.

"You know, I washed my hair on Thursday," Lee says.

I remember the time Lee asked if I would wash her hair. Leaning over the laundry sink to do it herself makes her too dizzy from her meds. I didn't understand why she didn't wash her hair in the shower. But I wanted to help. Sort of. And I felt bad that she was so sad because she couldn't wash her own hair. The nurses wouldn't do it as often as she liked. Except, I didn't really want to get my hands on some lady's scalp. I was also afraid that she would fall while I did it. I wonder if she remembered asking me to help her. I stand there, feeling guilty and like the worst person ever.

"Your hair looks really, really good," I say, each word

bursting with light and a lemon freshness zeal I didn't know I had in me.

"No, no," Lee moans. "It looks filthy already. I sweat so much. I just don't know what to wear anymore. I want to wear something cooool," Lee drawls. Her voice sounds like when you sit in front of a fan and open your mouth. Let some sound you never knew you had inside come floating out and away on the flickering air. I stand pinned on Lee's sound, stuck in the hallway. Not sure where I can go or how to get there.

October 11, 1999

Terry got discharged today. Terry, with long, dark, greasy hair and no shoes. Holes in her socks with her big, dirty toe poking through. Terry, who kept peeing on the lounge chairs so I couldn't be sure where it was safe to sit. Who said she didn't need shoes because her brother would just pick her up in a car when it was her turn to get out of this dump anyway. Terry, who still has my lighter.

I have this idea for a painting of Terry's discharge. Four panels, all of Terry's door to her room. The first would just be the door to Terry's room with the label that read, *Terry*. The second panel would be a picture of Terry standing in front of her door, blocking her name, with her eyes kind of vacant as always, her greasy hair falling in her face. The next panel would be the empty door. Terry out of the picture. No name tag. The last picture would be the door wearing a new name tag. I don't know whose name it would be. It doesn't matter really, just someone who replaced Terry.

The discharge and replacement rhythm reminds me of this old Dominion grocery store that used to be at Yorkdale Mall, where I went as a kid with my parents. The staff used to put all your groceries in these green, plastic buckets and roll them on this metal conveyer belt outside the store to where you could load your purchases into the trunk of your car. I still remember the swishing noise made by the metal pins on the belt as the buckets rolled along. That's almost what it's like watching patients get discharged and new patients getting signed in on the floor. Except we don't make tiny, metal clinking noises.

We cry uncertainly about where we are going or over the friends we are leaving behind. We blink wide-eyed or shuffle to the door holding our stuff white-knuckled. Not sure where to put our excitement. We are the crinkles of the shopping bags holding our belongings. The drag of suitcases on the floor. One girl leaves and another comes just as fast to take her place. The girl who just left was never even here.

Swish, swish. Here comes another one. *Swish, swish.* There goes another one. Is it dinnertime yet? Goodbye, Terry. I hope wherever you are going, you get some shoes and they don't mind if you pee on the chairs.

Swish, swish.

Whose name's on that door now?

October 12, 1999

Here's a list I made after Sadie's visit.

1. **Be The Bitch**

Sadie wants me to connect to the aggressive, femme top energy that I had before I got sick and let it loose against Jamie. Draw my lines in the sand and all that jazz.

2. **The Nurses Are Going To Get Me**

This wasn't advice. This is something I told Sadie. I'm

getting scared of the nurses' homophobia. I think they're about to turn on me and Jamie. I can tell they disliked seeing two women flirting. Even though Jamie pretty much looks like a guy, so much so that she confuses all the other patients on the floor. The nurses aren't as confused as the patients. They know Jamie's a woman and belongs on this floor. They just wish she didn't have to be there. This piece of broken that doesn't even fit in the catch-all basin of the ward. A piece they wish they could toss back. Make everything smooth again.

3. **No Clever Subheading**
Sadie reminded me again that my primary concern should be to feel better and get off the ward.

4. **Breaking Up Is Hard To Do**
I told Sadie that if I do end things with Jamie, I'm afraid about how to tell her. Partly because it was all so intense. Despite everything wrong about it, it still feels hard to end. I don't know what to say. If Jamie is abusive, what reason am I supposed to give her that won't aggravate her? I didn't want to cause problems for myself while I was locked on a ward with her.

Sadie's recommendation was to be EVASIVE. She laid out this strategy: "DON'T lay out your cards for the boy to take advantage of. Be smart. Be assertive. Play the teary femme."

I don't even know what Sadie's referring to by the phrase, "teary femme." She needs to bone up on her gender stereotypes. If I wanted to talk with someone who didn't understand my gender, there are plenty of people to choose from on this ward. Everyone. None of them understand the first thing about what it's like to be a dyke, never mind what a femme is. Maybe Leah would get the dyke thing, but we never talk about being queer, since on the ward being queer is some sort of crime. We just pretend it doesn't exist as part of our lives.

Maybe Sadie should go play a teary femme. But only if someone has underlined all the important parts for her in yellow highlighter first. To explain to her that EVERYONE cries. Not just femmes. I wanted to tell her to work through her misogyny. But I just sat there.

5. **Sadie's NOT Weird Advice**.

After the above advice, I was more than ready for Sadie to go. But it seemed rude to say so. Why I was hanging onto etiquette in a mental hospital was beyond me. It wasn't like I had invited Sadie to a tea party I was hosting. I felt like going to my room and crying. Of course, I realized the irony in that. It would make me the teary femme, realized in the flesh. I was too despondent to care.

"DON'T GET STUCK IN THE WARD WORLD!" Sadie said as she leaned in. "There's the world outside. And eventually you're going to get to see it again. Reconnect. There's the outside world, and then there's the world on the ward. And they are two totally separate things. You're getting sucked into the world on the ward. Don't forget there's a whole other real world out there you're going back to." Sadie smiled and I ducked my head.

I am going to go back.

October 13, 1999

I am one of the only ones who has off-floor privileges now, which means I am the one who goes to Coffee Time, which is just beside the institute, to get coffees, even though I don't even

drink coffee. Caffeine is really bad for my anxiety. I'd do anything to make the other women's days a bit better, infuse even a bit of comfort. Of course, I get a bit confused when I am ordering more than one coffee — who wants what and who gives me what money and who gets what change, so I have to write it all down to keep it straight. I have pages and pages of lists in my diary of coffee orders from whoever is in the smoke room when I decide to leave the floor to do a coffee run. Today's list:
Kate: jumbo regular milk, bring Sweet and Low
Tammy: jumbo, triple milk, lots of Sweet and Low. $ 1.35
Mary: Jumbo, triple triple. $20.00
Martha: medium, a little bit of milk, bring Sweet & Low. $1.25

Their faces are so happy when I come back up fumbling with the tray of coffees and their change, desperately thankful and relieved. It almost makes up for the fact that they aren't allowed to go and get it for themselves. This is something that weighs heavily against us, separates us. Something none of us can forget. I just hand out their coffees with nervous cheer, trying to pretend it is like some kind of fancy room service and that is why none of them can leave the floor to get their own. We all know the truth.

October 13, 1999

I wanted to be given more fancy boxes of chocolates. People keep bringing plants. I put them in the common area because most people don't get visitors. Everyone on the ward waters them too much and they just die.

October 13, 1999

I am at the payphone in the basement of a bar. The cabaret is going on later than I expected, later than when I told the nurse I would be back when I left the ward. I really want to stay to the end, but if I do, I definitely won't make curfew. I'm eating humility through my Bell calling card. Sharp edges that cut into the corners of my mouth. Calling to beg to stay out later.

Nurse Rhoda answers. She is usually very tough. Over the loud backdrop of the bar, I plead with her to allow me to stay where I am, at least until it is over. There is silence. At least, I think it is silence. I can't hear that well because of all the noise from the bar. I am praying she won't just order me to come right back, ASAP. I tell her it won't be that much later. I don't want her worrying that I'm going AWOL, or on some kind of bender.

"As long as you are safe," she curtly answers.

"This is a healthy place for me to be," I implore.

"As long as you are safe," Nurse Rhoda the robot repeats.

"I'll take a cab home… I mean to the institute," I supplicate. As if it really makes any difference how I get back. The issue is that I am coming back late. I was given a pass, went out, and will not be coming back in time to meet my curfew. I wonder in a panic if this might be the last pass I will get. If I'll no longer be allowed to go anywhere off the ward since I failed to meet my curfew.

I can almost hear her shrug. "Fine." Nurse Rhoda hangs up on me.

I don't want to go back tonight at all. I'm so fucking sick of living there. Tired of every part. I want my own bed, not one shrink-wrapped in plastic and so high off the ground I feel like I'm stranded on a ship sailing the ocean every night. I'm tired of it.

debra anderson

Why do I have to call some stranger named Rhoda, beg to stay out one more lousy hour just to hear a woman read at a microphone while I sit at my little table smoking cigarettes and sipping ginger ale? I realize I'm living in a mental institution and everyone gets to dismiss me as "crazy," but who's Rhoda to me? In the large scheme of things, why does Rhoda get to determine what I'm allowed to do with my evening? I haven't had a curfew since I was fourteen.

I try not to think about Nurse Rhoda. The curfew. What it will be like to slink back in late tonight. If there will be repercussions. Being here tonight has made me realize something I hadn't thought about. When I leave the hospital and run into people I haven't seen since I got sick, I have to come out all over again. Not as queer. This time, I'm coming out as crazy. Less than and starting all over.

People don't really like crazy people. Even if you aren't really crazy anymore. It sucks when your reputation precedes you. Or when someone uses that special tone of voice people only use to talk to crazy people. Like the person is speaking through latex to protect themselves from contamination.

When I was on the ward, I couldn't wait to get out. Talk to all the people I missed. I was starved for conversation, eye candy, hot girls to flirt with. For people to do that three minute, *Hi, how are you* little conversation as you passed. Hungry for anything.

Now that I'm out, I feel like hiding in a corner. Wishing for a secret decoder ring with invisible powers so I can stay and watch, unseen. I don't want to talk now that I see how differently people speak to me. Now that I'm wearing my, *I'm out on a pass from the mental ward* film coating me with a neon sheen. I want to record it all. Shove it at them so they can't back away.

Especially the ones who see me across the room, and instead of coming over to say, *Hi*, act like they've smelled someone take a giant crap. They make the hugest effort to stay far away from me the whole night. People who, before, would have sought me out to talk.

Instead of trying to socialize, I want to wrap myself up in a blanket with "Hospital Property" printed on it. Being around everyone is tiring. The noise. Trying to act like I'm having a good time and I don't care what people think is exhausting. Even if sometimes I am and I don't. I never thought I'd be saying this, but I want to go back to the ward. I've had enough for tonight. Except I basically sold my first-born child to Nurse Rhoda to be here, so I guess I'm staying. I wish I could buy a real drink. Just one. But, I'd bet all the coins left in my change purse that Nurse Rhoda will lean in for a whiff when I get back. Spot check.

One of my exes from a thousand years ago came to say goodbye when she was leaving. I guess that's a good sign. She could have just avoided me and left. When she went to hug me goodbye, I was too tired and filled with nervous energy to stand. My legs were shaky from sitting so long. We did one of those half-standing, half-sit down hugs. It was kind of lame. But not entirely without style. She gave me her cheek. The softness and swipe of girl-cheeks. So sweet. I miss that. As she straightened herself up, she smiled a real smile at me. Not one of those polite things. Or a half-smile. Not even a, *You've been in the mental ward and I have to be nice to you,* kind of smile. Genuine.

She turned to leave. And then she made the phone signal with her hand, which against all my better instincts I wanted to hold for some reason, after all these years and awful things between us. Then I wondered what was wrong with me. I knew she'd never call. She could pretend, if she wanted to. Try to make me think she would call me, for whatever reasons that made her feel good. But she'd never call me. I didn't even fucking want her to. All of a sudden, I'd gone mental and was stuck in the attic. Poor Alex was some sort of loser charity case, desperate for phone calls she didn't even want to fucking answer. What bullshit.

In spite of everything, what was wrong with me that I still wanted to hold her hand, just for one, single second? No words. Just touch her cheek one more time, softly, quickly, before I slipped back into my cell, late for curfew, ready to face Nurse Rhoda.

October 14, 1999

Jamie keeps sliding artwork into my room. The nurses don't seem to care as much about us since we stopped desperately trying to stake out any tiny spot on the ward to be alone in.

If only I'd thought to use cheap, reverse psychology on them when I had wanted to be with Jamie. Under this newfound freedom, Jamie's sent me handfuls of frantic letters. Thick, creamy pages with ragged edges torn out of her bound, black, leather-covered sketchbooks multiply daily. Inside of makeshift envelopes that she seals at just the right spot with ingenious adhesive. Stolen Band-Aids or the beige masking tape that has framed so many of the paintings she's made for me. I run my finger over the raised beige line, sealing her note like a scar.

Her pièce de résistance is the note with many tiny, slitted holes punched into the bottom. Through each hole, she fastened a string from a tea bag stolen from the kitchen. The Red Rose tags hang like elegant little tassels on a tiny window blind.

CODE WHITE

A beautiful miniature window in the palm of my hand, closed. Jamie pulled the blind down, putting everything between us behind it. Privacy I can hold in my hand. I haven't had any since I got here. And now, it's been given to me with a lot of care.

I've already told Jamie I want my space and my privacy. That's got me a lot of meaningful sideways glances and a shitpile of letters and drawings. The letters won't stop coming. Jamie will always be there, silently creeping up to the other side of my door, persistent. She'll quickly check for a nurse or a psych assistant, then insistently slide those strikingly decorated pieces of herself through the gap under my door, again and again. It doesn't matter what I say or do.

I wonder with what sharp object Jamie mastered poking the tiny slits? How did she cut the strings off each tea bag? "Sharps" are confiscated on entry. Jamie is extremely resourceful. I look at those shimmering Red Rose tea tags dangling from the bottom of her letter, picture her in her room when no one else is around. She's cutting at the paper, at strings, with a very sharp knife. She stashes it in her big, black duffel bag. Something she got past them. No one but the two of us knows she has it. A shiny secret.

I've never gotten love letters like this before. From anyone. Even before opening them they are breathtaking pieces of art. She covers them in whatever she can get her hands on from Arts & Crafts: artfully placed feathers, glitter and beads. Watercolour paint. Colleen's ecstatic that Jamie wants to participate in something, so she doesn't care.

But I couldn't keep accepting them. Today, I told Jamie to stop. Two hoods, like the heavy, silver faceguards on an old knight's helmet, slammed down fast over her eyes. So quick only I could have noticed. Her hands curled into fists beside her hips. Pink glitter at the end of her fingers and under the tips of her shortly clipped nails. Not a new butch fashion statement. I didn't want to be this person. Having to keep closing a door. Watching her bite her lip.

"I just don't think your letters are really working with the whole thing of us not seeing each other anymore," I said.

Jamie nodded and stared at her shoes. I tried to look at her face and noticed over her shoulder that Doug the psych assistant was staring.

Already, there's been a couple more letters today. One speckled with the pink glitter. And some others. All with her slanted, prickly, tightly bunched handwriting. I'm really hoping that tomorrow there's no more. That this is the end. But there's nowhere really for me to go in here if it's not.

October 14, 1999

We're in the smoke room and Leah is cackling. I could listen to her smoky, raspy laugh all day. It sounds corny, but when Leah laughs it's like the sun's shining right inside the smoke room, inside this crappy place where that never happens. The sound of her laughter is a diagram unfolding naturally. Reminds us we know how to do it, too. Even if we thought we forgot. Even if none of us has anything to laugh about. She still finds something to smile about after every shitty thing, every defeat, every mean word out of a nurse's mouth, every time no one comes to visit her and every rejection from a rehab centre she's trying to get into.

She sees the shit in her life. We barely see anything else now in ours. We sit in our corners feeling sorry. Leah must cry sometimes. But in front of us, she feeds courage. The biggest woman on the ward. Golden. When she smiles, something feels possible. Even if maybe it isn't. Even if maybe it never will be. Even if Leah's never going to get into a rehab centre. Always going to be looking for her next fix, shunted from one institution to the next. I want everything to turn out three blazing cherries for her. Lights flashing. Loud music. Big payoff.

"Hey, Alex," Leah said, exhaling a long stream of smoke. Even her greyness sparkled like a shimmering ribbon trailing out of her mouth, curling around the room.

Last week she told me how she learned to French inhale cigarettes. She was in her teens and was put in a mental hospital for the first time. Leah told me that story one afternoon when we were the only ones in the smoke room. The air was thick with grey smoke. She sat on the ground with her legs sprawled out in front of her and flicked her ashes on the floor, a reckless non-pattern speckling the tile. I worried about a nurse coming and giving Leah hell for not using the ashtray. Leah didn't seem concerned. She'd just finished a conversation with her mother that had gone badly. I'd heard the tail end from my room as she had crashed down the phone. She strode forcefully down the hall into the smoke room, each leg effortlessly pushing a heavy stack of weights.

When it was safe, after I thought for sure Leah would have been finished her cigarette, I made my way down the hall. Leah was still there, pacing the box of a room, hand in a curled fist around her smoking cigarette like she was charming a snake. I felt like I was intruding, but when she saw me, something in her exhaled. She paced a bit more and then sprawled on the floor. Flicking ashes in a way that was made to look careless, but I knew she was missing the ashtray on purpose. She was thinking about the conversation with her mother, being on the ward, all of it, *Fuck you* and *Take that*. No matter how immature, it made us both smile. *Flick, flick.*

She demonstrated French inhales, doing marvelous, round smoke rings that looked like life rafts. *Please get me out of here,* I thought that day. I couldn't French inhale very well. I kept coughing like a high school kid who just tried her first ciggie. But I had a lot of fun sensuously pouting "O"s out of my lips and pretending we were having some sort of debauchery filled sleepover. It didn't matter. I was having a good time. My ass had grown numb a long time ago and I wished we could leave the ward and go out for drinks somewhere together. My "O"s weren't round at all, but misshapen, pathetic things that floated out of my mouth and hung in the air between us. Sad little ovals. Made us both howl.

"Hey, Alex," Leah said again, and looked directly into my eyes. She rested one of her desert boots on the edge of the metal bench that sat in one corner of the room. The bottom of her jeans rose to show me a few fingers of bright, yellow sock. It felt oddly intimate. Almost like a panty shot, but without the sexual innuendo.

"Don't let the sun go down," she said and laughed loud. Her husky smoker's voice rattled comfort within four small walls. And for reasons I didn't feel like analyzing, I didn't feel so lost. She blew a huge, cushy smoke ring. I watched it rising to the ceiling, whose tiles were comprised of tiny dots. I wanted to grab hold of that ring. Lay my hand on the puffy edge. Let it take me somewhere. The sound of wind through the fan in the smoke room sounded like waves on the beach.

"I was on a jet ski when I had my first nervous breakdown," Leah started her story. Tapped a long ash on the floor. She always liked to tell lots of stories. That was just Leah. If you listened closely, all the pieces didn't exactly snap together perfectly, like they do in a puzzle. There was lots of overlap. Details didn't quite add up. Repeated stories with new endings. I didn't care. I liked it better that way. Stories that glowed in your hand as you held them. Left a mark when you passed them around. Whatever stayed was true enough.

"I was twenty-five at the time. I haven't been out of hospitals since. That was the real coast, it was beautiful. I wish I could go back. It was a real sunset that night. Gold dripping into the water as far as the eye could see. I circled round this big yacht to bum a smoke cause I was bored of zipping around and then we all went out for drinks," Leah concluded.

A lot of her stories ended like that. Getting drinks. I kept listening to the waves lap in through the fan. The air in the room was golden. I could almost taste the fancy champagne Leah drank that night, over twenty years ago. On a really big yacht. Lanterns glowing on the deck. Swaying gently in the breeze. Hundreds of dollars slipping down her throat. It tasted good. I didn't want any of it to stop. I smiled at her.

six

October 15, 1999

Nurse Susan walks in my room. Pauses to make a light tap on my doorframe, as if it's a real knock. I'm lying on my bed.

"Can we talk, Alex?" she asks.

I don't want to. When I really need something, she can never spare a minute. It's always, *Later Alex. I'll come get you.* I, too, used to be someone whose time was important. Now, I've become someone to dump to the bottom of the list, nudge over to someone else's work shift.

"Can we talk, Alex?"

"No," I say, and wait for something bad to happen. Wait for all the horrible things that have happened to me during my whole life every time I ever try to say *No.*

Nurse Susan looks surprised. "Well, it's your choice," she says.

They're all about choices here. Except when they don't want you making any. She gets off of my bed and leaves. As soon as she's gone, I'm curious what she wanted to talk to me about. But, unless she'll remember what it was and track me down another time, I'll never know. I think about every stupid thing the staff has ever talked to me about. I doubt it was important. It's not like I missed some secret tutorial on how to get out of here by tomorrow.

October 15, 1999

Sadie came to see me today and made me write down questions to ask the nurses:

CODE WHITE

1) *What are the names of my meds?*
   I don't really know what they're all called. I recognize most by their size and shape. By what colour they are. A few of the pills have writing on them. Tattooed on an industrial conveyer belt at the pharmaceutical company. The markings are never a full name, only a combination of letters and numbers. Or else the code is carved into each pill, like letters dug into a tombstone. It helps me keep track. I still don't really know what they are. I try not to think about it.

   I think about the little black tattooed letters and numbers on each pill I swallow dissolving in my stomach. Ink wriggling off each pill. Each letter and number adhering to my stomach lining until months from now, if someone cuts me open, the redness of my bowels will be an inky, peppery black pharmacological alphabet soup. Tracking every pill I've ever swallowed.

2) *What are the side effects?*
   Stuff like how my hands won't stop shaking. Or how I sweat all night and wake up with the sheets plastered to me. Or that my pants keep getting tighter and I'm thirsty all the time. And piles of other stuff.

3) *How long am I supposed to take them?*
   I'm scared to ask this. I have a feeling they aren't going to answer, *Oh, just for a little while.* As if the handful of multicoloured pills they give me every day and watch to make sure I take are like Tylenol, and when my little "headache" is over I can stop. I'm guessing they think it's preventative.

As long as I swallow their pills, I'm safe in their eyes. Safe from myself.

4) *How long can I take the pills without damaging myself?*
This is my secret fear. I want to know what long-term damage they're causing. Part of me doesn't. Sadie wants to know what kind of natural remedies I can use to solve my "imbalances." And while I appreciate her kefir madness approach to some things, the right blend of essential oils I burn three times a day in my diffuser is not going to cure bipolar disorder. While Sadie understands what's happened to me is serious, she's so anti-psychiatry, so anti-"medical model" as she likes to call it, she doesn't get that Burt's Bee's lip balm isn't going to caulk up the cracks in me.

One of Sadie's favourite discussions is how I need to "educate myself" to avoid making the institute a "secure place." I want to explain to her the hands-on education I get here everyday. Like a high school co-op placement. My ward *is* my placement. I learn from all of the inpatients every day. From seeing what everyone goes through. What I go through. Despite how close we were before this happened, despite how much I truly appreciate every visit, things have changed. Sadie walks out the door after every visit. I stay, she goes home. And the longer I stay, the more this becomes my home. This is my education, Sadie. Bye, bye. Visiting hours are over. You can go home now. I'm already here.

I clutch the round yellow tin of Burt's Bees lip balm she gave me in the palm of my hand. Rub some minty tingle on the cracked dryness of my lips and hope it will take. I'm highlighted natural menthol. I feel the compact roundness of the tin against my palm. A bright, hard yellow. I close my fingers around it; hold the past in the form of a circle. Press it close. Hold it harder than I've held anything on this floor for a long time. The tin makes a mark on my hand. An indented circle. I stare at it, moving the balm to my other hand, between two fingers like I'm gripping a quarter, like I'm about to get up and go make a call. Call someone. But there's no one to call. I am on my own. Completely. I know this. I sit very still. I think about how when Sadie left, she reminded me that I can survive.

Some days, I think I know this.

October 16, 1999

Jamie basically leaves me alone now, other than the wounded looks she can't seem to help shooting me whenever we're in the same room together. I try to make it so I happen to be leaving if she's coming into a room. It's just easier that way. Even though I don't really want to do that. And it's hard to keep making it look natural. Like it's one big coincidence that I'm evacuating a room when she's entering it. Even if I'm in the middle of a smoke.

I just can't stand her looks. I don't know which is more intense: her love letters or the looks. At least with the letters I can read them without her staring at me. Alone in my room. I hate how suddenly I am this huge asshole because I didn't think us seeing each other was any good. Even though she's the one who whipped things around, I'm the total fucking jerk. It's not like she doesn't have an inkling this isn't the best idea. We're on a goddamned mental ward.

The nurses walk around close-lipped whenever they're near either one of us. This whole thing like they're thinking, *I told you so.* Or, *Perverts. You get what you deserve.*

debra anderson

None of this is how I wanted things to go. Even so, I can't keep hiding in my room.

October 16, 1999

"I want my sharps, my complete medical supplies! I want to clip my toenails. I can do it myself, I don't care," Jean demanded marching up and down the hallway by my room this afternoon. She nodded at Abigail as she walked past and said, "She's lovely, isn't she? Thank you dear. Honey."

Sharps. A privilege. Will there ever be a time when I look at a pair of scissors and just see them as a functional object I could pick up and use on a whim if I felt like it? Instead of something withheld. Something that flashes. That says, *You can't be trusted.* Imprinting me with the label, *Dangerous.* Sharps.

October 17, 1999

The nutritionist is one of those blonde bitches that looks like she belongs on the Brady Bunch. She's totally skinny, like all she eats is styrofoam and a few shavings of pencil eraser for protein. She sat at one of the little grey speckled kitchen tables with me. The ones that look like they're supposed to be the surface of a stone. No stones look like these tabletops. Every time I look at my dinner on its plastic plate, on an industrial cafeteria orange tray, against the backdrop of grey, phony stone I lose my appetite. But I guess I haven't been losing my appetite. Not really. I'm sad and hungry for anything. So, I eat. The pills make me hungry, too. My pants keep getting tighter. I'm glad they have no good full-length mirrors here.

I had to bug the nurses for days to see the nutritionist lady. She sat across from me and I described specific culinary incidents, assaults, really, on my ability to heal. I watched her staring at my stomach, face and upper arms. All the places I'd put on weight since being here. All the spread. I demanded more healthy foods. More vegetables! I knew she was thinking, *Why bother? All you're going to do is stuff your face with chocolate bars.*

"I need more greens," I told her. Didn't tell her I wanted the dark green vegetables to fight off the cancer being on the ward was opening me to. Seeping into me like my fellow patients' constant crying, screaming and fighting. I knew how paranoid that would seem. I just asked for the vegetables. Something, anything healthy. I needed air. Less gloppy chicken stew. I needed to get out.

She looked at me for a second. And then at my stomach, which is where her eyes stayed. I tried to guess how small her waist was. Tried to measure whether I had ever been that small. Had ever been her size. I knew that I had, but it seemed a long time ago. I couldn't figure out why that was important. Her tiny waist a little rodeo rope, encircling me. But, it was important. Her figure was hollow. She was empty, flat. And I was starting to carry weight. Size bulging forward from me on places it never had before.

"Vegetables," I said to her. "More dark green vegetables."

She looked right through me. I knew she was thinking, *It's you. It's not this place. It's not what you get served for dinner. It's you. That's why you're turning fat. And that's why you're a failure. You're crazy. Your life is ruined. Whether or not you get green vegetables, nothing's going to change.*

She looked out the dirty, streaked window. I squeezed my hand into a tight fist under the table. I hadn't bothered to cut my nails in a while. The loud, red polish had flaked off in ugly, jigsaw puzzle-like pieces. They looked ridiculous in front of her. My nails were long enough to bite into my palms when I pushed. I tried to see green.

Miss Brady wrote one sentence in my chart. I tried to say something, but she closed my chart and stood. The chair's metal bottom scraped noisily along the floor. Andrea was in the lounge watching daytime TV and turned her head sharply at the noise. She grinned nastily at me, at the fact I was meeting with the nutritionist. She stretched leisurely in her cube on the couch to showcase her stick-like, eating disorder-ridden body to highlight it against my bloated one, and then turned back to her show. Miss Brady handed me a photocopied, colourless page on Canada's four food groups. A guide to healthy eating. And then she left.

The next day with dinner I got my own little plastic plate covered in see-through plastic. Underneath was an array of raw, wilting, cut vegetables: broccoli, cauliflower, and a stick or two each of celery and carrot, and a gloppy tub of Kraft Ranch Dressing. I figured the next day would bring something fresher or different. But, the plate arrived with the same tired vegetables, celery brown at each end, carrot dried and whitened, browned cauliflower. I tried to eat most of the vegetables each day, hoping they would supplement vitamins I wasn't getting and fight off the cancer.

Sometimes I couldn't finish them. I'd eat my regular meal and then these vegetables. But none of others got any extra plates. Suddenly, I was even more all mouth and stomach. But also too guilty to throw them out. This started a stockpiling situation in the patient's fridge. I was sure I would get to them. I almost never did. The plates would just stack on top of one another and the gross thick Kraft Ranch Dressing sent with each plate. A fatty cubic time capsule.

CODE WHITE

October 17, 1999

"I'm going to be discharged next week; it's about fucking time," Tammy tells me. "But I still don't have any privileges till next week. It doesn't make any sense. I guess they think if they let me have off-ward privileges I might disappear early and no one will ever find me again."

"How long have you been here, Tammy?" I ask.

"A while... since June I think. I think I got out for a week in August."

"And then you had to be readmitted?"

"Yes."

I don't ask why.

October 18, 1999

Today I had to say goodbye to Jamie. Once Jamie is discharged, she won't be allowed to visit. NO FORMER PATIENTS ALLOWED. That's the rule. I wasn't going to arrange any secret visits with Jamie on my out passes, receive any calls on the Inpatient payphone. No dates when I was discharged. Whenever that was. This was goodbye. For good.

Nurse Emma summoned me to the activity room to say goodbye. Waited in the hall, just outside my room. A pinched look on her face. Like I smell and she wishes she could be anywhere but here. I wanted to tell her to wait. I'm not ready. I don't know what to say to Jamie. I wish I looked better. But the nurse won't wait two seconds for me to change or even comb my hair. Lipstick's not going to happen. Why didn't I shower earlier? Then my hair would hang pretty around my face instead of stale and pushed the wrong way. Nurse Emma taps her French-manicured nails against my door jam. *Click, click.*

Nurse Emma is important. She has vital things to attend to. I wonder if the nurses drew straws for this task.

As we walk down the hall, Nurse Emma's shoes sharp-click against the floor like her nails on my door. *Click, click.* The rhythm is slightly hypnotic. Though we walk together, someone listening would only hear Nurse Emma. Her footfalls ring like shots in the hollow hallway. Her soles announce her presence, a professional and efficient personage. Beside her, I'm silent and invisible in my soft-soled Birkenstocks. Nurse Emma's shoes are shined. Outdoor shoes. Shoes to wear to work. My sandal-slippers are wide with thick straps and buckles so big they look like they were made for a baby. *Goo-goo ga-ga,* I think.

And then I'm in the activity room feeling less than and Jamie bolts off her chair and reaches up to give me a hug. There's too much last-timeness to it. Her arm is strong around my back, gripping my shoulder blades. Her head has found that pocket between my shoulder and my neck. I smell her hair. Men's pomade, laundry driers and, underneath, the faint scent of damp earth. I know I won't remember the smell by the time I walk out of the room. I won't be able to hold the scent. It's bizarre to get close to someone in a place where you were so watched you had to skip all the steps that unveil the details of a person. The wonderful, mesmerizing and mundane details I've previously taken for granted with other lovers. Not realizing how lucky I was to get to know them in the entirety that I did.

I start crying somewhere inside me deep. Try to ignore it, but I can't. A shake coming from far away. From a hollow, towards the back, from my spine. It's near the bottom. As if the whole trunk of me is a wishing well someone's thrown their pennies into. Small change people no longer want. Rattling around inside of me, a copper ricochet bouncing off stone walls, dropping faster. I am dropping faster, crouching somewhere small. Somewhere I can't even see. I can't remember what to wish. I've been here too long. Watched a parade of women trapped in their own pools. They tell us we can dream. But it won't come true. It will always be the shortest straw plucked out of the bunch. Discarded and discharged. So far, that hasn't been me.

I'm shaking a copper glare in my eyes. Taste the tang of metal. The wall I had resolved to keep up has sunk. Embarrassment like acid in my throat. Then I realize I'm not the only one shaking. Part of the reason I'm shaking so fierce is Jamie in my arms, jerking back and forth. She is, uncharacteristically, sobbing. Hot tears land on my skin, running wet tracks down my neck, into the collar of my shirt. They pool in the small bowl my collarbone makes. The salt burrows; lays claim to a space on my body that is hers, at least for today. Her back is steamy and heaving under her dress shirt and sweater vest. I smooth the wool, gently, in circles. Try to rub the sad out of her. Coax the scare out. We're leaving something behind today. It doesn't take a genius to see she doesn't know where she's going, only that it's different than what she's known since she's been here. The pennies rattle. Something pinches and lands. I hope she'll be okay.

Earlier today, I found out I'm supposed to stay for three or four more weeks. Again. When I finish that time, staff could recommend another month instead of discharge. I know better than to think this means I get to leave in a month. I know better than to get excited. To think I will go.

Jamie's still crying.

"It's going to be okay," I tell her.

"I don't want to leave you. I love you. I want us to see each other once you get out. I'll take you on dates. For fancy dinners. We'll stay at beautiful hotels. We'll have such a good time. You can make me your boy. I don't want to leave the ward. I'm terrified. I don't know what's going to happen to me," Jamie says in one hot rush, letters tripping over one another like the air out of a balloon. My skin itches.

"Alex?" she pleads and nervously clenches and unclenches her fists. Gives me that look that used to get me all open between my legs and hard in my chest. Push and pull her anywhere.

"I don't want to go," she whispers and there is so much I have to say. Caught in my throat like backed up vomit. And in the end it amounts to just as much as we stand there in silence. She thinks I'm still in her reach. I understand. I think of her holding a handful of my greasy hair tight in her fist in my room, pinning me on top of her, our breath ragged. The feel of her lip, swollen and thick inside my mouth as I bit down, hard. I'm heavy with pennies. Full of old dates weighing me down. I watch tiny girl hands shaking on a woman who wants to be a boy. Most of the time. Who throws plates and probably punches.

I finally mention the plates. It sounds like a circus act instead of what it was. Now that she's no longer an immediate threat, the plates transform into cartoon discs spinning harmlessly in the air, wearing smiley faces. Under the bright fluorescent lights of the activity room, I'm suddenly the unreasonable one. A drama queen. I search the wall of Harlequin romances across the room for help.

"It wasn't a big deal," Jamie says and smiles. "It was actually pretty funny the way that cake flew."

The room is too bright. I don't want to bother trying to say what I'm trying to say anymore. I'm glad she's going for so many reasons. Even though I'll miss her. I touch the inside of the ring she gave me with my thumb. I have to get out of here.

Jamie's face tightens. Nurse Emma must be cueing her to say goodbye, for real this time. There's no choice. Jamie will have to leave any second. She starts crying again, bawling. Her wet eyes slid right through me. Circled down. A heavy bag of copper wishes. Then I was crying my eyes out, too. This goodbye suddenly turned into the most raw gift she'd slipped under my door. Something I'd never seen before. Something I'd wanted then. But now I didn't want any of it.

"Remember all this," she says and steps closer. I wonder if Nurse Emma will come and separate us like we are at a church dance. "Always remember me by the ring I gave you."

I can feel it, heavy on my finger.

"How could I forget?" I answer.

"Remember me," she says, the words a heavy wax stamp on one of her envelopes. The last one.

"I'll wear it. Think of you. You don't have to worry. Even if I didn't have it, there's no way I'd forget any of this. You know that," I take her hand and hold it. "You'll always be in my heart because of the time we shared here. Even if we can't be together."

None of it felt right. All of it was how it should be somehow. Then she left, looking at me over her shoulders.

Back in my room there was a drawing from Jamie stuffed under my door. Done in a Valentine's Day style. Red heart, white lace trim. A portrait of me as an angel touching Jamie's cheek. On the back she wrote her phone number and address on it. I didn't think I wanted to use them, but part of me wasn't sure. I knew I'd hold on to it. The picture was beautiful, even if it was wrong. I was no angel. And we didn't belong together.

seven

October 19, 1999

Woke up today with another bad backache. I can barely move enough to make my mattress crinkle annoyingly through the hospital issue sheets. My spine aches as if someone has laid heavy slabs of concrete across each vertebra to keep me in my place while sleeping. I know better than to tell a nurse. None of them will believe me. They'll probably think I'm med-seeking painkillers or some bullshit. I'd love to see one of them sleep on this excuse for a mattress. Take the medications I take every day. Then see how they feel each morning. A science experiment.

I will not nap today.

October 19, 1999

Tammy and Mary and I were sitting in the smoke room today when Tammy blurted out, "I wish I had a cigarette the length of this room. My parents are waiting in my room for me, which makes it kind of hard to take a nap. I want to go to bed."

"That's one way of dealing with it," Mary said wryly, exhaling.

I watched Mary bounce her white sneakered foot, bobbing it up and down at the ankle from where she sat on the floor, leaning against the wall. Tammy stretched out awkwardly over the railing separating one seat from the other on the metal two-seater bench. *Bounce, bounce, bounce.*

Tammy doesn't get along with her parents. They never come to visit. But they were here now, and Tammy was hiding in the smoke room.

CODE WHITE

"I'm ready to sleep all day and all night," Tammy said. "Without any PRNs even."

"That's one way of dealing with it," Mary repeated.

"It's the only way," Tammy answered. None of us said anything.

Tammy's parents loomed through the wall. Tammy's room was on the other side of the smoke room. Her face was a weird shade of grey. The contrast made all the white scars on her skin stand out. The plastic ends of Mary's shoelaces made a tiny tapping noise as they bounced against her shoes. I could hear it if I really listened as she bounced.

October 19, 1999

I'm sitting in the dining room peeling an orange. I offer Jean some.

"When we get married I'll try oranges, until then I'm sticking with apples," she says, picking up an apple out of the fruit bowl. "Should I wash it?"

I tell her, *Yes*, as she peels the blue sticker off her Granny Smith.

"Will you watch this?" she asks and gestures to her drink.

And it weirds me out. It's because of patients like her I don't like to leave open cups lying around.

October 19, 1999

Leah: large black coffee. Du Maurier Light, King Large, $20
Sharon: small double double, sugar and cream, Du Maurier Light, King size Large $10
Kate: Large Craven A extra light or light king size, $5

debra anderson

October 20, 1999

    I go to the nursing station to see if my 11:30 a.m. appointment with Dr. Johnson has been cancelled or rescheduled without anyone telling me. These things happen all the time here, but no one tells us anything. They just efficiently mark it down in our orange charts. Crisp lines and unwavering ink. Permanent. I exhale my agitation in the smoke room. Delicate grey plumes. Elegant feathers tremble anxiously off the perch of my dry lips. I've been holed up in the smoke room off and on for hours now, waiting to see this specialist.

    Dr. Johnson is the head of the Bipolar Clinic at the institute, a few floors up from our ward. He's agreed to give a second opinion on me because I don't seem to be getting better. I don't really have any other options. I'm not climbing out of this depression. The huge crash on the other side of my grandiose climb. My doctor on the ward, Dr. Fieldstone, who I don't see very often, is concerned. Dr. Johnson is the one who will offer me a rope. Rescue me. Dr. Johnson is supposed to be an expert. Except Dr. Johnson doesn't seem able to keep appointments. *Maybe he is not an expert in time management,* I think to myself.

    Around the edges of grey I feel something else. A sharp, red outline. I'm angry. I don't really know where to put that. There's no place for that on the ward. No place for outrage. I can only sit. Wait my turn. Even though my turn has passed. Leah sees me fingering the red. It bites into my finger, presses in close, pierces the tip that I would point at someone.

    Nurse Emma opens the door and notices there are too many of us inside.

    "Some of you will have to leave. Only the appropriate

number of patients can sit in the smoking room," she tells us in her official voice. Shuts the door.

There's no sweet-talking our way around the rules with her like there is with a few of the other nurses. No joking. She puts us into place. Human file folders. I'm not going anywhere. Someone else can leave. I don't want to do anything except smoke. It's a stupid rule, anyway. Only allowing a select few of us in here at a time. Are we going to plan a mutiny if our numbers become too great? The door opens again and Nurse Emma turns to me. I know she's looking at me, because her head is directed at the space in the room I occupy. She stares at me. A cold blue wash. I no longer feel like I'm there. Nurse Emma opens her mouth.

"Alex, Dr. Johnson is ready to see you," she says and turns away.

After meeting with Dr. Johnson, I'm a scraped out grapefruit. I need to go somewhere. I want so badly to smoke a joint. My fingers itch to break it up, like pretty little beads, the sticky resin on my fingerprints tainting me familiar. All I want is to disappear. Remove myself from under the microscope. Take all eyes off me, including my own. Turn everything off. Stop.

In my room, I hope for quiet. So I can feel what it feels like to be Alex. Only Alex. Not Alex-in-a-mental-hospital anymore. I want to be still. Feel my feet. Each toe. Each nail growing. I want to feel they're mine. Run my hands over my legs. Feel each hair growing, soft against the palm of my warm hand. Palms moist, sweaty. I am without every single piece of this ward. I am Alex.

I come down the hall to my room and there's a gang of patients in the activity room listening to a tape of Cat Stevens on the tape deck in the corner. One of Leah's favourite musicians. When I discovered this, I was surprised. I don't know what I expected her to listen to. It wasn't Cat Stevens. Leah turns around. Sees me. I don't go to my room right away. I stand awkwardly in the doorway of the activity room. Watch everyone. The song *Morning Has Broken* is playing. Jean is accompanying in a falsetto voice that provides creepy comfort.

I don't know where to go.

Dr. Johnson had very long fingers with even longer, thin black hairs. I kept staring at them as he talked. He would clasp his hands together and rest his head on them, like they were a mini-hammock. Then he'd lean back in his chair. The buttons on his white dress shirt pulled hard against his belly. I thought they might pop off and hit me in the face. On one finger his long black hairs disappeared for a shiny breath underneath a plain gold wedding band. I wondered about his wife. Did he have a kid?

Later, I wondered what those long hairs on his fingers would look like wet, when he pushed them inside his wife. I felt sick, picturing those hairs sticking slickly to his fingers. I couldn't stop. I couldn't concentrate on the words droning out his mouth. Each a disconnected object slowly being laid out on an assembly line. Was he dipping into the nursing station's Ativan supply?

To distract myself, I looked at the books haphazardly falling all over the shelves in his office. He definitely lacked organizational skills. Every question he asked was insulting. Made it seem I was broken. And he was the great thing that could fix me. The "expert." An "expert" about poor pieces of shit people like me. People who had to live in a mental ward, of all cruddy places.

He was five hours late for our appointment. His fingers were coated in scary hair that looked like dead beetle legs. He sounded like an Ativan junkie and he couldn't organize his office for shit. The place was a complete wreck. It was a waste of time. I knew I had too many problems to be fixed by any of the stupid pills they were serving in their little cups. Something was fucked up in me that I could sit in this expert doctor's office who was trying his best to help me and, instead of trying to make the best of this situation and answer his questions, I chose to feel invaded and hostile. While he tried to learn my case history, I fixated on his stupid hands. Thinking one perverted thought after another until he got bored of my pouty silence. Ended our meeting. I staggered out of his office. Left a few pages of his scrawled notes about me on top of his chaotic desk. Waiting to be filed away.

October 21, 1999

Jean came up to me in the hall and pushed her face real close. I tried not to back away too fast. She smelled like piles of old, curling newspapers, the kind you would find in a hermit's house. Musty homemade pasty glue. And a bit like pee. I was scared of the collection of froth at the corners of her mouth. I didn't want any of it to land on me when she started talking. The whites of her eyes were kind of yellow and had clots of red in them. I didn't want to look anymore. I wanted to back away slowly and disappear into my room. I knew Jean couldn't help any of it. That's just who she was. I could help who I was. I could stop being an asshole.

Jean leaned in closer and I tried not to flinch. It seemed

like she was going to tell me something important. A secret. Something earth shattering. Jean smiled. Partly sweet, but mostly scary. A little demonic, actually. I tried to focus on the sweet.

"I was up at five o'clock this morning," Jean whispered. "Time to feed the chickens."

Then she leaned back. Looked at me hard. As if she thought, out of everyone on the ward, I was the one who would know what to do with that information. I finally breathed again, filling my ribs and belly with air. Filled in the space between us. My whole body tingled like someone had poured those little packets of Magic Rocks popping candy down my throat. Volcanoes erupting inside. Then Jean lurched away. She's always fairly unsteady on her feet. I tried not to notice the huge stain across the bum of her pants. Another of a different colour on the back of one calf. I wondered why her nurse, or any nurse, didn't get Jean to change into a clean pair of pants and wash the ones she was wearing.

October 21, 1999

Tammy: two Oh Henry, Jumbo coffee three milk, Sweet and Low on the side
Sharon: sea salt and vinegar large potato chips, $2
Leah: jumbo black coffee, bring sugar packs, $2

October 21, 1999

Put my hands on the table and felt the warmth left behind by mac and cheese comfort.

October 21, 1999

I went to go ask the nurses something, but it was the "wrong time." I've always hated asking anyone for anything. It's different on the ward. Here, you're not allowed to get things for yourself. Everything is off limits. Still, it never feels like the right time to ask the nurses for anything. Whenever I ask, I'm always putting one of them out. Sometimes though, it's even more the wrong time. Like just now. It's one of those times when their shop is closed. They won't help anyone no matter what we need. I guess if someone was choking on their own barf or if we saw someone trying to kill themselves and ran to report it they might deign to help. But otherwise, helping was off limits.

They put up a pink sign that says, "Progress Report" in black type on the glass window of the nursing station during their time out from us. They sit on chairs with wheels in their sealed off box. Trade papers and eat cookies or donuts. Laugh and wipe off what's on the huge, white dry erase board that takes up almost one wall. Then they write new stuff on the board with smelly squeaks. So they know all over again which patient is which nurse's responsibility. Who is under whose wing.

When they put up the pink "Progress Report" sign it's actually a changing of the guard. One shift ends and another begins. The baton has to be passed off. Red alert situations highlighted. Who threw a tantrum or had a Code White called. Anyone who's been really demanding gets demerit points on their chart. In between filling out forms and making new notations in our confidential charts, the staff catches up on each other's weekends, husbands, kids and the sore ankle one of them suffered from last week. There are lots of reports to finish.

October 22, 1999

"Are you a musical genius?" Alice asks Jean, who is sitting at the piano in the activity room.

"I'm no genius," Jean answers, too sincere to be bashful. Today, her eyes are open a little too wide for her face. Like someone gave her a special assignment: make sure to keep your eyes stretched as wide open as possible. It gives her face a constant look of surprise, or like bad plastic surgery. I try not to look, but I'm drawn. Like picking at a scab.

"Wasn't that you I heard playing before?" Alice asks, insistent.

I want to explain to Alice that Jean plays the piano every day on the ward. This is something that has escaped Alice's astute attention until now.

"Yes, that was me," Jean answers.

"Will you teach me?" Alice asks, jumping up and down and clapping her hands together, suddenly five years old. I can almost see her hair in pigtails. Flip-flops transformed into fuzzy bunny slippers.

Jean breaks into a rolling rendition of, *Morning Has Broken*.

"How'd you know I wanted to hear that!" Alice chirps.

I groan inwardly. "It's the only song Jean's played on that piano since she's come here, Alice," I said.

They both look at me. Alice, a child stoned on birthday cake and make-your-own sundaes at her own slumber party whose parents have just brought out the wet blanket of bedtime. And Jean, who stares wide-eyed, her fingers poised, ready to take it from the top. I try to catch her blink, if only once.

CODE WHITE

October 23, 1999

I have this reoccurring nightmare. A nurse calls a Code White on me. Every time I'm doing something different, but never anything to really get me in trouble. One time, I'm in the smoke room, huddled on the metal bench. One of the night nurses, Katya, comes in.

"You've smoked more than your share of cigarettes! You've gone over the ward's official allotment. You've broken procedure."

"What procedure?" I ask innocently.

"You better enjoy those last few drags. I'm calling a Code White."

"Wait," I call. My desperation stops her. I have her undivided attention. I'm innocent. I know there's no "official allotment." I've done nothing wrong. But, I don't want a Code White. I don't want those men coming at me. I can't be restrained. So I insert each putrid cigarette butt I've smoked into my mouth. The hard ash of burnt tobacco and filter cuts against my cheeks. My mouth is grey.

"What are you waiting for then?" she asks. Motions to the ashtray.

"Please," I utter, and a few butts fall out of my full mouth onto the floor, near a coffee cup someone left overturned there. Nurse Katya sternly points to the waylaid cigarette butts. I meekly pick them up. Poke them back into my mouth. Try not to gag.

"I'm sorry. Please don't call a Code White. I'll behave." Butts spew out of my mouth into my lap as I speak.

"It's too late," she sneers. She leaves the room. I'm too scared to move. I hear her voice calling the code. It sounds tinny and far away. I feel the hard metal of the bench as if it's under someone else's ass. Faintly taste the charred cigarettes from a great distance. The door rips open and slams against the wall. I worry it will leave a mark in the paint. A stampede of men rushes through the open door. They grab me all over. I am not here, so I do not resist. They drag me to my room, but I am not really there.

Restrained, my pj buttons have ripped off in what must have been a struggle. I don't remember. I want to cover myself, but I am in four-point restraints. I can't defend myself. I stare at the ceiling. Try to count the holes in the white tiles there. *One, two, three, four.* I shrink myself down so tiny that I can slide right into one of the small holes in the ceiling.

"We can't trust you to keep quiet," Nurse Katya barks. "I have to keep you quiet myself."

Nurse Katya pushes a floppy paper plate from breakfast with a giant, greasy fried egg on it toward me. The yolk is runny and quivers when she shakes the plate like the new fat on my belly. I wonder where she got the egg. They only serve scrambled for breakfast, and only on certain days. There must be a secret nurse's kitchen where they get everything they want that patients don't get to have. My last thought, as I feel the sharp pinch of the needle in my ass cheek sliding in deep, is how did Katya know I hated slimy eggs? Her big hand with the chestnut nail polish and the ugly cameo ring comes at me with the rubbery egg. Then she stuffs it in my mouth. I can't stop gagging.

"From now on you had better be a good girl," she cajoles.

I am filled with hate like I have never known. All I can feel is the pressure in my limbs being pulled by the restraints and the bite of the restraints themselves. The yolk spills out my mouth. Runs down my neck and chin. Coats me sunny slick. All I see is yellow, dripping hatred. I vow to get out of here if it's the last thing I do. I have to leave this prison. A light switch flips. Black.

I wake up. A flashlight blares in my face. A nurse doing night checks. Rhoda. She closes my door. My chest heaves. My pjs and sheets are soaked in sweat. There's a funny taste in my mouth. I could go to the nursing station and ask for something to help me sleep, but I'm too terrified to leave my room. I lie in bed and shiver, unable to fall back asleep. I mark the rest of the night using the quarter hour checks from Nurse Rhoda. I desperately want a cigarette, but wait until morning. I know nothing happened. It was just a nightmare. But I don't want to leave my room. Even with the light from my window it's too dark to count the holes in the ceiling tiles for comfort. Only raw, cold skin against the wet sheets. A crinkle against the plastic mattress.

October 24, 1999

"How are you, honey?" Jean asks everyone in the lounge and the kitchen in quick repetitions, like she's skipping rope.

"Tired," Mary answers.

"Half-asleep," Tammy answers.

"Bored," Leah says.

"That's good, that's good," Jean says. "Stay that way the rest of your life. You'll feel less pain that way." Jean shoots out of the room like a hockey puck gliding gracefully across the ice. She walks quickly down the hall, like she is point A and she needs to get to point B fast. I watch her map out an efficient, straight line to nowhere.

debra anderson

October 24, 1999

The paper toilet seat protectors are in a box labelled "Rest Assured." After I flush, I watch the protector swirl down the toilet into a peaked cap. It looks like a fancily folded cloth napkin at a restaurant. Except it's covered in shit and piss.

October 24, 1999

Someone brought up one of those red plastic children's fire chief hats from downstairs. It's "Fire Safety Awareness Week" and a couple of people in business clothes have been giving them out free in the lobby and flashing bright, white smiles. Why there's a table with children's fire chief hats and fire safety cartoon books in a building where most people live under lock and key and can't get out even if there was a fire beats me. Not much in this building makes sense. I guess whoever was on a coffee run and took one from down there thought it was funny. Left it in the smoke room for a joke.

It's been here a long time now. Sits on the little coffee table next to the huge apple juice can filled with dead butts. A fire hazard. Right next to where every overflowing, sparking ashtray gets dumped. The red colour stands out. Festive. Even snowy with grey ash. Today, Leah proposed that anyone with off-ward privileges has to wear the hat. Even for a few seconds, like some kind of signal. We all burst out laughing at how arbitrary and ridiculous Leah's new rule was. Just like everything else on the ward.

"Are we supposed to put the hat on in the smoke room only? Or wear it around the ward?" I asked.

Leah pretended to ponder the dilemma.

"Because if anyone who has any privileges actually wore

this hat around the ward, staff would automatically assume that person was fucking crazy for wearing this stupid red hat. They'd take away your privileges," I said.

"And with no privileges, technically, you wouldn't be able to wear the hat anymore," Leah smirked and we all exploded.

Leah shook the ashes off the hat. Anointed me with it. It perched at the top of my head, tiny. Like I was at a children's party, wearing a party favour on my head, elastic biting into my chin. Everyone was laughing so hard their faces were red. For a moment, something tight in Leah loosened, too. I watched her smile and crack more jokes to keep everyone going. I kept that tight plastic band around my head just a little bit longer. Stretched it out a tiny bit more. Even though I didn't really want it there. It felt so good to see everyone smile.

October 24, 1999

Her legs were so open. A wide A-frame, soft and sturdy. A hole I didn't want to fall into so fast, didn't want to feel the heat of her. Still couldn't believe I had just met her on the street on a pass recently, eyes hooking each other.

"Hey, where are you going?" she'd called, bold, after I'd tossed her a grin that said I meant something, but then turned my head and kept walking.

"For ice cream," I smiled, antsy that I only had fifty minutes and counting left on my pass.

"You look determined," she laughed.

"I am."

"Wait a sec," she said while I stared at the traffic and couldn't believe I was managing a pick up. Again.

"Take this," she said shyly, and deposited a scrap of paper into my hand that she had just scrawled across. "I don't usually do this, but you look like someone I should get to know."

I stuck the paper in my purse. I now had only forty-five minutes to get the ice cream I'd been craving for days and get back to the ward on my pass. And now a phone number to deal with. For later. I smiled.

"Thanks. Good to meet you…"

"Rachel. My name's Rachel," she'd said.

"Alex. Sorry, but I have to go."

"I know. Ice cream," she smiled and I wondered what it would be like to explain things to her later, on the phone. If she would still want to talk to me. Date me.

"Call me?" she asked, her blush reaching her neck.

Tonight, after dinner that she paid for, we walked. I didn't have any money or time left on my pass to do anything else before I had to get back.

"Can I kiss you before you light that cigarette?" she said.

It was the most adorable thing. Sexy at the same time. I'd been lighting a cigarette because I needed somewhere to hide my face. Something to hold. She cut through. We kissed. Hard, hot tongues and sharp teeth. I had to strain to reach her. Lean my head back, she was so tall. We didn't want to stop, but I had to get back. We said a new goodbye every five paces or so. I forgot about the crick in my neck. Wished I could take her somewhere instead of signing myself back in alone.

On the walk home, in between kisses, all the farts in me kept popping out like rancid sour firecrackers. Sulfur badness. Bad date behaviour. Very unlike me. I was petrified Rachel would notice the raunchy smell. I was a horrible liar. I couldn't think of anything to pin it on. I kept hoping somehow Rachel didn't get what was happening.

CODE WHITE

October 25, 1999

In the smoke room, Mary said she's being discharged Friday. She's supposed to go live with her brother. For how long? A while? The rest of her life? She doesn't want to. Doesn't want anything, she's so depressed. Except a smoke, a coffee and to kill herself.

What about her apartment? She pays rent with her ex's alimony payments. It's been empty so long. It'll stay empty. How would Mary decorate her space? I can't ask. She already thinks I'm weird. I don't want to pry. Even though I know what her left inner forearm looks like. The old cut that reads *Help Me*. Round, bumpy burns, as if butts had been poked into her skin like you'd dab a napkin at the corner of your mouth if you were trying to be well-mannered. Layers of cuttings and scars. The newest one is cross-hatched to look like Frankenstein stitches.

A few weeks ago Mary was sprawled in the smoke room in her white bathrobe, holding the coffee I'd brought her because she isn't allowed off the ward. Talked nonchalantly about cutting. *Everyone has their hobbies.*

I picture Mary applying for a job. Even though I know she's too sick for that, despite being discharged. See her print *Cutting,* on the part of the form where they ask you to list your extracurricular activities.

Apparently, Mary's ready to leave here. She never got full privileges. Made two suicide attempts. But her burns have stopped oozing pus. Now they're only scabs. Maybe that's how her doctor, Dr. Graham, measures progress.

October 25, 1999

"Sometimes, when I look down, I see something wobble in

front of me, but don't tell anyone," Jean said to our table at dinner.

We all kept eating. Jean didn't seem to mind.

October 25, 1999

I've finished my zombie walk around the gym, which involves me rhythmically dribbling a basketball around the gym's perimeter. Each time I slap the ball, I pretend its orange bumpy surface is a girl's ass I'm spanking. By the time I spank the girl (or the ball) around the gym thirty times, my hand is red and sometimes swollen. It's a good thing the institute doesn't allow therapy. If I told a shrink what I'm pretending with the basketball, they'd take away my gym privileges.

After I'm done, I sit on the wooden bench in the hall by the gym. A bunch of male patients storm past me with two attendants. One guy lags a little. Cases me out. I've seen him in the elevator before. Today, he's wearing the same pjs I wear up on the ward. The blue, wide-legged bottoms with "Hospital Property" stamped all over them. My eyes narrow. I'm about the only one who wears them on my floor. I feel like they're mine. It's as if it's the prom and we've shown up wearing the same dress.

He's in the gym now, but I can still smell him. Fresh and clean. No cologne. Pure boy smell. I'd forgotten what that smells like. I feel guilty for liking it. The boys are exploding in the gym, as if on fast-forward. They are firecrackers. I watch one guy wrap himself in the volleyball net. A pysch attendant approaches him.

I remember coming to the gym with two psych assistants a couple of months ago, when I was still manic. I spazzed out with a basketball, roughly throwing it around everywhere. I didn't bother keeping track of where the nets were. There were other patients in the gym, from a different floor, with their own psych assistants. One patient was older than me. He had a black fingernail. I asked him if he'd painted it or slammed it in a door. He said he'd hurt himself. I got on my high gender-revolutionary horse and told him I wished he'd paint all of his fingernails. That he should try it. That day I had either an orange stuffed down my underwear or my pink soapbox. He stared at my bulge. I thought he was envious. Now, I know he was just weirded out. He hollered. The psych assistants all came running. Pat and Ralph took me back up even though the other patients said they hoped they'd see me soon. They thought I was fun. My gym privileges were revoked for a long time.

These guys in the gym are bouncing balls off walls, dunking balls into nets, scooping plastic pucks with hockey sticks, running in crazy circles. They expel all this energy I don't have, or remember ever having. Pj Bottoms runs out the door after a sponge ball that's rusted. He throws the sorry-looking thing against the wall a few times. Doesn't look at me. I don't look either, but I can tell when he's gone back inside. The bottoms of my feet are burning. My hand's shaking. The left one again. He comes out and sits on the stairs. Spits into the garbage can at the bottom without getting up. Gross, what if he missed? He doesn't. He scratches his back. The top of his underwear shows. They're grey. And remind me of Jamie. He sits in a chair by the fountain. His head is shaved. When was the last time I saw a dyke with that haircut? I think about how good a shaved head feels under my hands, against my thighs, between my legs. I blush when he speaks.

"I know you," he says. "You went to my school. Did you go to Northern?"

I look at him firmly, and meet his eyes. They are grey, like his underwear. He looks crazy. Whatever that is. I want to stop this before it starts. Even if he does smells good. He's a boy. I'm a dyke. We're both locked up in here. I hate it that part of me wants to take him to the water fountain where the psych assistants won't see and kiss him. I hate it even more that he's here and Jamie's not.

"You don't know me," I say. "I didn't go to your school. I'm a lot older than you."

"No, you're not. I'm twenty-four, how old are you?"

I'm actually twenty-four, too. I know he somehow knows this, but I don't want to answer him. He starts doing this musical thing with his mouth, *Da-da-da TAAA daaaah!* He does it over and over. Punctuated with squelching noises. We stare at each other while his mouth makes noise. When I stare at him, all I can think of is Jamie adjusting her tie. Jamie underneath me on the floor beside my bed, on the side furthest from the door so we're hidden from a nurse. Shoving hospital pjs down around my eager thighs. I look at his wide hands. Somehow they're Jamie's small hands on my ass while I'm straddling her and sliding her big cock inside me after I'd ordered her to lube it. I look at his fearless eyes. Remember how afraid I was that Jamie and I had mistimed. That a nurse would be by any second doing rounds, and I'd get caught with this butch's dick inside me. Afraid because I was letting her fuck me. Afraid it would never happen again. Mostly scared I'd never get to have her. And I didn't. Jamie's a bit of stone, a bit of something else. Something so boy, there wasn't enough room on the ward for her to let down the guard she held. I didn't have enough time or space in between those relentless checks to flip her. And then she was gone.

The boy winks at me. I don't know why I don't just leave. Or why I'm wet. Or why I wish he were closer, so I could smell him again. Then his psych assistant comes out.

"Are you staff?" he asks.

Pj Bottoms smirks. I should have said, *Yes*. But I say, "No, I'm a patient."

They all leave. As he walks away, I picture Pj Bottoms blowing me a fruity, flouncy kiss over his shoulder, but he doesn't. He's not wired that way. I go back into the empty gym and stand in the spot where I first saw him throw a basket. Aim and shoot. The ball doesn't even hit the board. My throw was too low and my arm sockets hurt from the effort. I sit on the ball. My ass bones hurt against its bright, tight orange. Out of all the pictures Jamie gave me, I think about the picture I wanted to draw for her. Help her find her balance. Stop being so scared. Be more open. Her legs spread and both my hands inside her safe. Everything in the same pink glitter that was trapped under her fingernails that day. A bouquet coming out of my hand. Everything pink. Ribbons, lipstick, garter belt, a pair of high heels, and of course, flowers. Her hands would be cupped around my hands. We'd both be holding the bouquet. Offering it to each other.

I go to the opposite basket, closer to the left this time. Then I zero in, aim at a spot on the board and release. The ball smacks the board and falls effortlessly through the net. Hits the floor. My arm sockets are fine. I hear clapping and turn to the door. At first, I think it's Jamie standing there. Then I think it's Pj Bottoms. But, it's just Ralph, saying it's almost dinner. They want me back up on the floor. I've been gone too long.

debra anderson

October 26, 1999

"My memory's all screwed up since that ECT. I keep remembering everything I want to forget and forgetting everything I need to remember," Lee whined in the smoke room.

Then, after almost forgetting to put out her butt, she walked out to ask the nurse for her homeworker this weekend. Unlike me, Lee gets to go home every weekend. It doesn't really matter though. She's too scared to go outside no matter where she is anyways. She just sits inside at home, too. Pacing and smoking.

October 26, 1999

Leah was talking to a few of us in the smoke room. And then she said, "How pathetic would it be if you came in here to meet someone?"

Everyone laughed.

"Desperateville," Tammy giggled.

I ducked my head. Took a few slow drags off my cigarette.

I thought of Jamie and felt twisted. I didn't come in here to meet Jamie. I came here because I had to. I was made to. I just happened to meet someone while I was here. Someone who was here, too. I met her despite the ward. We couldn't look away. Is that pathetic? I don't know.

I took another drag. Tried not to feel like Leah was specifically making a direct jab at me. I couldn't remember if she was even here for the whole thing with Jamie. For any of it. It didn't really matter.

Later, I tried not to think about Jamie. As much as I knew we should stay away from each other, my fingers itched to call her. But I kept my mouth shut. I didn't want Leah to know any of it.

We all take love where we can find it. That's not pathetic. Is it?

October 26, 1999

Tammy had a new pad of gauze on her forehead. Held on by sanitary tape. Ambled into the smoke room wearing two hospital gowns. One in front and the other to cover her ass and back. She was wrapped in a long white, hospital blanket. The kind with tiny holes. Knit to breathe. Her bare legs were ribboned with old scars. Nurse Emma, who was wearing her usual crisp pair of slacks and an aubergine blouse, lit Tammy's smoke.

"Don't you have something else you could put on that would keep you warm?" Nurse Emma inquired.

Tammy ignored her. Padded into the room like soggy waffles were stuck to her feet. Nurse Emma hovered in the doorway.

Murmured, "Fire hazard," then left.

Tammy sunk to the floor after grabbing an ashtray. I laughed. It was nice to see resignation on the face of a nurse. Not on one of ours.

October 26, 1999

Lee's new white sneakers say "Bionic" on them.
I'm starting Lithium tonight.

October 26, 1999

Alice tells me she's getting discharged tomorrow. It's like a sick joke. She still seems incredibly ill. I can't believe they're letting her go. She tells me like she's won some competition. Who is worthiest to be discharged. Alice is Number One Mental Patient Extraordinaire because she got chosen to leave before me in the ward sweepstakes. I don't care. I don't remember signing up for that contest.

"I'm glad for you, Alice," I tell her. And I am. I have no clue how long she's been here. I just know it's been a really long time. And it wasn't her first time. I wonder what will happen to her with no nurses to look after her? And if I'll still be here when they bring her back for her next round.

October 27, 1999

"So I'm working on this plan. Hopefully, they'll decertify me tomorrow. I'll go to the bank and withdraw a hundred bucks. I figure I'll leave Thursday. Why stay the weekend?"

"Where are you going to go?" I ask Tammy. Tentatively, like pulling the sheets up gently over someone who's sleeping.

"Back to the group home. I'm scared. They want to evict me from there last I heard," she says.

"Didn't the nurses give you any other options?" I ask.

"Nope," Tammy exhales the word in front of her on a long jet of smoke.

I can't believe they are just kicking Tammy out.

"That's fucked up," I tell her.

"And they told me I can't come back here," she says. Each word in Tammy's story is a dart she's throwing at herself.

"What were you supposed to do to make it 'work'?" I ask.

"I dunno. Go to group. Fuck. I can't even get out of bed, never mind go to group," Tammy says. There's a whole line of darts lining her skin. Prickling like porcupine quills. Rankling.

"They have no other suggestions for you?"

"Nope," she taps her ash. It falls in her lap. A grey smudge. "They said if I come back it'd be on another floor."

"What will another floor do for you that this one couldn't?" I ask. I think of the sharp pleats in nurse Emma's pants. The crisp click of her shoes along the hallway. The slashes outlining her eyes. Hard.

"Nothing. Keep me safe for like three days and then release me. Then I can be someone else's problem again," Tammy says.

I look closer. She's sinking into the bench, her shoulders hunched forward. Round like bowls of pudding melting on the counter from lunch. Unwanted.

"Then what's the point of doing this?"

"There is no point." Tammy clears all the ash off her heater. Makes it into a clean, sharp point against the ashtray. "I'm pretty freaked. I'll pack my stuff and shit. I haven't even been on the subway in forever. Maybe six or seven months. And now they're going to kick me out and expect everything's going to be okay? When this whole time they've told me it isn't?"

The bandages on her head are bright and white. Her scars glisten all over her face. Lie across her arms. Her legs. I wish I could hold her.

"I'm going to take a taxi home. Then I'll go to bed. Fuck all the rest. Sleep. That's all I want to do," Tammy says.

She finishes her cigarette. Pause. Maybe I could have said a lot of things. I wonder about everything that comes into my head. Would any of it, would all of it just make things worse for Tammy? Would it cram into the tiny space she's managed to eke out for herself and take more of it away? I want to try to instill some shine. Not steal her privacy. Shit on her dignity. Wasn't my chance to take.

"Hey, I'm sorry," I say. "I'm going to miss you," I tell her. Try not to get all choked up. Make it worse.

"Yeah, well, it doesn't really matter, does it? See ya."
Then she walks out.

October 27, 1999

Sharon is voluntary on the ward. She has full privileges, which means she can go off hospital grounds for walks or to get a bagel and coffee. Often she does. Tonight, Sharon and I are the only ones in the smoke room. Most of the other patients are in bed. Sharon doesn't usually talk, but tonight she tells me she is pregnant.

"Don't tell anyone," she says.

"How far along are you?" I tentatively ask.

"I have eight weeks left," she answers shyly.

Sharon is a rake. Long bony fingers and toes. Tall body with not much padding. I assume she means eight weeks left for an abortion. There's no bulge in her belly. All she ever drinks is coffee. She smokes even more cigarettes than me.

"I'm pregnant, you know."

She pours over what looks like an oversized telephone book. A medical book with very thin pages covered in heavy ink. Scanning for information about the effects of drugs she either has been taking or is supposed to start taking on her unborn baby.

"The Epival gave me seizures," she says.

I stare at her belly. Sharon has extra long nails on her fingers and toes that she never cut. I'd seen her toenails because she always wore black strappy sandals even though it was October. Like she could stop the seasons from changing if she kept wearing all her summer stuff. It's quiet for a bit while I smoke and she reads. Then her head snaps up. It's newly shaved.

"I want this baby so bad I'll go crazy if I abort," she says. Her eyes pin me to the bench. That her meds could cause an accidental abortion is unstated. The book flaps open in her lap, which holds her diagnosis and its corresponding meds, becomes a huge boat, as wide as the smoke room. A boat that holds all three of us: Sharon, me and the baby. And the diagnoses and pill bottles of every patient on the ward until there is barely any room for any of us. None of us know exactly where we were going because none of us is navigating the boat. I can hear the wind howling through the smoke room fan.

"I want this baby so bad," she says again. Sharon didn't really talk to anyone ever.

Then she gets up and walks out of the room in a long white nightgown someone brought from home for her. Her skinny shoulders poke through, the narrow negative "V" space between her legs shines in the light.

She left behind a red delicious apple, bruised in two places and the only spot of colour in the room. And her empty styrofoam coffee cup. She took her Diet Coke with her when she left.

By the time I woke up the next day it was early afternoon, and Sharon was gone. A new girl was in her room. Mindy.

October 28, 1999

I heard Leah on the payphone outside my room. I wasn't eavesdropping, but Pat the psych assistant left my door open last time he did rounds. Leah was talking with her mother. It sounded like her mother didn't want to take her back between the time she got discharged and when Leah got into a rehab place. Leah was crying.

"I have no more friends left. No one to ask, or I wouldn't be asking... Fine. Thanks a lot," she said and hung up.

The phone call before her mother was some distress centre. As soon as they heard she was an addict, they wouldn't take her.

"I feel weird," Leah told me in the smoke room. "I'm off everything now."

"Congratulations," I said and meant it.

I wondered if she could tell. I held her eyes. They were trying to slide under the metal bench. Leah was sort of crumbling. Like always, I wished I had something good to give her. A marker of what she was accomplishing. I couldn't even give her a hug because of that stupid, NO TOUCHING rule. Also, everyone knew I was a dyke and so I was self-conscious about trying to get away with casual touching like a pat on the back or a squeeze of the hand or whatever. Especially with Leah, since she'd once told me that she was a dyke, too. Then she never really talked about it again, unless it came up in one of her infamous stories. All the gorgeous girls she got wild with and stuff. I didn't want her to think I was hitting on her when that wasn't the point. I only wanted to make her feel better. It was too bad I didn't have anything squirreled away in my room. She really looked like she needed something.

"Congrats," I said again. Wished I could say something else. Not sure what.

"Thanks," she said.

Her foot couldn't keep still. It twitched like a tic under the eye. She ground out her cigarette even though there were more than a few drags left. Whispered, "Going for a walk," as she left the smoke room. She could only pace the same bit of tile in the hallway. All that was left.

CODE WHITE

October 28, 1999

I'd photograph the silver payphone cord, if they ever allowed cameras on the ward. There's something about that payphone cord, the way it's ridged from beginning to end, connected to the black plastic receiver and the heavy black rectangular box of the phone, screwed into the wall. As if any of us would try to drag it into our rooms. As if any of us wouldn't.

I watch the cord sometimes when I'm on the phone. Lose track of the conversation I'm supposed to be having. Sometimes I stare at it from across the lounge when someone else is talking. I watch it move. Sway back and forth. I'd love to take a photo of the cord in motion. Each ridge blurring. Into the air around it. Into space. The silver line tear-stained like so many conversations. A cord. Connection to everyone on the other side of that door.

October 28, 1999

Lee always says, *Take it easy* to me when she leaves the smoke room. Ever since my discharge date's been set, she says stuff like, *I wouldn't bullshit you, there's something sweet about you. And that's from my heart. You're your own person. You stand out.* Her hands shake a little. The polish is pretty old and chipped, so I offer to do her nails before I'm discharged. She can't believe it. Lee rubs at her two fingers where they are yellowed. Worries how to get the stain off so the polish will look pretty.

She's pacing. Again. Asks when I'm getting out. Again. She's asked twice today. When I ask, she can't remember how long she's been here. I know it's longer than me. She can't remember a lot of things. The shock treatment blanks it out. Her favourite topic since she started the treatments has been her weight loss. She forgets she's complained about the awful headaches shock gives her. How nauseous she feels all the time.

"It's time something went right for me," she says. "I'm so happy," she drawls. "Another ten pounds and I'll be there. Whaddaya think?"

"I think you look good now, Lee," I tell her. And it's true. There are enough eating disorders on the floor.

Five minutes later brings new cigarettes for each of us. She talks about her weight again, after asking, "Really? You'd do my nails for me? Oh Sue, you're something special."

"At last something's going well. I have no appetite anymore. I've lost ten pounds already," Lee says. She tells me as if it's new news. As if I haven't heard it before. I pretend I haven't.

"I always liked you, Alex," she whines, then calls me Sue in the next sentence.

I don't take it personally; it's the shock therapy that's removed my name. I don't bother to correct her anymore. At first, I'd set her straight. She'd look mortified and apologize forever until we'd both had enough. Then she'd pace down the hallway. She's decided somehow my name's Sue. So when Lee calls "Sue" down the halls, I always turn around.

Lee tells me it's her birthday on Thursday. "But don't ask me my age, I won't tell," she adds as quick as a price gun in full minimum wage tagging fever. I wish she wasn't so bloated with the shame of how old she is. That she didn't want to keep that secret. She's told me so many other things it seems silly. Almost as silly as everything else that goes on in this ward. She gives me a hug and my eyes glisten. I hug the new her. Less body and less memory. So little space. Why do all of us girls want to get so small?

eight

October 29, 1999

I'm in my housecoat: the one Mary thinks looks like Aquafresh without the cinnamon. It's after breakfast. I'm trying to get my vitamin from the nursing station while I still remember. To my left there's a new patient. She's wearing stained, cream-coloured stirrup pants, running shoes and an orange blouse that looks like it's from the Bi-Way. I'm so tired my eyes keep shutting. It hurts to keep them open. An effect of the sleeping pill from last night.

"Why do you look at girls like that? You shouldn't look at girls, you should look at boys," she screams at me.

Why did she say that? Does she know I'm a dyke or is she just paranoid? I should stand up to her, but I'm stunned. I think she might physically attack me. I have to live with this crazy bitch until I'm discharged. I doubt she'll be going anywhere for a long time.

I calmly say, after purposely not looking at her, "I'm sorry you feel like that. I wasn't looking at you in any way."

Then I dissociate into numb TV snow. Try not to remember there was a time when I was a proud, out dyke. And then I go to group in the activity room. My nurse signed me up. If you don't show, they hunt you down all over the ward. There's never anywhere to hide.

In group I pretend I'm not there.

"Do you want to share that?" Priscilla the social worker chirps.

I pretend harder. I do a count. Patient Total: 6. Slipper Count: 3 (plus 2 patients wearing sandals). Full Pyjamas Regalia: 4 (plus

2 patients wearing sweatsuits). The social worker, social worker student, med student, and doctor are all fully clothed. Dr. Graham gives us a form to fill out. Priscilla the social worker hands out pens. A ping-pong ball resting on the piano ups itself and bounces on the piano several times, then falls onto the ground. We all watch until the social worker tells us, "Focus girls," in her fake cheery voice. I want to throw one of her pens.

October 29, 1999

Tammy's leaving today. For good. I slept until 11:45 a.m. and caught her in the washroom coming out of the stall. It smelled like she'd just taken her last shit on the ward. We gave each other a huge hug. Then we were in the smoke room with Christina. Tammy was freaking out because her mom was late.

"Like geez, is she getting her hair cut or what?" she joked.

We all laughed. Then a phone call came for Tammy.

She came back and said, "It's my mom. She's downstairs, gimme a hug."

Christina got a huge hug. I got a smaller one. Was it because I'm a lez? Or because I already got one? Maybe she was just nervous because her mom's here. Everything happened fast. I took mental snapshots of Tammy standing with her mother, who was tall and thin and super-coiffed in a red coat that matched Tammy's new windbreaker set that Christina bought her. Whenever Christina gets money, she buys stuff for people. When she sees someone needs something, she wants to give it to them. She bought me a funny little caterpillar made out of sparkly green pompoms. The bottom had a waxy sticker backing you could peel off. I haven't peeled mine yet. I'm waiting for someplace better than here to put it.

Tammy was short and fat and bald. Covered in old and

new burns and cutting scars everywhere. She said she'd put on over a hundred pounds from the medications she'd taken while she'd been here. From the weight I'd gained since I'd been here, I believed her. Already two pairs of pants were too small on me. The waistbands cut into my new padding with an unfriendly bite I'd learned to ignore. Tammy's been here, on one floor or another, for over eight months. One of her eyelids drooped from when she banged her head on the corner of her bed until a Code White was pulled.

Tammy's mother held the collage Tammy made last week out of magazine photos and glued onto white bristol board in Arts & Crafts and two black garbage bags full with Tammy's stuff. I clutched the green beaded anklet Tammy made and gave to me in the smoke room last night. I grabbed the bracelet so hard the seed beads bit into my fingers. I didn't care.

Tammy's mom disappeared. Tammy waited against the cream wall outside the smoke room. I stood beside her and said, "Is your mom coming back up to get you or is she waiting downstairs?"

I said it twice without an answer because Tammy was already gone. That's when I started crying.

October 29, 1999

The woman who screamed at me today about how I should look at boys and not girls, has a name. Donna. Donna freaks me out because she's so high in her manic place. I wonder if I used to be like her. Plus, she is just plain scary to be around. Donna keeps pacing the hallway between the nursing station and the smoke room and repeating the phrase, "Can I get a toothbrush and some toothpaste?"

"No one's listening to me," she observes loudly. And then

repeats that observation a few more times. "What do I have to do to get someone to listen to me?" she yells in a panic.

Then bitchface Nurse Dee says politely, yet firmly, "Do you need some medication?"

I hate it here.

October 29, 1999

Last night on our date, Rachel and I passed an alley. We both walked by a little slower. I was cruising for future sex possibilities. I told her so a block later because the alley looked hot. All that dirty exposed brick. Rachel got all red and stammered. An erratic jump rope skipping out of turn. She stumbled even though her eyes were on the pavement.

"I was checking out all the cool bikes parked along the fence," Rachel blushed. I nodded. I hadn't really noticed the bikes. "You're such a dirty old man, Alex," she said and I could feel the heat coming off her face when I leaned in to kiss her. I wondered what her ass cheeks would feel like in my open palms. I still couldn't believe we were dating. Or whatever it was that we were doing. That she still wanted to see me even though she knew my story. Knew where I had to go back to at the end of each date.

When it was time to say goodbye, I ordered her to jerk off once she got home. Today on the phone, I asked if she had followed my instructions. I had a feeling she wouldn't remember. Or she'd pretend she had no clue what I was talking about. She said, *Yes,* without missing a beat. I was stuck on pause. Not sure what the next song was supposed to be. I don't think Rachel felt the empty space as I tried to figure out what I wanted. I thought of Rachel touching herself when she got home after seeing me last night. Maybe she'd been planning on doing so anyways, but I'd told her to. I wondered if she waited until she got home. Pictured her burying her hand down her waistband as the elevator doors inside her building shut. I asked if she enjoyed herself.

"Yes."

She didn't sound as shy as she usually did. I heard the beam in her voice. I wondered how Rachel jerked off. Tried to imagine what that looked like. I couldn't. I wondered if she was lying.

"Did you?" she asked, tentative. "Did you do it?"

"Yes," I breathed into the receiver. I didn't tell her I'd actually jerked off between nurse checks mostly thinking of Jamie, with a ripple of Rachel. She didn't need to know. It would dim her beam. And she was just starting to shine.

October 30, 1999

When I get to the activity room for the Women's Support Group I have been wrangled to like a lost sheep by the nurses, Mindy is crashed on the piano bench in her blue ruffled party dress. She looks like she's been on a brutal bender for at least a week and has chosen this particular spot to hit bottom and black out. Even though the piano doesn't look comfortable, she's managed to drape herself over all the keys. Her legs sink beneath the piano as if a fierce undercurrent has her.

Everyone who enters takes note. Mindy doesn't hear any of us laughing or calling her name. Priscilla, the social worker, comes and tries to get Mindy to move. Mindy's too out of it. And too comfortable. In all my days of heavy partying, I've never seen anyone crash as hard as Mindy. Each time the social worker pokes her, grabs an arm or barks Mindy's name, Mindy moans like she has the world's biggest hangover.

CODE WHITE

"Mindy, you have to move now, please. It's time for group," Priscilla the social worker explains in her clipped voice.

"NOOOOOOO. I'll just stay right here," Mindy screeches.

Mindy isn't well enough to be forced to go to group. Priscilla tugs Mindy and Mindy pulls back, sprawling across the piano again. I wish I didn't have to be in the room watching this tug of war. I wish for the trillionth time that I was somewhere else. I wonder what drugs they've pumped into Mindy, but I know better than to ask. *Focus on your own recovery. Stop caretaking others. That's not what you're here for.*

I try to ignore the social worker unsuccessfully attempting to get Mindy out of the room. I pretend to be engrossed in each turquoise nub of carpet. I'm afraid to look at the other patients. I can't do my usual pj and slipper count to see how functional group is today because of the awful howls coming from Mindy. Every inane, public servant-y thing Priscilla says just to kick Mindy out of the room. How is this Women's Support Group supporting Mindy?

"Don't walk into the wall, Mindy. You need to open your eyes to see," Priscilla chides.

"No," says Mindy stubbornly.

Priscilla is guiding Mindy, who is as limp as overcooked pasta, off the piano stool and to the door. It's a slow, painful process, because Mindy refuses to open her eyes. Every one of her body parts is rubber. Earlier in the week, Mindy was bright and gleaming. Stayed in the activity room in her glittery party dress and played ping-pong for hours. The sound of that ball speedily hitting the table drove me mental. I wanted to go in there during the five second window when she ran to pee and steal it so she couldn't play anymore. The spark in her felt off.

Too dazzling and fast and loud. Intense ping-pong. Flashy party dress that she refused to change out of. Singing and dancing for hours in the activity room by herself no matter what anyone else said.

"Fun is fun," she said. And Mindy was fun. She was also pretty scary. But now she's worse. A shiny balloon someone poked a hole into. Everything sags. I wish it didn't have to be this way.

October 30, 1999

Jean came up to me in the hallway and cornered me. When she does that there's no way to get out of it. I'm not sure how she does it, but I can never walk away from her. I listen to her weird stories instead. Today, it was about some friend of hers that basically lives on the floor.

"My friend does everything on the floor. Not just sleep," Jean insists. "She sits on the floor. Watches TV on the floor. She eats on the floor too, from a miniature TV tray."

"Does she have Meals On Wheels delivered?" I asks.

Jean takes two steps back; totally offended I'd assume her friend would need help from anyone.

"She cooks shepherd's pie, everything, right there on the floor, Alex! It's the darndest thing! Her legs are wrong because she fell off of a swivel chair. And she has cats!"

How does one end up with "wrong" legs from falling off a swivel chair? In Jean's world, anything can happen. Part of me wishes badly that there really is this friend who has to live on the floor. As Jean speaks, each word in her story is one tiny light bulb in a pretty string of delicate Christmas lights, shining and glowing. The longer Jean talks about her swivel chair friend, the more lights there are, draped all over her. The sheen is mesmerizing. And then suddenly, it isn't very important anymore whether there really is a woman carrying on her business in some tiny apartment in Toronto where she can get to everything she needs with the reach of an arm. I don't feel pinned by her anymore. I actually want to stay. Watch Jean unfurling. She seems bigger now. Her shoulders wider. Feet planted more firmly on the floor. She's stopped wavering for the first time. Her eyes have almost lost their glassy glaze. They meet what's in front of her. Direct.

"I was in there one time helping her. She was making one of those fancy cakes. It was layered and it looked like a football! She was doing the whole thing right there, on the floor! Can you imagine?" Jean asks and giggles. "With homemade icing, even! Can you imagine that?"

I can. I want to giggle with her. And then I do.

October 31, 1999

"Are you okay?" Mindy asks Donna in the lounge. "What's wrong?" Mindy inquires in a maple syrup-coated school nurse voice. Mindy is more awake now; she's able to sit up and talk sometimes. I don't know if the nurses gave her something or if whatever they had given her is wearing off. Like watching full body Novocaine fade.

"I'm worried about my housing. There's a woman there who belongs here. NOT me," Donna explains loudly.

"Is it your daughter?" asks Mindy. She looks all of fifteen. Her family visits in a big pack. They bring baskets of food like they're going on a picnic, except they forgot Mindy can't go anywhere. Mindy doesn't realize that not everyone lives in a house with their family, equipped with mothers and fathers and brothers and sisters. Mindy doesn't realize that homes house all sorts of configurations.

"NO!! She isn't my daughter," Donna says. I can see the red line in her thermometer rising. "Weren't you listening? I'm worried about my housing. There is a lot of tension in the house right now —"

"— I know, because I've been bullied at school a lot and trust me —" Mindy flops a sympathetic hand on Donna's leg. It looks like a soggy potato peeling stuck to the side of a sink.

"— DON'T TOUCH ME!!!"

"Sorry," Mindy says, and withdraws the hand slowly.

"I'm trying to tell you there's this bitch who's living in my house. She's out to get me. She's been trying to turn me in for weeks. Maybe even a couple of months. But SHE'S the one that's really sick. And now I'm stuck here. She's still there, poisoning all the people in the house against me. I gotta get back before there's no place to get back to," Donna sputters. Tall sparklers that give off tiny, bright white sparks you're afraid will hurt as they fall onto your skin.

"They'll look after you here," Mindy says with professional assurance. She sits up straight like someone's put a hook into her and is pulling on it from the ceiling. "They'll take good care of you here."

I check to see if Mindy is holding a clipboard. Taking intake notes on Donna's case. She isn't.

"You think so?" Donna asks, wavering. Mindy nods.

"I need some potassium," Donna declares. She goes to ask Doug the psych assistant for oranges and comes back.

"No, bananas are for potassium. Lady, bananas are for potassium," and then Mindy touches Donna's arm to emphasize the point.

CODE WHITE

"Don't touch me," Donna snarls and looks at Mindy's hand.

"Oranges is vitamin C, not potassium…"

A nurse wanders by and Donna runs up to her. "I'm scared. I need to make sure I have housing. I need to make sure I have housing."

The nurse says something I can't make out from where I'm sitting. I can only hear Donna, who is really loud. Tattooed woman in a convenience store buying lottery tickets and cigarettes on her way to the bingo hall kind of loud. The kind of loud the nurse doesn't like. The look on her face says she smells something really bad. Her whole body fights to stand exactly where it is and not back away.

"I have to make sure I have housing. You have to help me —"

The nurse's face tightens. Words pop out, but I can't hear.

"Don't tell me not to repeat myself," Donna yells. "When I'm anxious that's what happens. I repeat myself when I'm anxious. Almost anything comes out of my mouth. You know, you'd be anxious, too, if you didn't think you were going to have any place to live," Donna yells.

The nurse threatens Donna. Tries to get her to "behave" and "calm down" rather than agree to help her or look into the housing crisis Donna seemed to think she was having. I moved closer to hear what was happening.

"Perhaps it is time for you to take some medication so you'll be less anxious, Donna," the nurse says.

Which wasn't what Donna had asked for at all. It wasn't what she needed. In the background, I could still hear Mindy, reciting all the different vitamins and minerals in every fruit and vegetable she could remember, true or false. It was like she had a little nutritional chart up there in her head from high school health class that kept unfolding.

October 31, 1999

    A few weeks ago on a pass I walked through the Philosopher's Walk with Sadie to go to Greg's Ice Cream. I can never make up my mind which flavour to get. The ice cream was an extravagance. We didn't have it on the ward. Their version of ice cream was cookie cutter flavours in small wax paper cups, tasting of the paper that housed it. A gross, gummy coating and freezer burnt snow crystals. Still, all the patients would fight for their little cup. On ice cream days, rows of melting cups someone had arbitrarily brought. So unexpected. So sweet. We never knew when these mysterious trays would be unceremoniously plopped down again. And if those mushy cups didn't melt, I could imagine how the women would angle to carry away everything they could in secret. Hide it in their rooms for later. When they needed another fix.

    Eating Greg's ice cream with Sadie on a pass is a planet away from those paper cups. I'm treating myself. Trying to undo a little of what's being done at the ward. After I made my choice and paid, we went back upstairs to the street. Sadie wanted to cross the street to the path behind the museum where we usually sit. Anywhere I wanted to go was too far. California or the beach or Niagara Falls. For a massage, a haircut, a drive-in movie. I didn't have a car. I wasn't even allowed to drive right now. I didn't have any money for any of it. I didn't even have enough for two subway tokens. Sadie kept nudging me to cross the street. I stood there watching my raspberry lemonade ice cream sink deeper into its plastic cup.

    "C'mon Alex," Sadie said. Took my hand. Pulled lightly.

The route back was a giant magnet drawing me to my rightful place. I stared at my mound of ice cream. I wasn't sure I wanted it anymore. I tried to feel my feet against the pavement. Uneven and dirty. Not like the smooth tiles in the hallway on the ward. Sadie tugged my arm again. I took a step forward toward the curb, even though I felt like being alone. I checked my watch to make sure I hadn't stayed out too long. I didn't want to get in trouble. I was early. I crossed the street with Sadie. Panic a sharp, pulsing light in my throat. Cars from both directions were going to hit me. The colours were bright. Paint shiny as they drove near me. Hurt my eyes. The dark grey of the road cut up with yellow dividing lines. Too sharp. I was unsure where it was safe to step. Where was the right place to walk? When should I be still? There weren't enough lines mapped. Like I was standing on a nurse's note page. A case study split in half; ready to be filled in with notes. Every word speeding. I was out of place. In the middle of traffic. Air from the cars rushing by. Music thrown out of passing windows. We made it to the other side safely. A weird part of me was disappointed I'd been wrong.

Sadie finally dropped my hands. We walked further across the sidewalk and onto the path. At last were away from Bloor Street and the cars. Onto a bench overlooking some flowers. And still, there's that tug in me. I looked at my watch again. Almost time.

October 31, 1999

Nurse Susan came into my room to talk. "I'm glad you're my nurse," I said when we were finished talking. It was true. She looked surprised for a minute. "Should I not say stuff like that?"

"I just think it's funny. You've really changed. Early, when you were manic, one time I let you know I'd be off for three days. You said, *Who cares, there are other nurses.*" She smiled at me. Every bit of me that I've shared while I've been here sat between us. Something no other nurse could just come in and pick up from. We both knew that now.

"I'm sorry I said that," I said. And then she left. What I didn't tell her was that back then I thought all nurses were interchangeable. All the same, and no help. I thought if one was gone, someone else would help if I needed it. That I didn't need help from anyone, anyway.

But that's not true. I realize that now. I do need help. Even if I don't want it. Even if I don't want to be here. I am. I don't know how my nurse doesn't hate me for all the crazy things I've said. I don't care if she's my Number One Fan. Inviting me out for drinks when I get discharged. It's nice to be helped by a nurse who doesn't discount who I am now by every fucked up thing I've done since I've been here. Nurse Susan tries to see me. Most days. I know it's not totally accurate. I'm still fighting a hangover effect of what I did yesterday or last month. But I don't think it's as bad as with some nurses. That refusal. Pinning you down as mental patient. Every last note in their binder as the definitive, rather than you standing there. It's definitely luck of the draw. The nurses are similar. Not the same. I could've done a lot worse than Nurse Susan. I was lucky. I wouldn't want her to take off now.

October 31, 1999

Halloween. And I'm still here. That in itself is the worst fucking trick I have had happen to me in my whole goddamn life. If I'd have broken my leg this summer I'd have had my cast off by now.

Instead, I'm still stuck in this place. Wondering where all the time has disappeared to. Swallowed in some weird institutional vortex. Every day rubbed off the nurse's dry erase board in one clean sweep. Not clear why this process needs to take so long. Why for some illnesses doctors seem to know what they're doing, while for others you're stuck on your own, treading water. Tough cookies, kid. I really got the short end of the stick this summer.

Even though my window's closed, I can hear everyone hollering out on the street. If none of this had happened, if I was still just my regular, old self, out there doing something to celebrate Halloween tonight, what would I have chosen as my costume?

I can't figure it out. I can't really remember what that would be like anymore. I look down at my lap and all I see are the "Hospital Property" pjs coating me blue.

nine

November 1, 1999

It's totally pathetic, but I have nowhere to live once I'm discharged. My parents are nice enough to take me back until I figure out where to go from here. They made me make a list of agreements. It was humiliating, but I understood their perspective. They want to do whatever they can to make sure I don't get sick again. So I made the list: Always take my meds. Stay at home to sleep every night. Provide a list of friend's names and addresses.

The list made me feel like I was fourteen. I have to collect all my friend's addresses. I don't even know the last names of half the people I hang out with. How do I explain why I need this information to people? For my parents' list, in case I go crazy again and end up missing? I don't want to sound like a spoiled teenager, but I'd rather stay in my room than collect a dossier about the person I'm going for coffee with. Explain my life story before we even sit down.

November 1, 1999

I've tried to call all the people I remember calling to attempt to undo whatever I did when I was manic. The crazy phone calls, everything wild that came streaming out of my mouth. Trying to wipe it away like attacking a dirty table with a clean sponge. The problem is I don't remember what I said to a lot of people. It's hard to apologize when you don't even know what you're apologizing for. Then there's the bigger problem. I know there are a zillion phone calls I don't remember making at all. How can I erase those?

My whole self is crumpled. I'm trying to fit into the smallest bit. Inside my belly button. Crawl inside and hide. I know there's no point in saying any of that stuff to anyone. In asking for forgiveness. Whatever I said was so fucked up it stuck. People don't just forget. My voice is probably going to play in their heads whenever they see me. That's all they'll see from now on whenever they look at me. The rest of me is lost. I probably made an even bigger ass of myself asking them to forget it. Reminded them of what I said in the first place. If I were in some feel good Movie of the Week, I'd be feeling strong and courageous now. Like I did something healing. Came to terms with my illness in a big way. But I actually feel worse now that I called those people. It's all bullshit. I never want to see any of them again.

November 1, 1999

Lee told me today she's going to be discharged in a couple of weeks once they finish her ECT. I'll be gone before her. She's already given me her number twice. Asked me to call. I'll call. Won't I? We both know she's not ready to be let out yet. As she walked out of the smoke room to find a nurse, she said, "I don't know how they pick a date, you know?" and then shut the door.

I do know and I don't know how they do it. It seems so random. Like picking straws. Or names out of a hat. Who goes when.

November 1, 1999

I'm bloated beyond recognition. Saturated past lines. There was a space that used to define me. A sharpness. Pants hanging off bony hips. A flat stomach I didn't feel ashamed of. Space I used to take for granted. All those angles used to add up. Then I came here. Swallowed so much. So many pills that made me want to swallow so much more. Turned me so much bigger than I ever thought I was. Which is actually somehow smaller than I ever thought I'd be.

November 1, 1999

"I'm baked, I'm done. I'm ready to leave this island," Jean called out, passing by the lounge and waving her hand goodbye. A hybrid of the Queen of England and chipper tour guide.

"Take me with you," Leah said, smiling.

"I'll look into it," said Jean, her brow knit. All tasks and to do lists.

November 2, 1999

The smoke room is the one room where all of us can talk unheard by staff. The only time the nurses come is if we've gotten too loud. If we laugh and have a good time, a nurse will tell us to knock it off. If there's a bunch of us in there, but we're depressed and crying, no nurse comes near us. No matter how loud we get. As soon as we find something funny and we're sputtering on the floor, clutching our stomachs and trying not to burn ourselves with the heaters on our smokes, a nurse is quick to open that door. Does a fast headcount. If there are more than the FOUR PEOPLE ALLOWED AT A TIME in the smoke room, she kicks people out. Tells us to be quiet. We try to figure out gracefully who's going to leave. It's an arbitrary rule. FOUR PEOPLE MAX. The staff only enforces it when they feel like it. That's why the two metal benches are only big enough for four people to sit on. Everyone always crams in here anyways. Spills on the floor like a torn bag of M&M's.

CODE WHITE

The nurse thinks she's done crowd control. We like to trick her. Shuffle a few women out of the room. Tell them to filter back in when the coast is clear. In this room, until a nurse comes in, nothing's off-limits. There's no rules. The grey air of the room is filled with shooting stars. Fragments of each woman's stories. They sparkle, rain down sharp. I collect everything I hear. Even what I don't understand. If you don't like it, all you need to do is walk away before it touches you. Reach the door. Get out.

November 2, 1999

"Good luck," Mindy said to me as they buzzed me out for my pass. I was meeting Rachel for a date. "Have fun! Don't come back to this place." She wore a lopsided smile the whole time. I wasn't sure what to say back.

"Thanks, I'll try," I said and slipped out the door before the nurses changed their minds and locked us both in. A new girl was wailing on the payphone by the ward door. She kept slapping the wall with her palm. The rings on her fingers made clinky noises with each thwack.

Walking to meet Rachel, I couldn't get Mindy out of my head. She'd been wearing a long, blue hospital gown. It hung in a ragged triangle from her shoulders to her shins. Like she was a women's washroom sign come to life. The ones with a stick person wearing a triangle for a skirt. As though that accurately embodied the entire female gender. The strings at the back were untied. Her hair was in a messy ponytail hanging out her scrunchy. It was hard to watch someone who'd come into the ward undone, unravel further.

Last night I was on the payphone, trying to talk to Rachel about our date tonight. Noise erupted in the hall like hot oil spattering against me. There was nowhere I could go because I was on the phone, unless I wanted to lose my call. It was Donna, yelling about someone who had insulted her. Crashing into the walls. Then the piano exploded in the activity room. Maybe Mindy. I jammed the receiver into my ear. Plugged my free ear with my finger to block out everyone else. That story about the kid with his finger stuck in the dam. Trying to block off all the holes. Except everything seeps in. Full force. It doesn't work. It's pointless to try anything on the ward. Rachel laughed at all the noise.

"I don't know how you do it," she giggled at the crazy combination of the pell-mell piano and Donna screaming. "*I'm* actually finding it hard to concentrate. You have such good focus, Alex!"

I guess I did. I knew she meant it as a compliment, but it seemed condescending. Like congratulating a dog for making a really great poop. Most people used their focus to concentrate on important things. A significant business decision. Writing that key memo. They didn't have to put all their energy into blocking out fucked up mental patients who made it impossible to do regular things like make phone calls. I used to do better things with my talents. I didn't think Rachel knew any of that. It pissed me off. That now, standing in this hallway, cowering, plugging my ear, this was all I was.

I didn't have a choice whether to focus or not. Rachel laughed again. She could hear Donna howling, "You bitches think you can insult me! Well, you can't. You don't control me. You'll be fucking sorry. You won't ever talk to me again."

It was sort of funny. So I laughed with her. But, it wasn't really funny. Rachel didn't hear the nurses say to Donna in a calm, formulaic manner, "You have to calm down now, Donna. There will be time to discuss this later."

Rachel didn't see that the nurses had no intention of discussing anything with Donna, ever. Or that the woman Donna screamed at smirked. The nurses don't bother her. Rachel missed the nurses putting their hands on Donna's shoulders. She crackled like they'd jumped her with electricity. Rachel couldn't see the nurses march Donna to the med station for the extras this outburst had earned her. There's a huge part of me Rachel's never met. I don't think she ever will.

November 3, 1999

I'm in the smoke room with Lee. She tells me again she's going to be discharged in the middle of November. She sounds worried, like there's an ache in her bones coming through her voice.

"I'm glad for you," I tell her. "Are you scared?"

"A bit," she says. She looks scared shitless.

"Are you worried you'll be in here past November?" Lee asks.

Lee doesn't remember I was supposed to be discharged at the end of this week. Then they changed their minds. She doesn't remember how often I've told her this in this very room over the past few weeks. Or how many times she's said she'll miss me. At least twenty times. She's also repeatedly given me her phone number.

"I'm being discharged early next week," I tell her. I've already told her this tonight. Her face falls. Before she can verbalize her dismay her nurse comes. Then I'm alone. The metal bench is cold under my ass even through pj bottoms and my thick terry cloth housecoat. Lee said on nights like this she wishes she were in a cabin. Curled up and warm in front of a woodstove. The fire crackling. Something good to look at.

I light another butt. Listen to the wind roar inside the room through the blades of the fan. Chill air billows in from outside without actually bringing in anything fresh. I don't know how that can be so. But it is. Everything on this floor is stale. The fan sounds like a ship tossing on stormy waters. Wind filling sails. Waves. I think of Leah as a burly pirate at the helm. Ocean water splashing across her feet as she turns the wheel. Intent on taking us somewhere good. Far from here. It's exactly like all of Leah's crazy driving stories. The ones where she gets behind the wheel of a car. Three days later she's an entire coast away and the car is totalled. Full of booze bottles and covered in a fine powder. Half-naked girls passed out in the back. In her stories, Leah always manages to walk.

I wonder where she is. If she's okay. There's no way to check. No one to ask. I hope if Leah isn't in a rehab bed somewhere, kicking ass and creating mayhem, telling all her stories to all the addicts there, trying to pull herself together, then I hope she's in a car. Driving far away. Driving herself out of this story. So deep into another one she'll never come back. A story so good she'll tell it for decades. It will shine so hard it'll make all her other stories pale. A story. I send out a flicker of white light. Hope for Leah. At the helm of something. Heading somewhere other than destruction.

November 4, 1999

I lost my job today. I probably lost it before today. I bet they were waiting until I was well enough to hear the news. I called the store to check in and tell them I'm supposed to be discharged next week. My luck Bob answered and not Hazel. Bob tells me they hired two people in the interim since I've been "away."

"We didn't know how much longer you'd take, Alex. You've been away for so long," he said.

As if that was my fault. Like if I just worked harder I would've gotten better sooner.

"The new people are really working out well," he said.

"What about me?" I said. I'd worked out well there for years. Until this happened.

He got all nervous. Didn't say much. I knew what was coming. I wanted to slam down the phone, but then I saw Nurse Dee accompanying Jean to her room. It distracted me.

"I've got a commitment to these new people. We hired them. We can't just let them go now," Bob said.

It took everything I had not to say, *Isn't that what you just did to me?*

I wondered about the pieces of furniture I never finished restoring at the store before I got sick. Maybe the new super employees finished them. I was going to be discharged soon and I had no job. For once, I didn't cry. I was glad. Instead, I mumbled stuff about how if they ever needed help to give me a call.

"Sure, sure," he said, which I knew meant, *No way.*

I went to my room and cried. And to the smoke room, and cried there, too. Kate and the lady with the fuzzy pink housecoat (who did up the zipper on the back of my dress yesterday) tried to make me feel better.

"Alex, this could be a good thing!" Kate crowed.

"You have to look at the positive, honey," said Pink Housecoat as she laid her hand on my leg. "It's really one door opening for you! Don't get bogged down in the door that's closing. Just look at all those open doors."

I appreciated their efforts, but it didn't give me my job back. And there were no open doors. Everything was shut tight. You didn't need to be crazy to see that.

November 5, 1999

I spent the rest of yesterday lying on my bed curled around the pile of clothes I can't seem to put away. And my housecoat. Shower stuff. I got really stiff after a while. I couldn't change positions because of all the shit on my bed. So I just stayed in that half-moon curve, curled up like the letter "C," spelling out "CRISIS" in bold, blazing letters. Tried to summon up courage to take the shower I'd avoided for days. But I was too afraid of the water. And of someone walking in on me. The washroom has no locks.

November 6, 1999

Graffiti sprayed in black. Big and messy across a wall. All the cars driving by could see it. Looked up from my book and saw it out the bus window as we sailed by. *Do you have ears in your hearts.*

Did Sunshine's roommate, Sage, put it there? The junkie graffiti artist. Fortunes she pastes on walls. Crumbs at our feet. Space she claims when there's not enough room to breathe. I wish I could have eaten each letter. Beautiful. Like she had iced the sentence on the top of a cake. Swallowed it slowly before my pass was over.

CODE WHITE

November 6, 1999

Donna's screaming in the hall, "Someone smoked a cigarette in the washroom. It smells like smoke."

What would she expect a cigarette to smell like?

She's slamming doors to rooms that don't belong to her. Her slippers smack down the hall. Is this big enough for a Code White? I decide to hide in my room for a bit. Until it's safe, although I never really know when that is.

November 7, 1999

Over the weekend they've installed carpets in the elevators. I'm momentarily happy I won't see the carpet coated in winter sludge. No salt stains creeping up like marks of a receding tide. Then I remember the six-week Day Treatment Outpatient Program I'm signed up for. I'll be seeing the carpets and this floor for at least six more weeks after I'm discharged.

At least I'll be on the other side of the unit. The Outpatient side. It'll still be group. Just one no nurse drags me to. All of us silent. Some people wishing the ones speaking would shut up. Facilitators and social workers and nurses will speak in placating tones. Cajole us to "share" our "feelings" while some dissociate and others leak tears.

November 8, 1999

"They're finally putting up curtains in my room," Pink Housecoat says to someone in the hall. I can hear her from my room. I remember Jamie telling me one time she wanted to disappear so badly that she ripped her curtain down. Except the curtain hooks weren't sharp at all. Foiled. Then she had to pull down the other curtain so it wouldn't look weird. Jamie ruined both curtains that night.

"It was so bright that morning," Jamie told me, her hands open in her lap. "All the light streaming in through my naked windows."

I held her eyes. There wasn't really anything I could say.

November 9, 1999

I get discharged in a few days. Time passes in fragments. Clouds running through my fingers. Nurse Susan sits on the edge of my bed at a respectable distance and says, "It's been good working with you, Alex."

"I'm really glad you were my nurse, Susan."

My face crinkles like a crumpled up Kleenex. There's so much more I want to say. Except there's protocol marked with yellow caution tape. A neat separation. Nothing explains why I'm so sad to say goodbye when all I've ever wanted is to bust out of here. But I am sad. I feel awful for everything I ever laid on her. Nurse Susan sees that. Or maybe she doesn't. Maybe I just want to think she understands. She nods and gets off my bed. Tomorrow there'll be a new girl in my room. With problems bigger than these small four walls. Larger than anything any of the nurses on staff can ever fix. I clench my thighs together. I don't want to think about the new girl. Her name on my door.

I'm getting out. I just don't know what I'm getting into. My fingers clutch the sides of the thin mattress for something to hold. I'm sinking. I want to say one last thing to Nurse Susan. Something that really means something. Except, everything is stupid and trite. What I want is to give her flowers. Brilliant petals. Soft and dazzling. A fragrance so special it will erase everything I've ever done. And notch a place inside her so she'll always remember me. It is stupid even as I think it. I have no flowers. I have no money for flowers. And it would be weird to give Nurse Susan anything. Especially flowers. But still I wish I could do something. Close this story. My heart won't slow down. I don't want her to walk out the door.

And then she leaves. She doesn't linger at the doorframe. Doesn't look back.

Later, I'm in the smoke room with Kate and Pink Housecoat. I thought they already knew about me from word getting around the ward or the whole Jamie debacle. Kate was here when that happened. But neither of them had any clue I was a dyke. Somehow, I accidentally outed myself. And it turned into this whole fucking huge deal. Kate was all betrayed. Like I had been planning some major lesbiano infiltration on the ward. Eyeing her lasciviously in her stretchpants, ballerina slippers and kitty sweatshirts. I didn't want it to be a big thing. Especially since I'm leaving. And I'd genuinely really liked talking with both of them. But I wasn't going to create a make-believe boyfriend so they could breathe easy.

After it came up that I was queer I couldn't just go hide in my room. What kind of statement would that make? I was trapped. A dyke trapped in a little smoke room with two scared straight women. Plus, I really did want a cigarette. It wasn't like I could just smoke somewhere else. After my second post-coming out cigarette, Pink Housecoat scooted over on the metal bench. Rubbed my cheek affectionately in a matronly manner.

"I'm going to miss you," she said. "You're great no matter what. No matter who you choose to sleep with. That's your business. I don't care."

I knew she meant well. Supporting me regardless of my apparently despicable sins. Kate was carefully inspecting the stitching on her ballerina slippers.

"You're an amazing person, even though you're *that way*," Pink Housecoat added into the awkward chasm.

If she kept this up, I'd have to hand her a miniature rainbow flag to wave around.

"Alex, you're leaving tomorrow. We all want to throw you a party!"

I didn't know about a party. Pink Housecoat was really full of spirit. Even if I was, *that way*. I could see all of us milling about in our pyjamas. A glass of apple juice in one hand. Saltine crackers in the other. All of us waiting for our night-time meds to kick in so we could stagger off to our beds. I sat smoking. Conversation, which had come easy among the three of us before, was now completely painful. I wasn't going to leave until I was finished smoking. Fuck it. Kate stayed quiet the entire time. She could barely look at me.

I thought of the little stuffed kitty I had bought for Kate while I was at a thrift store on a pass. Couldn't resist. Washed it in the tub in the laundry room in secret to freshen it up. Let it dry in my room for days so I could give it to her as a present during one of those spells when she was too sad to peel herself off her bed. How much she loved that stupid thing because she missed her real cat at home. Kept it on her pillow. Named it Taffy. All the coffees I brought when she wasn't able to get privileges to go off the floor and buy them for herself. She didn't mind me getting her coffees with my queer hands before she knew what I was. She had lots of conversation for me then.

I put out my smoke and left the room. Nowhere else to go

really, but soon I'd be gone. For the thousandth time, I couldn't wait.

November 10, 1999

"I'm sorry to always make you cry," the woman with the fabulously perfect eyebrows says.

How can I ever hope to get better and have eyebrows as precise as hers? She's Mona Camu, the Community Care Worker. She hands me a green packet with a drug card. The card looks more like a file folder than a card. There's no laminate officiating anything. I could drop it in the sink by accident and it would melt.

"When you get discharged, a homeworker will come to see you every week to help you with things," she tells me and ignores the fact that I cry harder at this news. She doesn't get that I don't want help. I want to be better. I want to work. I want my job. I want to be able to pay for my own drugs. I don't even want to take these drugs. And I don't feel ready to leave even though I hate it here.

Before I got sick, I was irritated with my job. I thought it might be time to find a new one. Now, I know how lucky I was, being able to work at all. Mona, gracious as ever, excuses herself.

"Well, I really must be going. Good luck, Alex."

And then those perfect eyebrows walk out of my room. She doesn't close the door all the way, which I hate.

November 11, 1999

Everyone knows I'm leaving tomorrow. I am change sifting through my fingers. Light reflecting off of every coin.

"I have something for you," Kate says and exhales her smoke. Eyes all lashes to the ceiling.

"Kate, you don't have to get me anything," I tell her.

"I want to. You've really helped me."

I hadn't known I'd helped her. Not exactly. I watch her pink ballerina slippers. Her feet flex up and down. She hands me a perfect beaded bracelet she must've made in Arts & Crafts. I hate to take it from her.

"Are you sure you don't want to keep it?" I ask.

"No. I want you to take it," she says.

I feel bad for leaving. Although I don't want to stay. The bracelet's made of tiny seed beads. Translucent ones that catch the light. Colleen the craftslady taught us how to string them so the bracelet was a linked circle of flowers. Like friendship bracelets we used to do at day camp. It was depressing to watch a group of grown women struggle with these tiny beads. Hardly anyone could find the little holes. Stabbing twine. The beads kept spilling off the newspapers on the table and onto the floor. All these plastic pinging noises we learned to ignore. The beads sparkle like candy. Kate would never in a million years allow herself to eat it if it was real.

"Will you help me put it on?" I ask and then remember the other day in the smoke room and feel weird. Does she think I'm coming onto her?

Her fingers encircle my wrist.

"Thanks," I say. I let the colour flash out from my eyes. I can tell she sees it. Kate rests her fingers on my wrist for more than a second as she ties the bracelet on. I pretend not to notice so she can keep doing it. I offer her a smoke when she's done, when she finally takes her hand back. It's the only thing I know she'll let herself take from me. The only thing I know she'll have.

CODE WHITE

November 12, 1999

    I'm discharged in what feels like a whirlwind. Except whirlwinds sort of go in the same shape and direction. I extricate myself in many return trips in the elevator. The new carpet is already dulled from dirt. To get to the elevator, I must pass through the locked ward door. All the patients lounging nearby watch. Or pretend not to. I get out the locked door by summoning someone in the nursing station to open it for me. Every time, the person looks suspicious, as if I don't have a right to leave, and is completely annoyed at being interrupted. I'm a dog at the pound. Each nurse scrutinizes my sweaty face to determine if I'm worthwhile enough to be let out.

    Then I push the button for the elevator. Wait with my heavy bags. I take them downstairs. Walk out the building. Every muscle coiled, thinking someone's going to yell, "Stop, get back in the building! They want you back on your floor."

    No one says anything. Not one word. They don't even look at me carrying bag after bag out of the building to the car. I root around for the keys. Panic each time. Think I've lost them. When I find them I open the trunk. Nestle my bags in like a life-size Tetris game. Then I have to head back upstairs to the ward and do every step in reverse all over again. I still have tons in my room to clear out. For the first time, I curse myself for being such a pack rat. I keep my head down as I go through the lobby. It makes me uncomfortable to see all the people. Doctors and nurses rushing back to their floors. Other patients. People milling. I don't want them to see my face. Where I've just come from.

    The locked door is waiting for me upstairs. Everyone is usually too busy to buzz me in. I have to stand by the elevator trying to get someone's attention. All the patients on the other side watch me through long windows framing the locked door. Finally, someone lets me in. I scoop up more stuff for another trip. Each time I leave, other patients swarm me.

"Are you leaving now?" Kate asks.

"Not just yet," I answer. "A few more trips still," I reply with a forced smile.

They say goodbye each time like I'm not coming back. Even though I just told them I'm not leaving just yet.

"Good luck," Kate says.

"We know you can do it," says some new girl I don't even know.

"All the best," Mindy chirps.

Their voices trail off at the ends of their sentences. Too tired for follow through.

"Angels have wings, use yours and you'll never look back," Jean stammers like she's handed me a Hallmark card. Each word written in an ornate curlicue. I don't know what that means. I smile.

Lee hugs me. We both cry. She kisses my chin. Her eyes say, *Call me*.

"I will. I'll call you," I say.

She doesn't believe me. I can tell. But, I know I will. Won't I? I ask Lee to say goodbye to Pink Housecoat for me. I haven't seen her yet today. She's having lunch with the head nurse for some special reason.

"Don't forget, okay?"

Lee nods eagerly. Then I stop. I remember Lee often can't even remember my name. She always calls me Sue. The ECT. I need to ask someone else to say goodbye to Pink Housecoat for me.

CODE WHITE

In the lounge it tastes like when summer camp is over. When all the girls from your cabin, even the ones who were mean to you all summer and you couldn't wait to get away from them, would get weepy-eyed. Suddenly, no one wanted to go. Except this wasn't summer camp.

On my next trip, I do see Pink Housecoat. Kate again, too. Hunched in one of the sofa squares in the lounge; legs draped over the armrest. I wonder if it's one of the squares Terry peed on eons ago.

And then I'm out for good. I can't believe it. I wait by the elevator when Pink Housecoat taps the glass. I want to ignore her. *Tap, tap.* I'm afraid if I turn around, I'll get dragged back inside. They'll never let me out. *Tap, tap.* What if when I turn around, there's a nurse? Saying they made a mistake. My room is ready. *Tap, tap.*

I can't ignore Pink Housecoat. Or any of them. A second ago that was me tapping on the window. I turn around.

"Alex, there's a phone call for you," she motions through the window.

I get a nurse to buzz me back in. Take the ward payphone receiver from Pink Housecoat's hand. Try to have a private conversation on the ward phone one last time. It's Ruth. I don't remember what she said. I'm trying to stop crying. When we are done it's weird to hang up the phone and think, *This is really the last time I will talk on the ward telephone.*

Ralph the psych assistant walks by as I hang up. Like a dream he says, "Good luck. You know, you're a great person. Truly. Even when you were manic. You could be stubborn back then, but you'd always listen to what others had to say."

It's kind of annoying. I haven't asked for a character overview. But, it's also as if he hands me a trophy. No matter how small. It's mine. It's been a while since anyone said something good about me. It feels like Ralph almost saw me. I hug all the patients. Walk out that locked door for the last time. I don't feel anything.

November 13, 1999

I've been discharged. I can't sit still. I want to fast forward to the good parts. It scares me how nothing is set in place except that homeworker. I don't have a job. I don't remember how to find one. Will Bob and Hazel even give me a good reference letter? What do I say on my resume about the huge gap when I was in the hospital? What do I fill out under "Extracurricular Activities"? *Sleeping. Smoking. Staring off into space. Manic spending sprees. Grandiose notions. Indiscriminate sexual activity.* I have no clue. I can't even wake up in the mornings. I keep hearing that lavender metal ward door click shut for the last time. Pink Housecoat waving goodbye through the window. Bye bye.

November 14, 1999

My drugs are assembled in front of me. Six bottles, varying heights and widths. Medicine to keep me on track. All very official looking. My pills are in bottles, piled on top of each other like people climbing over each other's backs, trying to escape a burning building. Way more threatening than the foil packets from the nursing station. Each pill was separate and contained. Robot-like inside the silver crinkling pocket. I still have to take the pills. Even if I don't have a nurse bursting them out of a foil packet. I wanted everything to go back to normal once I got home. For everything that happened to miraculously disappear. Be exactly the way I was before I got sick. Like it never happened. Part of the ward followed me. A depressing Hansel and Gretel path to all these ugly bottles on my desk.

November 15, 1999

One of the worst things is that I can't make conversation anymore. Not with people I know. Not with people I don't know. People ask, "What do you do? Where do you work?"

I don't work anywhere. People want to know why. It doesn't make a good impression to explain, "I had a mental breakdown. I had to be hospitalized for a long time and lost my job. I'm still too sick to find a new one. What do you do?"

Easier to stay home and hide.

November 16, 1999

I used to think it was noisy on the ward. The TV always on. Someone playing the piano or ping-pong. Or both. My room across from the payphone. Always hearing patients crying or yelling. Slamming down the phone. Slippers shuffling down the halls. Fights. Now that I'm out, it's noisy. Everywhere. Bright colours. Always seems like rush hour. I don't want to do anything but sleep. Feel guilty for being so lazy.

"What did I do today?" I ask myself. Most days, just like on the ward, I'm not sure. I'm not ready to find a job. Or start a course. I feel too stupid and out of it. But when I'm on the bus I look at people who are resting. Their eyes closed in complete exhaustion. I'm ashamed I no longer know what it feels like to be tired after a full day of work. I'm just tired now after doing nothing.

November 17, 1999

The cabbie's radio crackles like a thousand drivers crunch

takeout wrappers into their receiver at once. In one of the cabs, someone lets out a high-pitched screech. It rattles over the radio like a key scratching deep into paint on the side of a car. Falsetto.

"You need medication, alright?" the taxi dispatcher bellows over the radio. "You forgot to take your pills today. Lenny, you loon!" he cries.

My driver laughs. I stare out the window. The houses pass too fast to see the details that make each one their own. A suburban blur. I picture the vials of pills on my desk at home. An entire skyline. A town of houses filled with the same possibilities. *Do I take this, or not?* The taxi driver's radio crackles. Passengers sitting in cabs across the city can hear it, too. Every other person riding a cab from this company heard that stupid dispatcher's joke. Aren't crazy people hilarious.

"Do you want me to go straight or turn left here?" my driver asks. Bored.

Pause. I tell him where to go.

November 18, 1999

I had another date with Rachel tonight. Not sure anymore how enthusiastic I'm feeling about the way that's going. But I went anyway. She'd rented a copy of that dyke mobster movie, *Bound,* before I got there. I'd already seen it at least two times before and for what it was, it wasn't the worst movie. I didn't mind seeing it again. Rachel had this glow in her eyes as we were lying down on her couch to watch it. It was actually really romantic. She'd lit some candles and even bought some snacks for us. They were spread out on her coffee table.

The whole movie, Rachel kept admiring Jennifer Tilly's figure. Her dresses and shit. And yes, Jennifer Tilly is completely hot. No question. Her cleavage in that movie was out of this world. And her little cupid lips? I'd love to be able to transform my mouth like that with lipstick. I was all about anyone admiring femmes. Especially dyke ones. Or, rather, actresses who play dyke femmes. Or anyone admiring anyone, for that matter. What the fuck did I care?

While Rachel was drooling over femme vixen Jennifer Tilly, I was lying next to her in jeans and a baggy T-shirt. Nothing special — we were only watching a movie. Tent-like fabric to cover my new, huge body that I was not used to. That I didn't find sexy anymore. Not like before I got sick. Now, no matter what hot outfit I tried to rig together, nothing would fit. Everything looked bad. And none of it looked at all as mind-blowing as any of the killer outfits Ms. Tilly wore that Rachel kept exclaiming over. I was definitely in another league now since I'd gained all that weight. The pity party league, yes. Some entire genre away from head turner.

It didn't matter that I thought other fat girls were completely sexy. That didn't stick when I looked in the mirror. Saw swelling where it used to be concave. Looked on the TV. Saw that annoying actress lisping in her babytalk voice and strutting around in her heels. I just kept feeling worse and worse about myself the more I watched the crappy movie. As if I'd turned into a person with three breasts, one long caterpillar for an eyebrow and a hunchback. I knew I was beyond ridiculous and being really fucking weird. But I couldn't stop.

I wanted to go home. I felt like being alone. Except part of me didn't want to be rude and I couldn't think of a good reason to tell Rachel why I was going. So I stayed. And Rachel kept passing me the bags of Smartfood and Pringles and Hershey's

Kisses she'd bought. There was this smorgasbord of snacks heaped on the table. Bags and bags of junk food.

"I didn't know what stuff you liked," she said and smiled. "So I thought I'd get a bit of everything."

"Thanks," I said, but didn't make a move for any of it.

I could feel my stomach spilling over the waistband of my jeans, suddenly too tight and conspicuous. I was a gelatinous overgrown bag of pus infecting Rachel's couch. I was sure Jennifer Tilly didn't get to look the way she did by stuffing her face with Miss Vickie's Sea Salt & Malt Vinegar Chips, alternated with Junior Mints. Didn't wash it all back with icy cola. Even though I knew I was being ludicrous, I didn't want to eat any of it. I felt oddly disciplined and victorious turning down each of the various snacks. Like it was going to make a difference. Get me somewhere.

At the same time, I was making myself sick. It's not like I slept in a cave my whole life. I was a feminist. Wore the armor of Women's Studies around me in conversation everywhere. Rachel looked confused. A bit insulted. I didn't want her to think I was rejecting her good host efforts.

"Don't mind me, I ate a big dinner at home," I told her.

This made me feel like more of a big porkie. Like all I did was stuff my face. Constantly. In my mind, now that I was fat, it was like I didn't have a right to eat anymore. I was just supposed to subsist on the fat my body already had. We watched the rest of the movie, but every time Rachel moved closer, I leaned further away. This was difficult to do because the couch was really small and I already took up more than my half. It became really uncomfortable. Eventually we stopped lying side by side. I scooted up to the head of the sofa and tucked my knees up. I didn't want anything touching me. I wasn't there.

CODE WHITE

My skin was hard. Everything felt shut off, like a thin stone exterior was covering my surface. My heartbeat ricocheted off the coating from the inside.

I felt a bit calmer behind that wall. Protected. I shouldn't have come to Rachel's. Everything about dating her felt as if I was coming from behind a big slab of concrete. Maybe not at first. But now I wondered if it was my meds. Or Rachel. Or just a totally fucked up time in my life and no matter who I was dating, I'd be relating to them from behind that thick slab of stone.

After the movie, I didn't want to talk or kiss or anything. I couldn't stand to be there one more second. I needed to get home where no one could see me. I tried to leave fast so Rachel wouldn't look at my round stomach. Rachel was confused. It was still early. For once, I didn't care what someone else was feeling. I just wanted to take care of me.

At home, I couldn't fall asleep. I lay stiffly in my bed. I kept hearing Jennifer Tilly's stupid baby *Bound* voice whisper into my ear. I wished she would shut up. Jennifer Tilly told me in her pouty, breathy voice, *So fucking what that you're at home. Where the fuck are you going to go from here? What's next? You can't live here with your parents forever. That's pathetic.*

After a while, the wall around me got so thick it mostly drowned out Tilly. Then there was this low buzzing of TV static filtering over top of her. I couldn't hear her anymore. By then I was all in knots over what she had said.

November 19, 1999

At the corner of Bloor and Bathurst, there is a woman pacing. Painfully slow. Like something bad will happen if her feet stop touching each other. A slow bride walking herself down the aisle. Her outfit is wrong for the processional. Windblown hair. Skin that looks like it's been out in the sun too long. Everyone who passes her stops to watch. She doesn't notice. She's focused. Lifts each medicated foot forward. Do I look like that when I walk? Can people see shades of her in me?

The bride begins to walk down the subway stairs. One foot down gingerly. As if it's being ripped from a band of safety. The other foot joins. She pauses. Clings to the railing with a dirty hand. The skin cracked. Everyone behind her sighs loudly. A rush of water pent up behind her. She is a dam. She is broken.

November 20, 1999

I'm afraid of ghosts. Of running into women from the ward. Ones who've also been discharged. I place the memory of them between pages of a heavy book. Press them flat. It doesn't work. They won't go away. I keep trying because I don't want them to see me. Anywhere. That spark of recognition will pin me on the ward forever. A curse. I'll never get my life back to normal. Back to before I had to be in that place. See a single one of their shining potato faces about to sour. It won't happen if I keep bumping my shins against the ugly twin bed with the plastic mattress in the middle of every room. Every time I leave the house. I'll never get to be me.

I see parts of them in other people. Eyes, mouth, jaw lines. A profile. Hair hanging lackluster or tied back tight. Back of a body tensed. Someone holding a coffee. The way someone lights a cigarette, inhales, puts it out. Feet. Shuffling. Nails bitten. Hard eyes. Vacant. I always want to hide. Each time a false alarm. The only ghosts are inside me. Fluttering persistent. Beating against my eyelids. Resting hotly on my tongue, kicking sharply in my sleep.

CODE WHITE

I thought I saw Sunshine once. For real. Her golden crown of dreadlocks blazed. Flower face pink from the cold. Upturned in a huge smile to the person she was talking to. Her white teeth a pearl necklace. Radiant in her mouth. Shaking silver bells on her tiny wrist. When I looked again, I wasn't sure. Should I say, *Hi*? What would we talk about? Organic vegetables and the miracles of hemp? The nurses we'd escaped from?

As much as Sunshine glowed, something in me cringed to see her. To think of speaking with her. I turned my back. Hunched to make sure she didn't see me. When I looked again, she was gone. The inside of my mouth tasted like dirt.

November 21, 1999

I'm on my way to a women's play party. You have to know someone to get invited. I was invited by someone from a small bunch of girls I occasionally played with or went out for coffee with before I got sick. I never thought of myself as a person who knows anyone. I guess I do. I'll know lots of women who'll be there. Not that well. Well enough to get an invite.

I made a couple of dates beforehand. It would be too awkward to just show up and try to drum up a date. I don't feel up to that right now. But now, I'm beyond nervous. I'm waiting for one of the women, Wanda, that I arranged a date with. We've gone out before. We met years ago. We mess up her sheets sometimes in between each of us seeing other people. She's really sweet.

Now I'm supposed to meet her at Wellesley station. I wish I hadn't made these plans. That I was home in my pyjamas. I always feel nervous when I make plans to go out. More acutely when the plans involve getting it on. I'm supposed to look hot in front of these other people. Foxy is the last thing I'm feeling. I feel fat and ugly. Not voluptuous like other large femmes. Not hot and solid, like the big butches I see around. I keep picturing my gut bursting out the really tight, pleather miniskirt I'm wearing.

A few weeks ago on a weekend pass, I went to a friend's house party. I had social anxiety that night, too. I didn't know who to talk to. Who would want to talk to me? I was paranoid that people were whispering about me behind my back, like a self-absorbed sixteen year old. I alternated between taking deep breaths to calm myself down and smoking almost every cigarette in my pack. Talking myself out of hiding in the washroom. Every time I smelled someone smoking a joint I wanted to ask for a toke. But I didn't. I had to be the new, sober Alex, monitoring her mood disorder. I felt like the only sober person there.

The small group I was sitting with started talking about bodies. Size. Gaining weight. I felt embarrassed not to say anything since it seemed like my belly was big enough to be the fifth person in our group.

"I have my first real belly now," I said, hunched over like I could subtly make it disappear.

"Bellies are sexy," a girl with a fauxhawk and bright swallow bird tattoos across her chest said. She had a glint in her eye. I wasn't sure if that's what it was. Maybe it was the light from the ceiling fixture reflecting off her Buddy Holly-esque glasses. Then she leered at me. No mistaking that.

"Every time I've seen you, Alex, since you've been at the hospital you've looked great," she said, playing with her tongue piercing.

I was embarrassed that she knew where I'd been. But what was she supposed to say? *Actually Alex, you look like shit?* Not likely. She was one of those people who I couldn't remember how I'd met. I just had, from years ago. A tangled dyke web of she-knows-her, she-slept-with-her, she-was-roommates-with-her multiplied by a few breakups, bar dramas, womyn's festivals and a second generation of women sleeping together (who all eventually knew each other) in a murky pile that somehow led to me.

Through the rest of the conversation, we all leaned closer than necessary to speak. Hands on thighs. A look that felt subtle, but wasn't. Fishhooks dangling. Sharp. Blood close to the skin.

I had to find that same thing before Wanda came. I tried catching it at home while I did my hair and makeup. I couldn't see it. I'm more in a smoke-every-cigarette-in-my-pack kind of mood. Hide in the washroom. Not exactly sexy.

"Bellies make the world go round," this other butch in our circle said that night, voice low and gravelly. Her words fell soft as stars. Hit sparks up my spine, even though I felt a sucker for it. I stared at her short hair. Crisp, bleached tips I suddenly ached to palm and soften. Wondered what she'd look like in the morning, messy and tired against a pillowcase. Slack. She leaned forward, her wide hands encasing her thighs. Repeated herself twice, in case I missed it. I heard her. It just didn't stick. I didn't deserve compliments anymore, now that I'd been in a mental ward. The stars she gave me, grazing that spot inside my ear that always made me inhale sharp, shining bright, I didn't deserve. I couldn't look at her. She could've said it five or ten times. It didn't matter. Couldn't feel the chair underneath me. Stared at the floorboards and wondered how much space there was between each slat of wood. How small would you have to be to fall through?

Tonight, I want to have fun. I don't have a curfew anymore. I can stay out as late as my agreement with my parents. I can't remember when I ever had a curfew with them. They think it's a good idea to have structure in my sleep schedule now. I'm not going to argue. At least I'm not back on the ward. Checking in with Nurse Rhoda.

I pull out my compact again. Check that my lipstick isn't all over my front teeth. My eye makeup hasn't crept too low. Fix my hair. Too much nervous energy. My fingers are filled with lightning. Nowhere interesting to strike. Everything looks good. I hope. Out of nowhere, I notice that I really need to take a shit. Why couldn't this happen when I was still at home? Fuck. Forget about regulating my sleep cycle. I have to work on regulating a whole bunch of stuff. There's no way now I can deal with this anywhere. Not exactly the hottest thing.

November 22, 1999

I'm still floating. Grinning like a total ass. I had the best time. My skirt didn't explode. I had normal conversations with people. No one looked at me strangely. Wanda didn't stand me up. She wore this very short mini-skirt. Super hot. Took off her long winter coat and modeled for me. Like she held sparklers in each hand as she curtsied and pinched each side of her skirt, swinging her cute little hips. Sparking light everywhere.

"Do you like it?" she asked shyly, gesturing to her outfit. "I went out shopping for something to wear for tonight. For you."

I nodded slowly, a huge grin riding my face. Trying to keep eye contact, but unable to stop checking it all out. I don't think Wanda identifies as femme. Somewhere more along the middle. Andro adorable. Regardless, it was very hot and fun for her to be dressing up. Now I knew what every girl I'd ever gone shopping for had felt like. Stuck in a grateful stammer. Wanda also wore this shiny, black bra I wanted to rub my face on. A truly stellar outfit. By the end of the night, her eyes were all glassy like her bra. Endorphins. She looked through the shine at me, her quiet smile leaping larger than I'd ever seen across her face.

I couldn't stop smiling when I got home. Or this morning. Last night was so amazing. It's nice not to sneak things. To take as long as you want. Nothing timed for under fifteen minutes.

My favourite moment was wrapping myself in my coat, stepping out the back door, down the porch stairs into the yard. My high heels gently crushed the thin layer of snowflakes that had fallen since I'd last been out for a lone cigarette. I walked softly. Left my carefully defined footprints behind. Stood in the yard and pulled out a cigarette. Held my unmarked lighter. Inhaled the red heat. All by myself. Tipped my head back and felt the cold, biting the skin of my face and fingers. Up my legs through my stockings. Felt the snowflakes nip my face, wet the length of my cigarette, dampen the burning tip. I stood alone in the quiet and surveyed the night sky. Hoped for stars. Exhaled until I was finished and ready to go back inside again. The only people who noticed that I was gone were people who missed me, people who wanted to see me. No one was keeping tabs on me anymore.

epilogue:
fall 2000

Fall 2000

Max is standing on the broken driveway in her favourite grey Joan Jett T-shirt. The one she usually falls asleep in whenever I stay over. From under her long, baggy shorts her legs poke out. Covered in a layer of hair that always gets me hot. I think about how Max told me that when she used to visit the ward, she was self-conscious about what the staff would think. She always wore pants. Even in the sweaty heat. Now both of us don't have people around who make us feel like covering up.

"Hey," I say. "You been out here long?"

"Just waiting for a pretty lady to come along," she says and finds pebbles that need rearranging on the driveway.

"I'll wait with you," I say. Grab her by the hips. Hold her studded belt and pull her toward me for a kiss. When it becomes apparent we have to stop or go into her apartment, Max pulls away. Her mouth and the area around it is smeared maroon. My lipstick. It's hard not to smirk.

"I know, I know. What, am I new here?" she asks and holds out her hand. "Kleenex, please."

"Sorry, fresh out."

"But you always have everything in your purse."

"Not today. I'm traveling light."

Max pouts and turns to head inside her apartment, the first floor of a house. She points, stops me from following.

"Stay out here. If you come in with me, we won't come out for days."

"And?" I put my hands on my hips.

"And there's the surprise still waiting."

"Which you still never told me what it is," I announce.

"Wait right there, missy," she says. I wish I had a camera. Snap a photo of her covered in my smile. While she's gone I fix my lipstick. I don't do surprises well. Max comes out carrying a scarf in between both fists, like a blindfold. A woolly one with a plaid print. Not exactly sexy blindfold material. I can't help but laugh.

"So that's the surprise. Shouldn't we go inside for that?" I tease.

"No, no," she says gruffly. "It's not like that. Let me put this on you so you won't be able to see anything until it's ready."

I stand extremely still while Max ties the scarf around my eyes. I wonder what kind of surprise Max could have for me. I focus on avoiding having my mascara-laden lashes crunched by the material pressing into my face. I don't want two black eyes whenever Max unveils me. She ties it tight, no gaps. She touches my back as she adjusts the scarf. Max always likes things to be exactly how she wants them. I like a person who does things right.

With my eyes shut, I think about the weekend. How we never made it to the party we were invited to. We got ready slowly, picking ourselves off her bed reluctant.

"Can I shave your legs?" Max had asked quietly, staring at a spot on the bare wall behind me. At the image of her holding the razor, lathering my calves, crouching at my feet, dragging the blade carefully against my skin, I felt a rush. Said, *Yes*. We headed to her bathroom, like we were going somewhere important.

I didn't know a trillion lights would blaze in me when I put a razor in someone else's hand — by choice. I'd gotten it back and it was mine again to give. There was something so beautiful about watching her do this for me. Holding the sharp edge against my skin. Cutting off every little hair that had grown. Trimming my excess down to nothing. She pared away at me. Tugged the blade down towards my feet and rinsed it for each new descent. Her face gleamed brighter than the flash of those twin blades. All the fine, sharp points between us collapsed in the sticky fog of her washroom. I stood naked. Watched that soft spot on the top of her head where her hair spiraled out and away from the defined order of her part. Out of her control. She held onto something that was mine. Knew exactly what it was. Right what she'd been asking for.

I would never ask for permission to have what's always been mine again. We sat a minute. The water ran down the drain. Steam rising. Until a tiny smile broke across her face.

"May I have your other leg?" she asked, a can of shaving cream in one hand, soft dollop of foam in the other. Staring like she was peering through a keyhole and she didn't care who caught her. Razor clenched between her teeth like a rose. Some kind of promise.

"Here," I answered, my feet flat against the bottom of the white, hard enamel of the tub. A hum constant like a generator. When she was done my legs were tingling. Max tucked me into the shower. Kept the curtain open a touch to grab the soap. Lathered me up. Ran some shampoo into her hand and really got at my hair. Her hands felt good on my scalp. The tips of her fingers sent shocks spilling through me. When I turned off the water, she was waiting with a big towel to wrap around me. Another to pat against my hair. She dried me off. Rubbed lotion onto my legs. Sent me into her room to finish getting ready for the party while she showered.

In her room, I put on my makeup. Wondered, *Which dress?*

Looked at the couple of options for shoes I'd brought and left there at Max's suggestion.

"No sense having all your things at home when you spend so much time here," she'd observed. I didn't argue. She'd made space for my things. Pink, frilled and femme against her plain, practical and buttoned. I didn't know what to wear. I put on panties and a bra for a start. Max came in, watched me put my lipstick on in the big mirror over her dresser. Tits spilling out of my red bra. We weren't going to the party after all.

Later, starving underneath hot sheets, we ordered chicken wings and colas from the take out place a few blocks away before it closed. Too lazy to get dressed and leave her bedroom to get it. We opened her blinds half-way, and the windows. Caught the thick breeze. Lazy feet against each other like socks tossed in the corner. Streetlights with fuzzy halos. Convinced we could see errant, tiny stars far away. Deep in the black ink of the sky. Pinpricks.

In the darkness under the scarf it's woolly. No stars. I feel Max's hand on my skin for a long time after her palm leaves. I can tell I'm standing completely alone on the driveway. The concrete's hard under my feet. All this air around me. I think I hear a car drive by. Tires crunching. I can't tell how close or far anything is. I don't know where Max has gone. Then I hear a very loud creak. It might be the garage door opening. Or someone aiming something large and threatening at me. I touch the fringe of the scarf hanging above the small of my back. I want a cigarette. I'm not sure if there's room between my mouth and the edge of the scarf. I don't want to set my face on fire.

"Max? Where are you?" I call like it's no big deal. It's not. Really.

There's no answer. I hear soft footsteps at the other end of the driveway, by the garage. A light *tick, tick* noise. Something spinning. Like on *Wheel Of Fortune*. It stops. And then hands on my shoulders. I jump a little.

"Shhh... Sorry, it's just me. Are you okay?"

"Yeah, you surprised me," I say.

"That's the idea. Are you ready?" Max asks. Something in her voice. That thing people feel when they see a fresh snowfall. Unspoiled whiteness stretching for miles. The thing I feel when I answer the phone now and it's Max. Her voice spilling into my ear. Asking me to come over days before our next date is penciled into our daybooks.

"Yes," I say, "I'm ready," and unclench my fists. Reach for one of Max's hands. I grab it close. She pulls the scarf off with her free hand, making sure not to ruin my hair. A butch who knows her femmes.

At the end of the driveway are two bicycles. The two most amazing bikes I've ever seen. The kind of bike that will probably get stolen in about two seconds the minute you lock it and run into the store. They're beautiful. And they are twins.

Lowriders. Hanging close to the ground with whitewall tires and sparkly spokes. Max's is black with a long banana seat. Mine's another story. A serious maraschino cherry that takes no prisoners. The finish is glittery metallic like a nail polish I'd fight dirty at a femme sleepover to walk away with. The seat is the same colour in vinyl, a whole boat of a banana to tuck your tush onto. Sparkly red streamers hang like two pretty pigtails, flipping in the snapping wind. At the back, the sissy bar. A giant, gleaming paperclip. Under the seat, someone's attached a crimson fringe of silky tassels. It's a total dream. And it's not my birthday.

"I wasn't sure if it's totally cheesy. If you don't want to ever ride yours, I won't be offended. Maybe it was a stupid idea. I could always resell it —"

"— Max. I love it! I have never loved a bike as much as I love this one. You shouldn't have."

"I love rebuilding old bikes, it's one of my things. I knew you had to have it. You'll look so totally hot on this bike."

She's cutting so perfectly into my heart I'm scared to move. Scared I'll break it. I think back to the ward. That line between the people who decided who could feel just the right amount and who felt it all wrong. Who was too dangerous to hold certain items, and who was too dangerous to be held. Who was allowed to keep all the sharpness behind their glass walls and decide who else wasn't fit to use it. Now the sharpness is all mine. The only one who can take it away is standing at the end of the driveway, yelling at me to shake my stuff and haul my ass onto the bike already. I don't know if she knows she has that power.

"Alex, come ON already. I already told you, you look gorgeous," she calls as I fix the tops of my boots and stockings.

She looks adorable when her eyebrows get all scrunchy. She knows never to rush me. She pretends to duck, as if I'm about to hurl something at her.

"Come ON, Alex," Max says.

I hesitate one more second. Partly because she's really cute when she hollers. It's so unlike her. And partly because I don't want to lose a single part of this. I don't remember being this happy. This is the way things are working now. I owe Sadie something really, really big for sitting me down months ago in front of that phone. Making me suck it up. Swallow everything I had and just dial.

"Are you done yet?" she asks with exaggerated impatience as I get settled on the seat of my new bike. Everyone says there's something about riding a bicycle you never forget. No matter how much time passes, you can climb back on and ride like you never stopped. I guess your body remembers some things.

And I will never forget. Any of it. But I have to keep going. Loosen my fingers. Leave room for everything that's supposed to come next. Whatever that's supposed to be. Not panic because I don't know what that is. I know I need space. A lot of it. Room in my purse for whatever I want to stick inside. Not just lugging old journals already crammed. Room to keep uncovering my shine. Fumbling fingers finding all those places that got buried. Stop being so scared of the light. Light just wanting to spill out.

I'm sitting on a throne with wheels. And tassels. Streamers. And glitter. A femme throne. Vehemently red. I want to ask one more time if Max is absolutely sure she wants to give me this present. If she wants to have me around. Instead, I listen to what my body already knows. Ignore that destructive voice that wants to fill the room with grey smoke. I think about how glamorous I look on this bicycle instead. Flaming red. Inside and out. Legs I'd drool over shooting down the sides. All this light inside. Beaming out. High gleam. A hum somewhere far inside only I can feel.

"You ready, Alex?" Max asks.

"Yes," I tell her. And I am. I really am.

And then we pedal off the driveway.

I lead.

Acknowledgments

A huge thank you to everyone at McGilligan Books and everyone involved with the project for taking such time and care, including Zoe Whittall, Suzy Malik, Heather Schibli and JP Hornick. Much thanks as well to Ann Decter for being such a fabulous editor and publisher. Thanks to Rose Cullis, Mike O'Connor, Susan Shipton, Elizabeth Ruth, Meryn Cadell, Richard Teleky, Frances Varian, Cindy Cohen, Susan Goldberg, Anna Camilleri and Stephanie Hill for your time and advice. Thanks to the *Stern Writing Mistresses* for all of your feedback and encouragement. A special thanks to Jodi Hoar for support and encouragement through the years. A key place in my heart to my friends: Susanne Illes, Maria Prattas, Jess Dobkin, Rebecca Rogerson and Leanne Gillard, for listening at every step of the way. And, thanks to everyone who saw something in what I was doing and let me know they were looking forward to the rest.

I am grateful for the generous financial support from the Ontario Arts Council received during the writing of this novel.

Debra Anderson is an award-winning writer, playwright and filmmaker. A recipient of the George Ryga Award for Playwriting, she's been a regular on the Toronto reading scene since 1997. Her writing has appeared in *Geeks, Misfits and Outlaws* (McGilligan, 2003), *Bent: On Writing* (Women's Press, 2002), *Brazen Femme: Queering Femininity* (Arsenal Pulp Press, 2002) and many literary journals across Canada. Her short film *Don't Touch Me* (1999), has screened widely at independent film festivals internationally. *Code White* is her first novel.

Visit Debra Anderson's website: www.debraanderson.ca.